I0778466

Harvest Island
by
Lissa Raines

Dedicated to Jeremie & Adriana, Josh, Nat & Bethany, my three sons and two daughters-in-law. And to Easton, Odin, Lennox, Jonathan, and Benjamin, my five grandsons. You all make me so proud. Thank you for your love and support.

Introduction

I'm a slow learner. The irony is I'm a teacher. I was at the top of my class in college, but in real life, not so much. And I had one critical lesson to learn. It took one of the hardest trials of my life to date and a series of dreams to discover what I should have figured out long ago.

Whether the dreams were the product of my overactive subconscious, too many late-night snacks, or the result of some supernatural experience, I'm not sure, but if pressed, I'd have to go with the latter. Knowledge beyond my natural understanding was revealed in the dreams. Either way, natural or supernatural, I'm grateful for the shift in my perspective—difficult though it was.

I'm no one special. No high-profile platform. No social media influencer with a massive following. I'm just like many of you, a flawed, insecure, and often fearful person on a journey to find truth. And I'm a woman who dares to be hopeful that I am finally on the right path.

Thanks for reading my story.
Blessings and Hope,
Samantha Anderson

Author's Note: This story, characters, and Seagrove, South Carolina, are fictional.

Chapter 1

Fifteen Years Ago

Boom! Pop! Pop! Pop! Boom! Boom!

I froze in place. When I could finally speak, I whispered to JoJo, "What was that?"

"'Uh, I'm not sure." JoJo edged toward a window and pulled back the blinds, just enough to peek into the back yard.

Pop! Pop! Pop! Boom!

About twenty of my birthday guests stood motionless, baffled expressions on their faces.

"It's fireworks!" JoJo announced.

"Ah! Phew! It sounded like gunfire," I said.

I joined the line of relieved guests filing outside and was hit with the overpowering scent of sulfur. Dad had set up haybales for seats around the yard a safe distance from where he was lighting fireworks. I sat down between my mom and JoJo. What an exceptional man. Dad was forever full of fun and surprises, and more importantly, he never let me down.

Boom! Boom! Crackle! Pop! Pop!

Dazzling red, blue, yellow, and green explosions filled the sky. I hated that John was missing this. Where was he? He promised he wouldn't miss my birthday celebration. I even made oatmeal chocolate chip cookies especially for him. Why did I bother?

Everyone at the party had already consumed Aunt Karen's mouth-watering sweet and savory hors d'oeuvres and four-tier, multiflavored cake, and now he was missing the spectacular fireworks show.

After the family party, I planned to go out with my two best friends, JoJo and Maria. They both turned twenty-one last year, so I'd been the designated driver on their big days. Tonight, one of them would have that privilege. But even more than going out with my friends, I'd been looking forward to seeing John at the party.

Logan Anderson, my newlywed husband, was traveling for work. He seemed genuinely disappointed that he would miss the celebration, but he couldn't get out of mandatory training in Florida. I'd comforted myself with the knowledge that John had promised to be there. I figured John's presence would compensate for Logan's absence.

A ringing phone made me jump. Mom and I both pulled our phones from our pockets. We had the same ring tone. "It's mine." I retreated into the house so I could hear.

"Hello, this is Samantha."

"Samantha Anderson?"

"Yes, and to whom am I speaking?"

"Officer Gordon, with Seagrove Police, ma'am. Have you seen John Garcia today?"

"No, I haven't, but I'm expecting him any time. Officer Gordon, what's this about?"

"What's your relationship with Mr. Garcia?"

"He's my father . . . that is, my biological father. What's going on?"

"We're not sure, ma'am. His calendar book was open on his desk. Your name was listed on today's date along with BDP21. Does that mean anything to you?"

"Yes, it's my twenty-first birthday. John was coming to the party."

"You call your father John?"

"That's right. I have a stepfather, Thomas Myers, that I call Dad. John hasn't been around much for me and my brother, Kyle, so John, is just . . . John to us." I'd probably given more information than he wanted, but I ramble when I'm nervous.

"I see. When was the last time you saw your biological father, John?"

"Um, let's see . . . probably about six months ago. He came back for my wedding."

"Is that typical? To go that long without seeing him?" he asked.

"Yes. John is a traveling nurse. What's this about?"

"Where was his last assignment?"

"He was in Springfield, Missouri. Right before that he was in New Orleans. Is he in trouble?" My heart was pounding. John was known for womanizing and drinking a bit too much, but he'd never been in any trouble with the law, at least, not that I'd known.

"We're not sure, ma'am. A neighbor complained that the music in his apartment was blaring, and they couldn't get him to answer the door. We did a wellness check and found the door unlocked."

"Really?" John had always been a stickler for safety and kept his door locked even when he was in his apartment.

"Yes, ma'am. When we entered, a gun was lying on the table next to his open appointment book. A lamp was knocked over, papers and books scattered around, and there was a massive amount of blood on the floor. Whoever's blood that was . . . uh . . . well, never mind, let us know if you hear from him." The phone went silent.

"Gun, blood. Oh no." The room began to spin, and I collapsed onto the floor.

Chapter 2

Present Day

I raced into the emergency room and stopped short. Three doctors were frantically attending to a dozen or so injured children. It looked like a scene from a television medical drama. The doctors shouted instructions to nurses and orderlies, requesting medications and sending a few kids off to surgery. Several children were crying, and one kept calling out, "Mommy, help me, it hurts. Mommy, help me."

Tears filled my eyes. My background in education was useless here.

"What happened?" I asked an elderly man with a sling on his arm.

"A semi lost control and veered into the side of a school bus. Then the bus slammed into several cars, mine being one of them. Then the situation went from bad to worse—"

"That's awful! Are you okay?"

"I might have a broken arm, but with several kids injured, they haven't had time for x-rays. I don't mind waiting. Others have a greater need."

"I'm so sorry."

"It's okay. The poor bus driver was hysterical. A nurse gave her a sedative and took her back to another room. The police headed that way a few minutes ago . . . probably taking her statement. Tragic. Just . . . tragic . . ." He stared blankly at the commotion.

"You said something worse happened?"

His gaze shifted back to me. "Uh, yes, when the bus clipped the other vehicles, it tipped and then rolled. I heard the driver saying she had already dropped off over half the kids, so at least they're now safe and sound at home. From what I can tell, no one was seriously injured in the vehicles the bus hit. I sure hope these kids are going to be okay."

"So do I."

The elderly gentleman continued, "The truck driver who started the mess didn't appear to be hurt. I heard the doc say they were going to keep him for observation because he didn't remember the accident. He and the bus driver had their seat belts on. The kids didn't. Not that I'd wish the drivers any harm. But those unfortunate kids were tossed around like a salad."

My mind started to race. Why didn't our school district require seat belts in school buses? It would only take a few more dollars to protect the precious cargo they carried. Besides safety, it would provide bus drivers with easier student control. I made a mental note to bring it up at the next school board meeting. After this accident, they should be motivated.

I thought about my ten-year-old twins, Jayce and Jazmine. Fortunately, they were safe at Spencer's home. Mom had called to tell me Dad, my stepdad that is, had taken a turn for the worse and been brought here to Seagrove General Hospital. I had called my next-door neighbor, Spencer, and he offered to keep an eye on the twins. He said he'd put them to work helping him paint his garage.

"Miss?" the elderly man said.

"Oh . . . stressful day. I need to go and check on my dad now. Thanks for the info . . . I hope your arm isn't broken!"

He nodded, and I proceeded to the information desk.

"Hi, ma'am. Can you tell me if my dad has been admitted, or is he still here somewhere in the ER? His name is Samuel Thomas Myers, but he goes by Tom."

The gray-haired woman scrolled down the computer screen. "Let me see. Yes, Thomas Myers, he's been admitted. When the accident victims came in, they moved him upstairs. You'll find him in room 444 if he's out of radiology. If not, you can wait in his room until they bring him back, dear. It's a private room." She smiled and motioned toward the elevators.

"Thanks, ma'am." I dashed to the elevators.

Waiting for the doors to open, I reflected on Dad's room number. I've always liked the number four—it was my favorite. I wasn't sure why, but the repetition of numbers was comforting. Is four, four, four a good omen? Or possibly, more evidence that I'm obsessive compulsive.

The doors opened, and I stepped into the elevator. A man in a trench coat and fedora joined me. He kept his head down and turned away. That was fine with me. No need to get into another conversation. I needed to see Dad and make sure he was going to be okay.

I arrived in Dad's antiseptic-smelling room before him and made myself comfortable in the overstuffed, red pleather chair by the bed. I wondered if they made it a 3X size, so people had a comfortable place to sleep while staying with loved ones.

Trying to suppress my panic about Dad, I thumbed through the unopened mail I had grabbed off the kitchen counter as I left my house. Bill—bill—credit card offer— satellite TV offer—postcard from a local dealership with a coupon for an oil change—I'd save that one. The last piece of mail was a large manila envelope with only my name and address handwritten in block letters. No return address. Hmm. The envelope was stiff, like it contained cardboard. I squinted to read the faint postmark. Dallas Fort Worth Airport, dated three days ago. Who would be sending me something from DFW? I ripped open the seal and took out the contents.

"What?" I gasped.

"Is everything okay, miss?" A young nurse had quietly entered the room. She began to fluff the extra pillows she'd brought for the bed.

"Uh, I guess so. I didn't see you come in."

"Can I get you anything while you're waiting for Mr. Myers? You look a little pale. Something to drink? Water or coffee?" Her smile appeared genuine.

"No, I'm fine, thanks." I took a few deep breaths to calm the throbbing in my ears.

A buzzer sounded in the hallway, and she headed for the door. "Let me know if you change your mind."

"Thanks." I appreciated her offer to go above and beyond.

I looked again at the photos and shuddered. Pictures from when I was ages 5, 14, 18, and 21--all taken at memorable occasions in my life. I pulled out a tattered photo from my purse. It was identical to one of the photos from the envelope--me and John on my fifth birthday, two years after he and Mom divorced and a year before she married Tom. John's arm was around my shoulder. My beaming smile revealed a missing top front tooth. I was clutching a shiny pink guitar. It was one of my favorite childhood gifts and memories.

Under the photos were a few newspaper articles taped to posterboard. One was from ten years ago when my twins were born--five years after John disappeared. Jayce was the first baby delivered at Seagrove General Hospital that year. Jazmine was the last baby delivered the year before. The local newspaper had written a human-interest story about the twins born in two different years. Jazmine has never let her brother forget that she's a "year" older than him.

Another clipping was from two years ago when I was named "Teacher of the Year" at Seagrove High School. The final article was written last December when the twins were in a play at Mom and Dad's church. The article contained several photos. One showed the twins in their angel costumes. Every clipping was from the Seagrove Times. I was surprised they were still printing the local paper. So many had shifted to online only.

I heard my parents coming down the hallway, so I stuffed the photos and articles back in the manila envelope. As I put them in, I felt a hard object at the bottom. I tipped the envelope and a key taped to an index card fell out. On the back of the card was a strange handwritten message: TINU EGAROTS GA 54321.

I laid the envelope on the table next to the chair with my other mail and crammed the key and index card into my pocket.

Chapter 3

The door burst open and in blew my animated parents. Dad was being wheeled on a hospital bed with Mom close behind. Dad didn't look good but was awake and bickering with Mom. He appeared lucid. I was relieved. As Alzheimer's progressed, he faded back and forth from confusion to reality more often. It was devastating to lose him this way. His mental deterioration was now being followed by major physical decline.

"No, Tom. That's not going to happen," Mom said.

"But I need to, Georgia. It's important," Dad said.

When they saw me, their faces lit up, yet I could see the weariness and anxiety in their eyes.

"They're checking for pneumonia," Mom blurted out.

"That's . . . that's not so bad," I said.

"Right, it isn't so bad," she said, but her tone betrayed her true feelings.

"Now you two don't worry. God's got this. I'm in His hands," Dad said.

The potential diagnosis of pneumonia was jarring, but it could be worse. Cancer or a heart attack or stroke would have been a lot more serious. But in his condition and at seventy-two years old, pneumonia wouldn't be a walk in the park. He may not have been worried, but I was.

At the assisted living home Dad had lost a significant amount of weight. His six-foot two-inch frame could nicely handle the two hundred pounds he carried when he was admitted. Now at one hundred and sixty pounds, he appeared gaunt and frail. His heart's decline weakened his physical strength. I hoped he had the stamina to fight whatever nasty enemy was assaulting him.

"Dad, it's so wonderful to see you awake and ornery enough to be squabbling with Mom. What's that all about?"

He glanced at my mom. "Oh, your mom and I were discussing how long I need to stay here. She says I'll be in for a few days, but I told her I'm fine, and I want to go back to Grand Haven with all the old dudes like me."

He hung his head and then mumbled, "They won't know what to do if I'm not there to help them beat the other team. It's a big dominoes tournament tonight . . . or is it gin rummy? . . . or backgammon? Hmm."

He looked up at us and said, "I know there's a big game tonight, and it's important. So don't let them keep me here."

Dad had been playing those games for so long, he could still play when he was confused about where he was and with whom he was playing.

Other long-term memories were still intact. His Vietnam War stories were usually fresh, as if they had happened yesterday, and it didn't take much to get him talking about his near misses with death. He felt blessed to have been spared when several buddies were gunned down yards away. He was proud of his military service and always said he'd have volunteered if he hadn't been drafted early on.

Dr. Gerald Graham, Dad's longtime family doctor and friend, stuck his head in the door. "Hey Tom, do you have time for a visit from a crotchety old doc?"

"No, we are a little busy here saving the world," Dad shot back with a chuckle.

Dr. Graham stepped in and firmly shook each of our hands. After asking about Jayce and Jazmine, he got down to business.

First glancing at me and Mom, and then

compassionately over to Dad, he said, "The x-rays confirm pneumonia, Tom. We'll up the dose of antibiotics, and hourly when you're awake, I want you to do breathing exercises with this." He showed Dad a plastic apparatus. "It's an incentive spirometer. The nurses are overwhelmed right now, so Georgia can help you.'" He looked at Mom.

"Of course."

"I'll show you both how to use it."

"Thanks, Gerry," Dad said.

Doctor Graham nodded. "Tom, even if you're not hungry, try to eat. And make sure you continue to drink fluids, but not too much, no more than thirty-two ounces. With your congestive heart failure, we need to strike a balance."

It was unlikely Dad would remember, but Dr. Graham addressed him anyway, rather than me and Mom, as he showed him how to use the device. It was a good habit that many of his colleagues hadn't developed. During office visits, Dad's specialists addressed us instead of him. Lately he hadn't commented about it, but early on it bugged him. He'd mention how humiliating it was to be treated like the family pet. Thankfully, Dr. Graham was all about esteeming each person's value, no matter their condition.

Then Dr. Graham turned to Mom. "Georgia, the nurses will help you to keep track of how much fluid Tom's getting, if you'd like."

I jumped in. "Yes, that would be good. Please have them do that."

Mom never wanted to be a bother, and she needed to focus on being a support for Dad, not his nurse or dietician. It seemed she had no choice about being on spirometer duty because Dad wouldn't remember when or how to use it, no matter how often he was reminded. Alzheimer's had taken care of that.

While Dr. Graham listened to Dad's lungs and took his vitals, I talked with Mom about who might be available to help with Dad's breathing exercises when we weren't there.

"I'll help as much as I can, Mom. Maybe I can take some time off from school. We can enlist Uncle Charlie and Aunt Karen too." Charlie Schmidt, Mom's brother, was a local attorney with a large staff, so he might be able to spare the time if we got desperate. And Aunt Karen owned the Seacoast Café and Bakery. She had enough employees to cover for her in a pinch.

"Maybe, we'll see," Mom said.

"And Brandon and Brian may help if they can get away from their business," I said. Five years ago, my twin half-brothers had started a construction company in Little River, a couple of towns over from Seagrove.

"Oh Sam, you know how busy they stay. And with Brian and Katie both working full time, they like to spend any free time with little Noah."

"But Brandon's still single. I can ask him. And I bet Kyle would help out too. I know he's busy with his doctoral thesis, but he could bring his computer and do some work here. If Michaela's not at the salon, she might join him."

Mom tilted her head. "Maybe Brandon . . . but Kyle and Michaela are newlyweds. I doubt they'd want to spend—"

"I'll stop by tomorrow morning during my rounds, Tom. Good to see you Georgia, Sam," Dr. Graham said.

He nodded and exited. No words of encouragement. No false promises. No long-term prognosis. Only the practical information we needed right then. I'd ask Doctor Graham, when I could catch him alone, Dad's chance of beating this.

An hour later, when I was ready to leave, Dad had become confused. "Please, take me home. . . right now! I want to go. . . I need to mow the lawn . . . and take out the garbage." Breathless, he continued, "We don't want the yard overgrown . . . and the garbage stinking . . . I have responsibilities . . . Georgia, please . . . take me home . . . so I can . . . so I can . . . what was it? . . . whatever . . . I want to go home!"

I saw the sadness spread across Mom's face like long shadows in the late afternoon sun. Dad was struggling to get out of bed, so he could go home—not his assisted living, Grand Haven home, but the home he and Mom had shared for decades. I'd rarely seen him that agitated.

Dad hadn't been home with Mom for a year, and even then, he wasn't mowing the lawn or taking out the garbage. He had no comprehension of how sick and weak he'd become.

The nurses sedated Dad, so he could rest. I had never liked the staff at Grand Haven giving Dad drugs to "calm" him. Maybe they were doing what was necessary.

My chest ached as the Dad I loved so deeply become a mere shadow of himself. His grey tinted skin and shallow breathing alarmed me. Yet when I had arrived, he'd been vigorously arguing with Mom. Stubborn to the end. His feisty personality still came through if only for brief periods.

Should I tell Mom about the mystery photos and articles I'd received? "Uh, Mom?"

"Yes, dear?"

"Oh, never mind. Let me know how I can help. Dad's going to be fine, I'm sure. I need to run home for a bit. I'll be back later with the twins." My words fell flat. I wish I was more like my half-brother, Brandon. He'd know what to say to bring real comfort. He always did.

~

As I opened the door from the garage into the house, I was greeted by Lucy, my two-year-old rescue dog, a white Pomeranian. Sweet and beautiful. As usual, she jumped straight up into my arms. I needed her comfort that day. Her unconditional love helped to ease the pain of the loss that was surely imminent.

I called the high school and requested family leave for the rest of the year. There were only a few weeks left, and my students would mostly be studying for and then taking the standardized state testing. Julie in HR listed the documentation I needed, and said she'd have the necessary paperwork ready for me to sign whenever I could stop by.

I called Spencer and asked him to send Jayce and Jazmine home. The twins hadn't lost anyone in their young lives, so they wouldn't fully understand the gravity of Papa's illness. I wanted them to see him again before it was too late.

Spencer accompanied the twins back. It was unnecessary, but I was grateful for an adult's presence. And a handsome adult at that. Spencer's tall stature, wavy dark hair, and hazel eyes reminded me of one the property brothers, including the dimples.

"How's your dad, Sam?" Spence asked.

"It's pneumonia. Dr. Graham's treating him with heavy-duty antibiotics, so we'll have to wait and see." I glanced at him and then back to the hamburger meat sizzling in the pan on the stove. I was afraid I'd melt down under Spencer's sympathetic gaze. And I didn't want to cry in front of the twins.

"Sorry, Sam. I'll be praying he pulls through."

I mumbled, "Thanks, Spence."

"Please call if you need anything. Even if you just want someone to talk to. I'm here for you."

I glanced up, saw his hopeful expression, and nodded.

After Spencer left, I explained Papa's condition to the twins.

"Is Papa going to die?" Jazmine's eyes filled with tears.

I didn't know how to answer. "I hope not, sweetie." I hugged her. "But it is possible." I didn't want to lie and tell her it was all going to be okay. It probably wasn't.

Chapter 4

When I arrived at the hospital with the twins, Dad was no better, but thankfully no worse. His few expressions of recognition helped to ease our pain. The twins talked to Papa about Lucy's obedience class they were both attending. Jazmine told Papa she wanted to be a veterinarian. That was news to me. Jaz had always been close to Dad. He held her hand and tried his best to follow her ramblings. She took after me. If you don't know what to say, say something, whatever comes to mind. Jayce appeared content to let his sister do most of the talking.

After we returned home, the kids watched the end of American Idol while I folded laundry. My attempt to distract myself from worrying about Dad wasn't working. Folding towels, sheets, and the kids clothes was too mindless. Maybe those photos and clippings? I grabbed the manila envelope from my dresser, took it to the kitchen, and carefully dumped its contents on the table.

Were these photos and clippings from John? Is it possible he's still alive . . . somewhere? Why wouldn't he call? What has he been doing all these years? Severely wounded, amnesia, another family, joined the mob?

John has always been a mystery to me—Navy vet, traveling nurse, womanizer, life of the party, collector of art and antiquities. Not your typical father. He had infrequently been part of our lives before that terrible night fifteen years ago when he disappeared leaving only a massive amount of blood behind. After all this time, I tried to wrap my head around the possibility that he was still alive. The amount of blood in his apartment indicated otherwise. The police confirmed it was his blood. I never wanted to believe he was gone because his body was never found. Deep inside I felt that the likelihood of finding him was a false hope.

Until the time he vanished, John sent postcards every few months from wherever he was. He enjoyed life on the road. The last time I heard from him was two months before my twenty-first birthday.

He'd called from a number I didn't recognize. "Hey kiddo!" He broke into a Sinatra style song--"Happy birthday to you, happy birthday my dear Sam, happy birthday to you."

"Thanks, John, but it's not for two months. It's been a long time since I've heard from you." I didn't try to hide my disappointment. He should know he'd hurt me.

"Sorry it's been so long. I got your email about your birthday party, and I'm calling to RSVP. I'll be there, kiddo."

"Don't make promises you can't keep."

"I'll be there, I promise. My assignment here ends a week or two before your birthday, so I'll be back at my apartment in Seagrove."

'And where are you now?"

"I'm in the whopping big town of Springfield, Missouri."

"Never heard of it," I said, even though I knew he'd been there before.

"You know, I've sent you post cards from here. It's the home of Bass Pro Shops, and locals say it's also the birthplace of Route 66. Ringing any bells?"

"No, still nothing," I lied, irritated he hadn't been in touch sooner.

"Never mind. I'll send you a post card soon with my address if you want to send your old man a letter or care package or something. You make a mean batch of oatmeal chocolate chip cookies," John said.

"We'll see. If you show up at my party, I'll have some waiting for you."

"Ah. Bribing the old man, huh? I'll be there. I promise."

Then in a more serious tone, John asked, "How are you doing? I heard that George Purnell passed recently. I know you two used to be pals."

My heart softened. George and I were close in high school, taking a lot of the same classes and hanging out with the same group of friends. How had John heard about George's death?

"I'm doing okay," I said. "It's been about three years since I've seen him. He went on the road and settled near Denver. I was shocked. An overdose they said."

"That's the story anyway."

"Huh, did you hear something else?"

"Uh, no. I just find it hard to believe he got mixed up with drugs. He was a pretty straight arrow, wasn't he?" John asked.

"Yeah, he was. But people change. Make bad choices. Poor judgement. Get mixed up with the wrong crowd."

"Right. Have you talked to his family?"

"I did. I went to the funeral and saw his mom. She was inconsolable. Had no idea he was into drugs. Such a waste. He was a talented musician and was an awesome friend too."

"Yes, he was. I'm glad you're doing okay, Sam," John said.

And before I could ask how he was doing, he added, "Sorry, Sam, but I've gotta run. There's a concert tonight at the Shrine Mosque, and I don't want to be late picking up my date."

I sighed. "I understand. Thanks for the call, John, and I do hope you make the party."

"I will, kiddo. I promise."

Those are the last words I ever heard from him. And the

promised postcard with his Springfield address never came.

For months after John's disappearance, Kyle and I had diligently searched for him, holding onto a slim hope that he was still alive. Though well loved by Tom and Mom, the itch to locate John was rekindled with the mysterious envelope containing those photos and clippings.

John had been employed with several travel nursing companies. Through my research, mostly phone calls back then, it appeared that he left the last agency when he left Springfield, Missouri, a couple of weeks before my twenty-first birthday. I never found the address where he'd been living in Springfield, so there wasn't much to follow up on.

I felt like a blindfolded kid trying to pin a tail on the elusive donkey. With a name like John Garcia, he wasn't easy to track. I didn't know his social security number, and Mom's repeated promise to find it for me was still unfulfilled. She thought she threw away any paperwork regarding John when they moved into the Myers Mansion, my nickname for Mom and Dad's huge home. That left me with a common name and a not so common occupation to go on.

In spite of a throbbing headache, I sat down with my laptop on the daybed in the guest room, a.k.a. my home office. I scoured a plethora of social media accounts. Nothing.

I pulled out a file from my four-drawer wooden file cabinet. It contained previously contacted travel nursing companies. I searched for any other agencies, found several I hadn't previously called, and jotted down their phone numbers to call during business hours.

I jumped when my cell phone rang.

"Hello?" I hoped Dad was not taking a turn for the worse.

"You'd better stop what you're doing." The voice was strange, like a robot.

"Huh?" I wasn't sure I'd heard right.

"Stop digging if you know what's good for you."

"Who is this?" I asked, but they'd hung up.

Did that just happen? My pulse pounded in my temples. How did anyone know what I was doing? A prank? A wrong number? Must be.

An hour later, a throbbing migraine completely overwhelmed me, so I took a prescription pill and fell into bed exhausted, ready for a respite from my pervasive anxiety. After tossing and turning for two hours, the intense pain and nausea finally subsided.

I didn't pray often but figured it couldn't hurt. "God, if you're real and you hear me, help Dad get better. Help me to cope with everything. Please let me find John. Please protect my children and help me not to be scared." After praying variations of this short, but direct and sincere prayer four times, I drifted off to sleep.

Chapter 5

Dream: The Island

A chilly autumn wind whipped through my hair as I walked down the narrow leaf covered path. I love the musky-sweet smell of autumn—dying leaves in crisp cool air. I inhaled deeply bringing back pleasant childhood memories. I was east of the Waccamaw River, close to Gregory Elementary School where I'd attended. I've walked these woods hundreds of times, but today was different. Everything felt more real, more vibrant. The birds chirping sounded louder, the hues of the fall trees appeared more brilliant, and the rustling leaves and the bubbling brook were more animated.

Anticipation filled my heart, but for what?

Then it happened. I was no longer crunching dry leaves under my Nike's but looking down at the path from fifty feet in the air. It was exhilarating. I was flying. I was able to will my body to go left, right, up, or down.

For the first time since . . . since . . . I couldn't remember when I felt this free. Free of burdens, free of worry, free of fear. The squirrels chased each other in the trees, the birds flew from branch to branch, and the tops of the trees swayed in the wind. In the distance the sun reflected off the sparkling river. What an incredible view. I was energized as I soared higher into the moist cool clouds. I felt curious and hopeful, like I was a kid again.

Life hadn't turned out the way I'd expected. I had a stable teaching job, but one in which I was overwhelmed at times, was divorced, raising two children largely on my own, and was plagued with migraines several times a month. Flying above the tree line, these gloomy realities faded into the recesses of my mind.

I wasn't aware how far I'd traveled until I no longer recognized the landscape below. Instead of autumn-colored woods and the flowing Waccamaw River, I was passing over farmland. Mile after mile of fields, a variety of hues and sizes. Farmhouses, barns, and outbuildings dotted the colorful rolling landscape. In the distance I saw the ocean— one of my favorite places on earth.

As I approached, the water was unexpectedly not the blue of the Mid-Atlantic, but tropical waters, a vast sea of aqua. I was amazed at the multitude of dolphins and sharks close to the surface. Seagulls squawked in the distance drawing my attention away from my path causing a near collision with a squadron of pelicans.

Along the horizon, lay a string of islands. A short distance from the largest one with craggy cliffs was a smaller colorful island that had an eerie, but captivating glow. Intrigued, I willed myself toward it.

It appeared to be about a mile in diameter. Around the entire exterior of the island was a sandy white beach with an abundance of palm trees. One circular wide cobblestone street marked the next tier of the island. It was the only street visible from the air, possibly the only one on the island. I didn't see any movement other than the swaying of the trees and vegetation but assumed there had to be inhabitants.

Sprawling homes on large estates covered the next layer on the interior side of the road, with only one home beach side. Rooftops of various sizes and styles suggested each home was a unique masterpiece. Although one building appeared to be more like a prison than a stately mansion. A high barbed wire fence enclosed that dwelling. From the air I couldn't tell if it actually was a penitentiary.

Finally, a circular field of crops filled the center of the island. It was comprised of different colors--one slice of pie behind each estate. Some fields were smaller than others with only a few thinly planted rows. Others were large with dozens of rows packed closely together. How peculiar.

I grew up in the small coastal town of Seagrove, South Carolina. Crops were grown further inland, so I didn't know what to make of this agricultural anomaly. Rows of richly diverse colors filled the circular field. Even more strange was that they all appeared to be the same plant, a type of leafy lettuce. Could there be that many varieties of this same vegetable? Flowers possibly, but vegetables, no. Not that I'd ever seen.

What a bizarre sight. I was circling the field again contemplating its meaning when a large radiant figure appeared floating next to me. He waved me down to the island below.

As we landed on the soft white sand, he said, "Do not be afraid. I am Him Who Does His Bidding."

"I'm, I'm Samantha."

"I know who you are. You seek answers about your father. I've been sent to bring you those answers and also to answer the cry of your heart. It is a soul cry that you haven't fully recognized, but it's been clearly heard and will be answered," said Him Who Does His Bidding.

"Uh, I'm not sure what you mean, but I'm listening," I said. "Who did you say you are?"

"My name is Him Who Does His Bidding. But you may call me Mr. Bidding if that's easier. For the mysteries you seek to be unveiled, you must visit the eight homes on Harvest Island, talk to the inhabitants who dwell there, and inspect each field. Learn as much as you can about them. As you leave each home, you'll be given a clue for your quest. You're allowed to visit only one home each day. After every visit, return here to the northernmost tip of the island. We'll discuss what you've discovered. Finally, after the last visit, you may choose in which house you desire to dwell," instructed Mr. Bidding.

He sounded like he was reading the rules of a board game. Choose in which house to dwell? It was crazy. But I was grateful for the opportunity to find John, so I didn't argue.

"I am anxious to find John, my biological father. If the clues lead me to him, it will be one of the best gifts of my life. Besides finding John, I'm not aware of any other heart cry other than my sorrow over my stepdad's condition. If you have any control over that and can give him his health back, I'd forego the clues about John. Tom's a wonderful man and doesn't deserve Alzheimer's, heart disease, pneumonia, or anything bad," I said.

"I see your sorrow over Tom, Samantha. His health is not part of my assignment. I've only been delegated the job of providing clues to find your father and your heart's cry through the residents of Harvest Island. The latter I'm not allowed to discuss at this time. All will be revealed in due time, Samantha. Have faith," Mr. Bidding said.

Sad to hear that Tom's health wasn't on the agenda for this strange little venture, I moved to the next item.

"I'm sure you mean well, but I can't imagine choosing one of these homes as my residence. I have a home in Seagrove," I said, hoping that conversation would never take place. I wasn't in the mood to move now and probably wouldn't be for a long time to come, if ever again.

My ex, Logan, and I had a custom home built. It took nine months, three months longer than estimated, and the process of building probably contributed to our divorce. I'm sure my OCD didn't help. We separated a year after our dream home was completed and divorced six months later. I got the house in the divorce because I have primary custody.

"No, Samantha." Mr. Bidding interrupted my thoughts.

"I'm not going to ask you to move into one of these homes, only to dwell in one."

Chapter 6

The alarm blared. It couldn't be 6:00 a.m. already. Groggy from the migraine pill, I pulled myself out of bed and stumbled into the bathroom.

Lucy looked up at me from her dog bed in the adjacent closet. "Do you have crazy doggie dreams, sweet girl? You wouldn't believe the dream I had. It was so vibrant, so real. But in the first part of my dream it was fall, not spring. Hmm. I didn't sleep through summer, did I?" She cocked her head and wagged her tail but didn't get up.

"You look pretty content right there. I'll shower and then get us breakfast."

I stepped into my teal and aqua tiled shower stall and closed the glass door behind me. The hot water washed away much of the fog but left the dream vividly intact.

Before waking the twins, I sat at the kitchen island and slowly ate a bowl of Cheerios and blueberries, drizzled with honey. Could that dream possibly have some significance? Or was my subconscious working overtime? Is there a Harvest Street in Seagrove? Or possibly an island off the coast of South Carolina? Maybe a remote island somewhere in the tropics? I made a mental note to look up streets and islands named Harvest on Google maps. Surely, the dream didn't mean I was itching to move. Not after enduring the ordeal of having my dream home built.

After breakfast, I walked to the mailbox at the bottom of the driveway and saw Spencer heading toward his car.

"Morning, stranger," he called. "You doin' alright?"

"Yeah, I'm fine. But I had a weird dream last night! So strange."

He approached. "How so? Was it about me?" He chuckled.

Shaking my head and smiling at his comment, I rattled off a Cliff's Notes version of the dream.

"You are the queen of strange dreams. It's been a few months since you told me about an ape taking over the high school. It's about time you had another whacky dream to entertain me," he teased with a twinkle in his eye.

"Very funny." He had me. I've always had a vivid imagination. Maybe that's all it was.

"See you later, Sam. I've got to run." He made a quick exit.

That day I dropped the twins at school. They could have ridden the bus, but after witnessing first-hand the results of that school bus accident, I felt it was safer to take them myself.

I wanted to see Dad, and hoped to cheer him up, so I stopped by Flowers Forever on Main Street. Dad always loved wild Tiger Lily's—a large blossom with bold orange pedals and black spots. He'd occasionally buy them to encourage Mom when she was having a bad day, but the truth was, he liked them as much or more than she did.

I grew impatient as the clerk waited on an indecisive customer. Did she want pink or red carnations, a combination of colors or multicolored white with red edges? How many, a dozen or two? How much did she want to spend on a vase, four or six dollars?

I wanted to scream, "I know exactly what I want. Wait on me!" But I exercised a little self-control and waited, not so patiently. One virtue at a time was all I could handle right then. Finally, after fifteen minutes, flowers in hand, I was out the door.

Pulling into the hospital's visitor parking area, sadness

swept over me like a heavy blanket. Would this be the last day I'd see Dad alive? What should I say that I haven't already said? Was there anything that I'd regret? I was lost in these thoughts as I circled the lot, looking for an empty parking spot. In my dream Mr. Bidding said otherwise, but I hoped that my unspoken heart cry was that Tom would recover, that I'd have more time with him. Was I actually putting credence in my silly dream?

While trying to stay positive, I felt an urgency to see him. After parking, I closed my eyes trying to compose myself and get my emotions under control. A picture of an hourglass with the sand running through it flashed through my mind. How much longer would I have with Dad? My heart pounded. I needed to see him before he passed. I got out, locked the car, and hurried into the hospital.

Waiting at the elevator doors, I overheard two nurses quietly discussing the bus accident.

"Have they found the cause for the semi driver passing out?" one asked.

"No. He has a cough. Says he's been weaker than usual and is having trouble breathing. His blood oxygen has dropped, so we've started supplementing. He's negative for the flu and Covid. His heart rate is elevated. Multiple blood tests have been run, an EKG, a CAT scan, and then an MRI. They all appear normal."

The elevator doors dinged, and the nurses' conversation halted as several people stepped out. The nurses stepped into the elevator. I followed. They continued the conversation in hushed tones.

"He said he passed out the day before the accident too. He woke up on the floor in his living room," said the tall thin nurse with a ponytail.

"Oh my. Why did he drive after that?" asked the shorter heavier nurse with her hair in a messy bun.

"He assumed it was from lack of food and drink. Said he had a long haul that day and didn't stop as often as he should have. But he'd eaten and hydrated considerably since he passed out at home, so docs don't believe that's the cause."

The elevator doors opened on Dad's floor, and I exited. As I entered Dad's room, relief washed over me. He was sitting up, trying to eat. At first his expression was one of delight, but soon changed to confusion as he struggled to find my name. It was lost in the tangled torment of Alzheimer's.

I reminded him, "It's Samantha, Dad. I brought you your favorite flowers. The flower shop had a batch with huge open blossoms."

"Yes, thank you. They are so cheery . . . I'll take them home with me later today. Then your mom . . . can enjoy them too." His words were labored and breathy, not his usual strong timbre.

Normally I would have told him he wouldn't be going home today. I strongly believe in facing reality, not wishful thinking. But his condition was anything but normal--both mentally and physically. I wanted him to know how much I loved him.

"I'm glad you like them." I left it at that.

Why upset him with the news he wasn't going home today? He wasn't going anywhere for several days. Until the pneumonia was under control, he'd stay put at Seagrove General. When and if he left, he'd be headed back to his Grand Haven home on Shepherd Island.

Remembering the sand in the hourglass, I wanted to take advantage of what time we had left. I needed to make sure Dad knew how much I loved him.

"Dad, I-I need to tell you something."

Softly, he answered, "Ok, dear." He seemed to know who I was even though he didn't remember my name. "You know . . . you can . . . talk to me . . . about anything," he deliberately articulated.

"It sounds trite, but I want you to know how much I

have appreciated your love and support all these years. I would have been lost without you, really lost. You have to get better. I don't know what I'd do without you," I blurted.

"Oh, darling. . . you are stronger . . . than you think," he answered barely above a whisper. In short wispy breaths, he continued as I strained to hear. "You are . . . who you are . . . because of choices . . . you've made . . . not because . . . of me. You have a . . . good heart . . . and you will do . . . perfectly . . . fine . . . when I'm gone. . . I'm an old man . . .not good for much . . . anymore." After catching his breath, he added, "Samantha, you have . . . been a joy . . . always a joy. . . in my life . . . Never forget it." His blue eyes sparkled.

I reached over and squeezed his hand. At that moment he was the Dad I knew and cherished. He'd remembered my name.

"Oh, Dad, you know how much I love you, right?" I held back the tears.

Quietly he replied, "Yes, dear . . . of course . . . and I always . . . will love you . . . and your heavenly father . . . will too . . . Now tell me . . . about the twins . . ."

Relieved that he was lucid, but worried about the deterioration in his breathing, I chatted with him for several minutes about the kids and our summer plans when school let out. For a minute or two he hung on every word, excited about the little events in our lives. I tried to do most of the talking, so he could save his strength, but our conversation was taking a toll. His eyes clouded over, and he became flushed and started sweating. I touched his forehead. It was warmer than it should have been.

"John . . . your father. I need . . . to tell you . . . not lost . . . close by . . . so close . . . so happy." He coughed, sighed, and then began coughing again. I helped him to get some water from the plastic cup on the tray by his bed. After a few sips his coughing subsided.

What was he trying to tell me? His rambling made no sense. I wanted to spend as much time as I could with him, but he wouldn't have a chance of recovering if he kept exerting himself.

"Try to get some sleep. We can talk more later, Dad. I brought my laptop, so I'll get some work done, but I don't want to keep you awake with the clicking on my keyboard. I'll be outside in the waiting room. If you need anything, buzz the nurse, and she can get me. I won't be far away," I promised and exited, hoping he understood and would get some healing rest.

Chapter 7

Dream: Daniel Dark

As I strolled down the cobblestone lane, I saw the buildings on the island from a new perspective. Instead of rooftops, I stood in front of homes that ranged from magnificent to peculiar, all with colorful fields behind them. Each dwelling was unique, unlike the cookie cutter neighborhood where I lived. The size, style, levels, and hue were all distinctive. The homes and field colors flowed together as a whole, so that the neighborhood didn't appear disjointed as one might imagine.

I stopped in front of the shabby, navy-blue Victorian with the gray field. I instinctively understood that the dilapidated, massive building housed three individuals. At the center of the gable was a cat gargoyle, black with piercing green eyes. A shiver ran down my spine. I didn't feel welcome. The shutters and door were the same gray as the field behind the home, like matching accessories to an outfit.

He Who Does His Bidding appeared next to me.

My heart skipped a beat. "You startled me."

"This is where you should begin the journey," Mr. Bidding said.

"What do I do? Ring the doorbell and tell them they are to answer the deepest cries of my heart?" I asked sarcastically.

Ignoring my comment, he said, "Go to the door and tell them your name. They will be expecting you. When you visit each home, observe the inhabitants carefully. In this house dwells Daniel Dark, George Godfree, and Harry Hardhearted. At the end of your visit, Harry will give you the first clue to find your father. Then take a stroll through the field behind the home. I'll meet you later to discuss what you've witnessed.

Timidly, I walked across the cobbled street to the stone path that led to the house. With each step, the clouds swelled, and the wind began to swirl behind me. It was like watching a storm video on fast forward. The thunder boomed, and the lightning flashed. In a matter of seconds, it was dusk. A smidge of daylight remained, just enough to light the path to the front door. I picked up my pace, so I wouldn't get soaked in the rain.

The black cat gargoyle's piercing green eyes followed me as I approached. The far-left gable housed a fox gargoyle, and the far-right gable was home to a devil gargoyle--oddly both were a little less intimidating than the cat. The outside of the house was in disrepair, reminding me of a haunted house, looking spookier with each step closer.

The cobblestone continued along the front walk to the sprawling Victorian home, up the stairs and onto the wraparound porch. I counted as I ascended the stairs. One, two, three, four, five. If I landed on an odd number as I did this time, I stepped down and up again, so I'd finished on an even number. Six. It wasn't logical, but it was comforting, the balance of even numbers. Every number had a match.

The storm became deathly quiet as I approached the large mahogany door with a small, hinged square in the center. The name on the stone mailbox fastened to the door was "DARK". Another mailbox to the left of the door read "GODFREE" and one to the right of the door read "HARDHEARTED." As I rang the bell, I heard it reverberate a four-tone retort like the large Taiko drums of

Japan. "Ta-Dum-Ta-Dum" It echoed as only a Taiko drum could. I waited for a minute and there was no answer. Surely if someone was home, they would have heard that. I glanced back to Him Who Does His Bidding, but he was no longer there. At least I couldn't see him.

I rang the bell again and waited. Finally, I heard shuffling inside. Someone was indeed home. What if they were sleeping or worse yet, in the bathroom? I hated to interrupt.

Out of breath, a middle-aged man, with soft features opened the center box and peeked out and said, "Yes, can I help you?" A strap over his shoulder held an object. I only saw part of it through the small opening in the door, but it appeared to be a rifle.

"Um, uh . . . I . . . uh, I thought you were expecting me?" I said, taken back that he was armed. I'd blindly trusted the word of Him Who Does His Bidding.

"How can I know if I'm expecting you, if I don't know to whom I am speaking?"

"Oh, I'm . . . uh . . . Samantha . . . Samantha Anderson."

"You sound a little uncertain," he snapped.

"Oh. I expected you to know. Him Who Does His Bidding sent me," I explained.

"Hmm. I see. Yes, I am expecting you. Please come in. I'm Daniel Dark," he said as he opened the door a crack and stepped back into the shadows.

Daniel stood about five feet, four, a few inches shorter than me. His dark hair, bushy eyebrows and equally bushy mustache outlined his delicate features and sad brown eyes. Though he had a boyish round face, his gravelly voice and creased brow revealed his true age. He looked Italian or of another Mediterranean descent.

Stepping into the dimly lit room blinded me at first. A sliver of light seeped in around the edges of dark velvet drapes that hung over the windows. No artificial lights were on, though I saw an old glass chandelier with unlit candles in the center of the high ceiling. A lantern with a tiny flickering flame sat on the ornate marble mantle. The musty smell and stale air choked me as I scanned the furnishings. I coughed and cleared my throat.

"Let your eyes adjust before you walk around. I don't want you falling and suing me," Daniel said.

The front room was filled with antiquities from around the world. All had a thick layer of dust blanketing them. Colorful tribal masks from Africa, ornate vases from China's Shang dynasty, beautifully carved wooden statues of King Tut and an emerald and diamond French tiara. Or was it Italian?

John's interest in antiquities had sparked an interest in me as a teenager. Hoping to gain John's approval, I spent hours in the library pouring over books, mostly picture books of many of the world's most valuable items. When it came to antiquities, I was an amateur hobbyist at best.

A stream of light fell through a crack between the curtains drawing my attention to the dark paneling where magnificent paintings were on display--Van Gogh's *Starry Night*, one of Monet's landscapes of a cliff overlooking the sea, and another of Monet--a vase of Sun Flowers. I loved that one—so cheery and bright but appearing dull in the dim light. The artwork surrounded the room like guards keeping watch over the inhabitants.

This room resembled a museum, but the earthy scent was like an old damp basement. Cobwebs adorned the corners of the ceiling, and I hoped that none of their inhabitants would find their way down to me. In addition to having OCD tendencies, I'm an arachnophobe.

How did Daniel come into possession of these masterpieces? I'd seen a few of these paintings in art museums when I vacationed in New York City, Chicago, Italy, and Greece during my college years. I always made time to visit the local exhibits. I had coordinated one trip with John's itinerary and visited his favorite galleries in

Chicago.

I was inspired by John's love for the merging of the mind and heart on canvas. What was the artist thinking? What emotion or message was he or she trying to convey? Such a love for art was in my genes. The collection in this room alone was worth a fortune. Outside a loud clap of thunder made me jump as lightning lit the room for a split second.

Daniel ignored the severe weather and started the conversation. "I'd like to welcome you to Harvest Island. Here we're all real."

"Um, thank you," I said. What did he mean? We're all real.

"We are what we are. No hiding. No games. Take us or leave us. When talking to *you*, we must speak the truth. It is one of the rules of Him Who Does His Bidding--on this we have little choice. Like us or not, what you see is what you get."

What you see is what you get, my favorite acronym, WYSIWYG. Truth and honesty. But would I hear what Daniel believed to be true or what was in reality true?

Daniel removed a pile of books from an antique Victorian, high-back armchair. "Here, come and sit." He patted the chair, and a plume of dust floated into the air.

I warily approached the chair and stopped in front of it imagining all the germs that lived there. I focused on my mission in order to ignore the dirty surroundings. Gingerly, I sat down.

"Ok. I'm here to learn, so tell me about yourself." I was curious to see what he'd reveal and what clue I'd be given to find John.

"I grew up in this house. My parents moved to another town, but I couldn't bear to leave this lovely old home and all its treasures. It's not the monetary value that keeps me here. It's the people each article embodies that intrigues me. Living with these antiques is a way to keep the past alive and enjoy it forever," he said.

His lackluster tone didn't sound as if he enjoyed much of anything. But I was trying to understand who he was and if there was a clue about my father hidden in his words.

"Please tell me more. What do you do for a living?"

Daniel continued, "I survive on the crops from the field behind the house. Of course, I, George, and Harry can't possibly consume everything that grows there, so they take the rest to market on the other islands—primarily Tahiti, and I live, for the most part, off the proceeds. George and Harry have other income. I treasure trade too. Last week I swapped a two-foot-high, gold Buddha for a thousand-year-old Koran. That was the best deal I've made in a while."

"How do you decide what you'll part with?" I asked.

"When I tire of an item or no longer hear its spirit, it's time for a new relic," he said.

So, this house didn't just look haunted, it was haunted. "Would you mind turning on some lights, so I can take a better look at your collection? I love museums."

"No," he barked. "I don't allow artificial light in our home, and I abhor sunlight even more. The light hurts my eyes, so I stay inside and keep the curtains drawn. I cherish my antiquities and doing what I've always done—puttering around the house listening to the spirits of those who are long dead. But every harvest season, I'm required to go outside to help with the crops. I wear dark—almost opaque glasses, and cover myself from head to foot, so I don't absorb any of the light."

"Doesn't it get lonely being by yourself all day?" I asked. What was I feeling? Pity? Empathy? Fear?

"No. In the evening George and Harry come home. We have a sensational time together. First thing, one of them will light a candle and put it on the other side of the room. Far enough away so my eyes don't burn, but close enough, so they can find their way around the house," Daniel explained. "George and Harry are understanding about my condition and don't force me into the light."

Fixer that I am, I asked, "Wouldn't your eyes adjust to the light if you gradually increased the amount you're exposed to?"

Daniel huffed. "Now why would I want to do that? I am perfectly content with my antiques and dark home. The light is a nuisance. I try to keep it out, not invite it in."

An hour later I was still sitting in Daniel's reception room listening to his story. He lived on Harvest Island all his life. Both parents were gone. He was an only child. Never married. Harvest Island was located on a small island in an Archipelago in the South Pacific, a few miles off the coast of Tahiti. I was confused about how I had arrived in the South Pacific. But my unwavering desire to get answers about John's whereabouts allowed me to put aside my concerns and continue my quest as instructed by Him Who Does His Bidding.

Though Daniel's responses were sometimes gruff and his disposition grumpy, I was grateful for his willingness to answer my questions. The dark shadows that permeated this home seemed to extend to his soul. I couldn't get a read on what made him tick. And I had discovered next to nothing about his housemates.

"So, what do George and Harry do?" I asked.

Daniel said, "I hear them outside. I'll let you ask them yourself."

Chapter 8

Dream: George Godfree and Harry Hardhearted

The heavy door slammed behind George Godfree and Harry Hardhearted as the wind blew it shut. The storm was still raging. I had been so engrossed in Daniel's story, I had tuned out the torrential rains and howling wind outside.

Apparently unaware of my presence—George scolded, "Daniel, you doofus. Why'd you leave the door unlocked?"

As their eyes adjusted, they realized Daniel was not alone. Wiping his wet face with an old towel from a coat rack by the door, George stared at me, hesitating, apparently not sure what to say.

"Sorry, Ma'am. I'm George Godfree. I didn't see you there," he said.

"Can I offer you some refreshment?" the other newcomer asked. I assumed it was Harry Hardhearted. "I see Daniel wasn't very hospitable. We don't get guests too often here on Harvest Island."

"Um--I uh—I um, I guess water would be good." I was parched. The dusty furnishings were likely to blame.

Harry disappeared and reappeared with a glass of filthy water. It was dark and murky, like the house.

"Oh, um, thank you," I said.

I held the glass briefly hoping they didn't notice I wasn't drinking, and then set it on the table in front of me. No way was I going to drink that water. I hoped they didn't offer any food. If they did, I'd tell them I wasn't hungry. I had glanced at their field when I approached the house, and it was full of grey shriveled crops. How in the world did they sell those at the market? And how could those crops possibly sustain them?

"George, Harry, tell me about your work." I tried to take the attention off the water I wasn't drinking.

"Sure, we do a lot of odd jobs around the neighborhood. Something always needs repair. With our tools and handy man skills we keep busy." George rocked back and forth on his feet.

Both men wore overalls with tool belts around their waists. George was taller and thinner than Harry. His gray hair was pulled back into a single braid which reached to his slim waist. He reminded me of Willie Nelson. Harry had a stocky build, bulging muscles, and a bald head--a stereotypical bouncer vibe. His brown skin stood in stark contrast to George's fair complexion.

Harry broke the momentary silence. "That's right. Every day folks need their homes repainted or roofs repaired. They're so gullible. We can charge twice the going rate and still get it. People are stupid. They get what they deserve."

"We hardly ever have anyone check up on us. We keep doing what we've always done, and they keep paying even though they could go elsewhere and pay a lot less. Kudos to us!" George exclaimed.

"And we tell people they're getting the materials at cost, but we always double or triple the price," Harry said, apparently excited by cheating people out of their hard-earned money.

George added, "Hey, it's every man for himself. You've got to look out for number one. No one else will. There ain't nothing wrong with that!"

I didn't know what to say. "Um--uh, I see. What else can you tell me about yourselves?"

George continued, "We love living here with Daniel.

His place is so comfortable. Darkness, dust, spirits in all this old stuff, and fights. We love to fight. Conflict feeds our souls. It's exciting. Never a dull moment around here. You see how weak Daniel is?"

"I don't know, maybe?" What was I supposed to say?

"Well, he is, and it's fun to beat him up. We do whatever we want to in the dark. Don't answer to no one. Nobody judges us or hassles us about doing the "right" thing. We all like it that way, except for Daniel. He whines about getting thrashed."

I nodded, a little shocked at what I was hearing. But I didn't want him to stop, so I didn't interrupt.

"I make up my rules for living as I see fit. Harry usually rebels against them and does the opposite, and Daniel acts like he never hears me when I'm announcing the latest rules. He's hard of hearing. That may be why. Daniel's deafness, Harry's attitude, and my random rules—they give us a lot of fodder for disagreements." George beamed and nodded in self-satisfaction.

"I see," I said, but I didn't see at all. Who was this person who loved conflict? Lived by his own rules?

"I know what's best for me, so my rules line up with what feels good at the time, you know, what is to *my* best advantage. Then I change the rules as necessary for each situation. It's a superior system and works for me. I live untroubled and without the heavy guilt so many people carry," George said. His voice grew louder. "I don't bow to a supreme being with constricting rules and regulations. Those who need religion are weak. God's a crutch. But I'm strong. I don't need no God or religion. Of this I am most proud. I am truly God free. George Godfree--and don't you forget it."

My mind swirled. Lives life by his own rules. Loves fighting and discord. It was hard for me to process because I prefer to find harmony and acceptance. And I follow the rules. I'm not particularly religious, but I respect people who are. George's existence was certainly not my cup of tea.

"Harry," I shifted my attention to the end of the sofa where he sat. "Tell me about yourself."

"Okay." He cleared his throat. "Ma'am, I came to Harvest Island as a child and have never lived anywhere else, unlike some of the neighbors who have lived in a lot of exotic places."

Exotic places. You are living in an exotic place, an island in the South Pacific. I kept my mouth shut, not wanting to derail him from telling me about himself.

"As George told you, rebellion of rules fuels the fire in my belly. It makes me feel powerful. I'm not the creative type like George, but I do like to push the limits. Whatever arbitrary rules George comes up with, I find a way to bend or break them. It's a wonderful challenge and helps me to feel alive--like I am making my mark on the world," Harry said.

He pulled out a box of old knives from one of the antique dressers and began to sharpen them. Pausing only briefly, he continued. "I come from a long line of British criminals—murderers and thieves who were shipped to Australia in the mid 1800's. Then my parents moved to these islands when I was two, so it's the only place I've ever known."

"And how long have you lived in this home?" I asked.

"About ten years. My dwelling is in the west wing of the home. George has the east wing and Daniel the main home in the center. There were a few other inhabitants, but they mysteriously disappeared." He stared at me without blinking and then slowly pointed one of the twelve-inch blades toward me, waiting for my reaction.

Fear replaced my curiosity and hopeful anticipation. I wanted to run but froze in place. Him Who Does His Bidding would protect me, wouldn't he? His promise to help me find John was spoken with such authority. More than that, he seemed to possess supernatural powers—knowing my thoughts and heart. Surely, he wouldn't let me be harmed.

If Harry thought his homicidal sneer would scare me away, he was mistaken. I said nothing as I donned my poker face. I'd spent my life hiding my true feelings from my parents, and I was rather adept at it. My bluff served me well.

I wished Spencer was there. He's the one person who would know how terrified I was. We had been friends and confidants for so long, he could read me like no one else.

Harry grimaced as if in pain, and then his lips curled slightly. "In reality it wasn't so mysterious--but you don't need to know about that. I'm not allowed to lie to you—but I don't have to tell you everything. Him Who Does His Bidding forbade me to blatantly lie to you like I do with my customers. We are unable to break his rules—a paradox in our little abode."

"I'm not sure I understand. Lying to me caused you pain?" I asked.

He relaxed as the pain subsided. "Can't blame a guy for trying, but Him Who Does His Bidding is stronger and brings excruciating pain in my gut until I tell you the truth. It's like magic. He told me it would be so and, unfortunately for me, he is never wrong. Imagine a life of always telling the truth. What a boring existence he must have. He could never succeed in our business. Lying, cheating, and making a killin'. That's what makes life worth living. Don't you agree?"

His menacing smile turned to a scowl when I didn't respond. I wasn't going to applaud him for such nonsense.

I'd heard from all three inhabitants but hadn't received my coveted clue that Him Who Does His Bidding had promised. I longed to know where my father was, but Harry's surly antics were enough to keep me from asking for anything else. I had discovered more about these three than I wanted to know. My desire to leave was about to overpower my wish for a clue.

As if reading my thoughts, Harry reached into his

pocket and pulled out an envelope with three gray seals on the back. The cat, the fox and the devil, representations of the gargoyles that adorned the front of the home. "This is for you! Here you'll find light. Take it and leave," he barked in his murderous tone. The hairs on my neck stood.

"Uh, thank you for your time and uh, for this. Thank you all," I called to Daniel and George who had retreated to the darkest shadows in a corner of the room. As I started for the door, I heard a maniacal laugh. Soon it was joined by the other two inhabitants laughing with blood-thirsty hysteria. Suddenly the whole room erupted in frenzied shrieks and howls. I darted for the door and let myself out without looking back. I'd had enough of this home and its inhabitants.

I stepped out into gale force winds, but the rain had ceased. I started running against the wind as fast as if I was being chased by a bear. After about a quarter of a mile, I paused to catch my breath. Instantly the wind died.

Mr. Bidding's words boomed in my head. "Inspect each field." Did I need to go back? I'd glanced at Daniel, George, and Harry's field on the way to their home, but hadn't 'inspected' it. I scanned the path I'd run and didn't see any evidence of being followed, so I snaked my way back to the field, staying off the wide-open road.

After arriving, I kept looking over my shoulder. Surely Daniel, George, and Harry wouldn't peek through the curtains or venture outside. I comforted myself knowing how much they loved the dark. They were unlikely to invite any light in.

Only a sliver of grey crop filled the small field. It was repulsive. I reached out and plucked one of the lettuce-like leaves. It crumbled to ash in my hand. How did that sustain them? And how in the world did they sell that produce at the market?

The wind picked up and a powerful gust pushed me toward the road and then to the north end of the island. After the wind subsided, I sprinted the last quarter of a mile to be sure I was safe. Stepping onto the beach, I stopped to open my first clue.

My palms were sweaty. What would I find? Trembling, I broke the seals on the fine gray parchment envelope and pulled out the card inside. Written in red ink or was that . . . ? Of course, it was ink, I convinced myself. In elegant cursive was the clue – "It Began in The Isle of Palms" Okay, what does that mean? And what did Harry say? "Here you'll find light." I sighed. Find light. That could mean a lot of things. John wasn't as messed up as Daniel, George, and Harry. At least he didn't used to be. He was a man with a few controlling vices, but not addicted to evil or darkness. Excitement was more of a drug to him than hatred and violence. John was, by my measure, a far superior human than Daniel, George, or Harry.

What did the clue mean? Where is the Isle of Palms? Was it in the South Pacific? Was he here collecting and trading antique lights? Or was he on an island somewhere else in the tropics with lots of palm trees? No, that didn't make sense. What a weird clue. It was too broad to interpret. With additional clues, I hoped I'd understand more.

The chirp of my phone pulled me from my dream. I hit snooze, hoping to get back to my dream and find answers about the clue. Though I tried, my mind raced, and there would be no additional eight minutes today, so I surrendered to a new day.

Chapter 9

Spencer offered to watch the twins on Saturday, so I could spend more time with my dad. My kind neighbor arrived early while I was filling the twins' backpacks with activities, snacks, and games to take back to Spencer's house. He had a few home improvement projects to work on, and said he'd enlist Jayce and Jazmine if they wanted to help.

"Sorry I'm early," Spence said.

"No problem. Help yourself to coffee while you wait."

Spence poured a cup of coffee while I finished stuffing the backpacks.

"How are my favorite twins today?" Spence called into the dining room where the twins were finishing up breakfast.

"Good. Can't wait to play with Riggs," Jayce said.

"No, I'm going to play with Riggs. I'm older, so I get to play with him first," Jaz said.

"You can both play with him. I have a few games that he loves. We can all play at the same time," Spence said.

"Yay!" both twins yelled.

Last year Spencer had adopted Riggs when the German Shepherd retired from the K-9 Unit. The twins had grown as attached to him as they were to Lucy.

"Jayce and Jazmine, go upstairs and brush your teeth and see if there's anything else you want to take with you today," I said. I hoped to have a few minutes to talk to Spence about the strange envelope and phone call. The kids ran upstairs.

"How are you, Sam?" Spence asked.

"I won't lie, it's been a rough couple of days. Dad's condition has me yearning to find John again. That's crazy, isn't it?

"Not at all. I understand how Tom's health is renewing your interest in finding out what happened to John."

"But Tom has been such an extraordinary father. He's the one who's always been there for me. He was at all my special events—gymnastic competitions, plays, concerts, and he was there when I was crowned homecoming queen."

"Homecoming queen, huh?" Spence smiled. "Of course, with your long wavy red hair, striking green eyes, who wouldn't vote for you?"

My cheeks burned. "Spence, you're incorrigible. As I was saying, Tom was there for all my important activities. He even tried to make every game when I was on the volleyball team."

"Team captain, you mean." Spence took a sip of coffee.

I didn't remember telling him that. Did Mom? She epitomizes the proud mama. Bragging every chance she gets.

"Yes, I was team captain. My therapist suggested that I was an overachiever because I was trying to win John's approval."

"Really? I've always thought you are exceptional at anything you put your mind to, Sam. Seriously." Spence's charming, dimpled smile warmed my heart.

"Thanks, Spence, but my therapist may be on the right track," I said. "Whenever I had a success in life, I was looking over my shoulder to see if John was there. And he rarely was. Crazy, huh?"

"No, Sam. I get it. You wanted him to be proud of you. And I'm sure he was. How could he not be?"

"I've constantly tried to be good enough. Why couldn't Tom's love be sufficient for me? I felt rejected, abandoned, and then my marriage, well, you know how that turned out."

"Yes, I'm sorry, Sam. You know that wasn't your fault.

Logan was the one who spent all his time at work. He didn't pay any attention to his exceptional family at home, and he still doesn't as far as I can tell. Has he caught up on child support yet?"

"No, after he moved to California, he fell even further behind. But the twins still want to see him, so I let them go every other holiday and half of the summer."

"That's generous of you, Sam. He's defaulted on his obligations, so there's legal recourse if you want to take it."

"I don't." I sighed. "He's their father. I don't want them to feel like I did growing up. Although he's missed several important events that he promised to attend just like John had. Did I subconsciously marry a man like John?"

"That's a possibility. I understand it's a common occurrence."

I stared at him. "And you know this how?"

"From my psychological expertise. You know, my Psych 101 class." Spence had a way of lifting the mood in a serious conversation. It was usually appreciated. Occasionally irritating. This time it was appreciated.

"I see," I said. "And what else did guru Psych 101 teach you?" I asked.

"Well, that awareness is the first step to change. So, now you won't make that mistake again, right?"

"I sure hope not. But sometimes what I know is not what I do. For a long time, I kept trying to win back Logan's affection from that bimbo assistant of his, Tammy. I really am sick!"

"No Sam, you were hurt. I get it. You fought for your marriage, but it takes two."

"Thanks, Spence. You're a good friend. Um, I've had a few strange things happen---"

"Hey Mom, do you know where my iPad is?" Jazmine called down as Jayce descended the stairs.

"Look on the bookshelf in the guest room, Jazmine," I yelled back.

"I'm ready to go, Mom," Jayce said as he entered the kitchen. He proudly held up his gym bag bulging at the seams.

"Good job. With everything you packed and everything I put in your backpack, you shouldn't run out of things to keep you busy. Have fun, but make sure you mind Spencer. Whatever he says goes. Got it?"

"Sure, Mom. Say 'hi' to Papa for me."

"Will do, sweetie."

Telling Spencer about the strange envelope and threatening phone call would have to wait for another time. Were the two even related? The envelope didn't appear threatening in any way, so probably not. And was the threatening call even intended for my number? Did the person mean to threaten someone else? Or was it a kid playing a prank?

Chapter 10

I arrived at Seagrove General Hospital early and found Dad sound asleep. I went to the nurses' station to let them know where to find me when he woke, and then settled into a comfortable upholstered chair in the waiting room, hoping Dr. Graham would be by soon. Mom arrived before Dr. Graham just as Dad was waking. She went into his room and spent a few minutes helping with the breathing exercise. After doing as much as he could tolerate, she rejoined me in the waiting room while Dad rested again.

Mom sat next to me. She'd recently started reading a book I'd read several years ago, *One Second After* by William Forstchen. We talked for a few minutes about the book's plot-- an EMP's (electromagnetic pulse) attack in America and how that would affect our lives if it were ever to occur.

"What would you miss most, Mom?"

"Gosh, I don't know. TV? You know how much me and Tom enjoy our shows. Or should I say we used to, until he went into Grand Haven." She fidgeted with her wedding ring. "How about you, Sam?"

"Of course, TV and tablets especially for Jayce and Jazmine's sake. But for me, warm clean water for showers and washing dishes and clothes." My mind jumped to another important part of my life. "And then there's computers and cell phones. I love being able to google any topic and find lots of information in an instant." *Almost any topic, except for John Garcia.*

"Spoken like a true teacher. Let's pray we don't ever have to experience anything like that. The pandemic was bad enough."

"Amen to that," I said.

I shifted my focus back to my laptop, and Mom resumed reading her book. It was an escape from the difficult reality of her own life right now. Mom and I shared the belief that a good book is one of the best distractions when life is challenging.

Over the next several hours, Dad rested, revolted, and rambled. Mom and I took turns checking on him every half hour or so. If he was awake, we made sure he didn't need anything and every hour one of us would help him with breathing exercises. It broke my heart to see him gasping, wheezing, and coughing. I felt helpless and a little lost knowing his days or possibly hours were numbered.

He had spent twenty-nine years being my stepfather. No doubt, he loved me more than my real father. Why couldn't that be enough? Why did I so long for the love of my biological father? Why did I need to know what happened to him?

Finally, at 11:00 a.m., Dr. Graham arrived on the fourth floor.

"Georgia and Samantha, so glad to see you both here this morning." His voice was a bit too cheery.

Before he had a chance to say anymore, I jumped in, "So what are Dad's chances? Please give it to us straight. Is there anything else he can be taking? The nurse said you are treating his fever, but he was still sweating and flushed this morning. Why is that?"

Surprised by my barrage, he calmly responded. "Let me go in and see how he's doing, and I'll be able to tell you more. Stay right here while I check on him."

Yes, of course I'd stay. I'd been there all morning, and I wasn't planning on going anywhere.

After what felt like an hour, but was probably only five or six minutes, Dr. Graham reappeared. His smile was absent, his countenance darkened.

"The antibiotics are not working. I've instructed the nurses to up the dosage and increase the Tylenol for his fever. His temperature is up to a hundred and two point five. We need to keep that under control before it gets any higher and causes other problems," he said flatly.

He looked at my mom and spoke softly, this time with a hint of compassion. "If things don't turn around soon, he won't have much longer."

My heart sank. While I appreciated Dr. Graham's directness and use of lay terms, rather than medical jargon, I had been holding on to a flicker of hope for better news. Mom leaned on my shoulder and began to sob. I wrapped my arms around her and patted her back.

I had to stay strong for her. "It's going to be okay, Mom. Dad's in good hands. You know Dr. Gerald is doing all he can. He'll make sure Dad makes it, right?" I shot a glance at Dr. Graham.

His impartial manner returned. "I'm doing everything I can. I must get on to my other patients." With that, he turned and left.

I wanted to stay in denial--to believe that everything was going to be all right, that Dad would be released from the hospital soon, and have several more years with us. But Dr. Graham's matter-of-fact attitude told me otherwise. He had a way of sheltering his emotions from reality. Mentally Dr. Gerald Graham acknowledged the facts but didn't allow his heart to feel the truth. Compartmentalizing my therapist called it. When Granddad died several years ago, Dr. Graham had shared with Dad his need to stay detached.

Dad had explained it to us. "Decades of doctoring make him appear aloof. Don't be upset with him. In his early years, he empathized with patients and families--weeping with those who wept. But after the first few painful years, he decided to take a step back emotionally when the prognosis was grim. He's naturally tender-hearted and so much sorrow was taking a toll on him."

I wasn't sure what I'd do in similar circumstances. When your life's occupation is to help those who can't always be helped, I'm sure it's overwhelming and depressing. I tried not to judge him knowing I would struggle with such a dilemma.

After calming Mom, I couldn't focus on the lesson plans for the new class I'd be teaching, so I resumed my online hunt for John. As the years have ticked by, more counties and cities have posted their public records. I held onto hope that something new would pop. I focused on areas of the country from which he accepted a lot of assignments when he'd been a traveling nurse.

He loved the rugged snow-capped mountains in the Colorado Springs area and the rolling hills of the Ozark Mountains. Springfield is part of the Ozarks and only a short drive from Table Rock Lake, where he and Mom honeymooned. His all-time favorite place was the quaint, historic coastal town of Portland, Maine, followed by the Florida Keys, especially Key West. And then there was New Orleans. He said the Keys reminded him of New Orleans. Because he enjoyed so many different places, I felt like I was searching for a lost guppy in the ocean.

I spent the afternoon rotating with Mom in and out of Dad's room. They were precious moments, though mostly incoherent that day, leaning over his bedside to catch his fragmented speech when he was awake and then returning to the waiting room to continue my search.

"Mom, Dad keeps rambling about John, but he's not making any sense. Has he said anything to you?" I asked.

"No dear. It must be his fever or Alzheimer's talking. You know how he jumbles timelines and events. Lately he's even come up with things that never happened. Don't pay any heed," Mom said.

"You're probably right, though I feel like he's anxious to tell me something but can't quite put his thoughts into a coherent sentence," I said.

My search for John was futile. I'd found no new leads that panned out. Lots of John Garcia's, but none were my father. His disappearance remained a mystery that day.

I headed home to see the kids. Spence had texted that they were back at my house to feed Lucy.

"Hey Spencer." I greeted my neighbor and hung my keys on the hook inside the front door.

"Hey Samantha, how's your dad?" he asked.

"About the same, but completely disoriented today. When I first got to the hospital, he was lucid but that went downhill fast."

"I'm sorry, Sam. Is there anything I can do?" Spencer asked and took a step toward me.

"No, but thanks, Spence. Where are Jaz and Jayce?" I asked.

"Upstairs working on school projects. Do you want me to call them down for you?" Spencer asked as he followed me into the kitchen.

"No, that's okay. I need to catch my breath. I haven't done much today, but Dad's condition is taking a toll. I'm exhausted. I'll make tacos and then head back to the hospital. I can take the twins with me. Interested in staying for dinner?" I sat down at the kitchen table.

"You look beat, Sam. How about I fix tacos for you all? You go into the living room, put your feet up, and relax. Watch TV, look at Facebook, play a game on your phone, or do absolutely nothing. And then I can watch the twins after dinner. I know the drill, Sam. That is if it's okay with you."

"That sounds divine. But, Spencer, you don't have to do that. And it's not your kitchen—I'd need to show you where everything is." I objected, but hoped he'd fight me on this one. I was spent emotionally.

"I want to, Sam. I know how hard this has been for you.

I'll find my way around your kitchen just fine. Vegetables in the bin or refrigerator. Meat in the fridge or freezer. Taco seasoning in the cupboard or pantry. Frying pan hanging on the rack. Last, but not least, water . . . Hmm. Possibly from the tap? Right?"

"Alright, you win. I'll spend a few minutes with my feet up and my eyes closed. Thanks Spence. You're a dear."

After a welcome break doing absolutely nothing, I heard Spence setting the table, so I went into the kitchen. "Hey, thanks for taking over for me. You really are too good to me."

"Not at all. What are friends for if we can't be there in tough times?" he said.

"I hope I can repay you somehow," I said.

"Not necessary and you already have. Remember all you did for me when my sister had that car accident?"

"Watering a few plants and walking Riggs is hardly comparable to all you're doing for us. And it was spring break, so I had plenty of extra time."

"But you offered to do more if I needed it. I want to be here for you, Sam, so don't worry. I'll ask for help when I need it. Deal?"

"Deal."

During dinner, I updated everyone about Papa's condition. I didn't want to talk about it, but they needed to know. I hated that he was suffering, and there was nothing I could do. I wanted to wake up from this nightmare.

Chapter 11

Arriving at Seagrove Hospital, I stopped at the nurses' station for an update. They said Mom was downstairs in the cafeteria having dinner and Dad had been sleeping for at least ninety minutes even through the last hourly vitals check.

As I approached his bed, I heard his shallow raspy breathing. Should I wake him for his breathing exercises? No, rest is what he needed, so I curled up in the oversized pleather chair by the bed and was soon dozing.

Dream: Mr. Bidding

My dream on Harvest Island continued as if no time had lapsed. I stood in the brilliant sun captivated by the swaying palm trees and glistening water. The sound of waves crashing on the shore was only interrupted by the occasional squawking of a sea gull overhead. A gentle breeze blew my hair away from my face and the sun warmed my skin.

After a few splendidly relaxing moments, I sat down, absorbing the warmth of the sand and contemplated my visit with Daniel, George, and Harry. They were terrible housemates, the worst of the worst. And what did that clue mean? I had no idea.

"Don't give up, Samantha!" Him Who Does His Bidding was standing above me.

"Where did you come from?" I asked as I stumbled to my feet.

"From I Am, of course!" He chuckled.

"Okay. Where is I Am?" I asked.

"I Am is everywhere. He is The Maker."

"Well, that explains that." I laughed knowing my sarcasm was evident.

"In due time, Samantha, in due time. All will be clear. Tell me what you learned from the owners of the gray field," he said.

"What I really want to know is what does 'It began on the Isle of Palms' mean?"

"I'm sorry, Samantha, but I'm not at liberty to discuss that with you. But I can talk to you about your visit. Anything in particular stand out?" His voice was gentle.

"Okay. I get it. Rules are rules. Let me see. What did I learn? Primarily that I don't ever want to go back," I said.

"I would imagine as much. What else?"

"That you should never drink their water. It was filthy, blah," I wrinkled my nose and stuck my tongue out, but my smart-aleck remark didn't faze Mr. Bidding.

"Of course, dear, anything else?"

I started silently counting the palm trees in front of us. Ten. Nice even number. Mr. Bidding waited patiently. I must have learned something useful. My mind went back to that bizarre visit. I shifted my weight back and forth in the sand. One, two, three, four.

"Hmm. They were a strange bunch, to say the least. Daniel, George, and Harry like living in the darkness with haunted furnishings. They thrive on conflict, each with their own agenda."

"Excellent, and what is their agenda?" he quizzed.

Was this a test? I've always loved school, so I didn't mind the challenge.

After reflecting for a minute, I answered. "For Daniel, the objective is to stay in the dark at any cost. He avoids the light like it would kill him. George's goal is to be completely independent from any authority, human or otherwise. And

Harry scared me--he appeared to be a murderous sociopath. He thrives on bucking the system and taking advantage of people to feel powerful."

I added my observation of their emotional state, though unsolicited. "Daniel appeared sad and confused, George defensively carefree, and Harry dangerously angry."

"Yes, yes, very good," Him Who Does His Bidding said. "Your insight is on the mark. Daniel, George, and Harry love living in the dark because it's what they're used to, what they consider normal and acceptable. Daniel has never known anything else, and you're right, he's terrified of the light. George likes the darkness because he can change the rules as often as it suits him, and without light, Harry's evil deeds can be hidden, or so he believes. They're all comfortable where they are."

"But they can't actually enjoy living in the dark, can they?" I inquired.

"It's all they know. The very thing they cling to is what is keeping them from their ultimate desire," he said. "They won't turn unless The Maker's Mighty Wind infiltrates their defenses, but as of today, they've resisted. The Wind wafts into the darkness to change their hearts. It woos, it beckons, it invites. The Maker waits. Patiently, He waits. The Wind blows harder on occasion. The offer stands. Yet, The Maker allows free will, so those that come into the light do so because they choose to, not because they are forced to. When they admit that The Maker's light is indeed far superior to their darkness, they can relinquish the darkness. But pride often prohibits . . ."

"Sam. Sam. Wake up, dear"

I heard her words but couldn't quite surface.

"Sam, you need to wake up, honey," Georgia prodded.

"Oh, hey, Mom. I must have fallen asleep." I stretched my arms above my head and tried to focus my eyes. Dad's hospital room. The big red recliner.

"How long have I been asleep?"

"A few hours, I didn't have the heart to wake you, but you were in such an awkward position the last half hour, I figured you may end up with a stiff neck if I didn't intervene."

"Thanks, Mom. Still taking care of me at my age. I'm going to get coffee and try to wake up. Do you want anything?" I asked.

"No, dear, I got back from the cafeteria a while ago. They have yummy desserts if you're not hungry enough for a meal," she said with a twinkle in her eye.

"Sounds good," I said. Mom knew I had a sweet tooth, even if I wasn't hungry. There was always room for freshly baked goodies.

"Go to the elevator down on the right. Take it to the first floor and then it's kind of like a maze to get there. A right, two lefts, another right . . . uh, or was that two rights, a left and a right? Oh, never mind. Follow the signs when you get to the first floor, honey."

"Thanks, Mom. Will do."

I took the elevator to the first floor and followed the signs toward the hospital cafeteria. The floor contained a row of white tiles flanked by beige ones. As I proceeded along the beige tiles, I counted. If someone was blocking my way, I'd pause and look at my phone pretending I got a text. I didn't want to lose track. If the tiles ended on an odd number, I'd count a step back and then forward, so I'd end that row on an even number. Then I'd turned down the next hall and start counting again. I did glance around to be sure no one was watching me. As long as I was aware that I was doing something crazy, did that mean I wasn't crazy? What's wrong with me?

Chapter 12

Over the next week in the hospital, Dad started regaining his strength. I spent hours each day visiting him, doing what I could to keep him from relapsing. Mom and Uncle Charlie helped keep a watchful eye on him too.

Despite the phone warning I'd received, searching for John became a primary pastime while Dad was sleeping.

I heard the familiar ding of a new email. It was from the ancestry company, Origins DNA, where I had submitted my saliva a few weeks prior. I reasoned that if I found relatives of John that I didn't know about, that could lead to finding him. Or if he had another family, I might find a half-brother or sister of whom I wasn't aware. They would surely know where he is or what happened to him.

The email contained interesting results. No real surprises--primarily Spanish and French descent, 41 and 39 percent respectively, with 20 percent German heritage. The list of DNA matches contained over 500 blood relatives, and that was just from their site. It was hard to comprehend that I had so many living blood relatives.

I recognized two names, my first cousin, Mary Botello, and her son, Julian. Mary was the daughter of Charlie, mom's brother. So, this DNA stuff actually works. I'd heard the stories of long-lost relatives and adopted children finding their families through DNA searches, even crimes being solved through familial DNA matches, but hadn't been completely convinced. I guess I'm a skeptic at heart.

Seeing Mary and Julian's names on the list gave me renewed hope that DNA might help me find John. If not today, then when more people were tested and added to the database. Other than Mary and Julian, the matches were all listed as 2nd through 6th cousins. But no first or last names that I recognized.

I searched Facebook for four of the names on the list with the most centimorgans in common and who lived the closest to the town in Mississippi where John was born, North Haven. Not all matches had posted their location, so I skipped those. John and his family had lived all over, but most of his aunts and uncles, cousins, and grandparents had lived within fifty miles of North Haven for decades.

I sent them private messages on Facebook, providing my phone number, and asked if they would call me to see if we could figure out how we were related. I didn't mention John. I would bring that up on the phone if they were his blood relatives. I also sent those four people messages through the Origins DNA system but wasn't sure how that worked. It would be a waiting game.

If those four names didn't prove productive, I'd keep moving down the list, four at a time. I'd wait for four more days, and then move to the next group. Surely someone related to him knew something I didn't. I could only hope.

Chapter 13

Two nights went by without another dream. The clue still had me baffled. I was stalled in my search for John and hoping for more clues. Were my silly dreams from an overactive imagination, or did they mean something? My dreams about Harvest Island were unlike any I'd ever had—they felt so real, and their memory didn't fade. It was as if I was recalling events that really happened--every detail crystal clear.

I only heard back from one of my distant relatives, and we quickly discovered we were related through Great Aunt Eloise, my mom's aunt. Eloise had twelve children, so it made sense that there would be a large contingency of blood relations through that branch of the tree. She was a second cousin or is it second cousin once removed? Either way, it was a dead end to finding John. At least I found a new distant cousin to connect with. She seemed nice. I promised to visit next time I was in the area.

I sent out four more inquiries, hoping for better results.

I was trying to be strong for Mom, and Mom was trying to stay strong for Dad. But we were both beginning to crumble. Though Dad regained some physical strength, he was slipping further from us mentally. I started to lose hope.

Mom and I sat in the hospital waiting room, so we didn't disturb Dad's sleep. I tried to distract Mom by updating her on my search for John. My motive wasn't completely altruistic. I secretly hoped she'd be able to help. I knew John wasn't an exciting topic for her, but years had passed since they split, and her relationship with Dad had brought a tremendous amount of healing. He loved her selflessly. Consequently, her wounds from John left only faded scars—at least that's the way it appeared, and what I'd always hoped for her.

New wounds of a different kind were being created and taking their toll as Dad slipped further and further from us. The pain was raw, and deep. Worry had aged Mom. New lines etched her brow and bags formed under her bloodshot hazel eyes.

"Mom, I've been hitting a lot of dead ends in my search for John. I told you I was hopeful, but I've been striking out," I said.

"That's too bad, dear. I don't know what happened to him. But the past is best left there, dear. If he's alive, I'm sure he's fine," she said unconvincingly.

I assumed she was trying to comfort me. But it didn't work. "Really? Even after that ghastly disappearance from his apartment?"

"You know he was never found, so we can only assume he's gone or didn't want to be found, right? Remember the story John told us about the man from Springfield who staged his disappearance to look like he was abducted or killed when someone robbed his business? Then he traveled several hundred miles away to be with his girlfriend who knew nothing about his family in Springfield. When he was found, he said he had amnesia. Some labeled it psychogenic fugue. But many people thought he was faking it because he'd been in a relationship with the other woman for months. I've wondered a time or two if your father needed to disappear for some reason and borrowed a page from that man's playbook."

"What an awful thing to do. John wasn't that callous. Was he?"

"I don't know what to think. But if he wanted a fresh

start or was in trouble, who knows?"

"Okay, let's assume he's alive and well. The internet has a lot of public information, and more is added every day. Why haven't I found any link to John since his work at the medical prison in Springfield?"

"I wish I knew the answer to that, sweetie. I remember he sent postcards from Springfield. Couldn't you start inquiring at his last address? Someone there may know what was going on in his life."

"He'd sent postcards from there on previous assignments, but even though he promised, I never received a postcard that last time," I said.

"Oh, I'd forgotten that. It's been a long time since you and Kyle were searching for him, dear."

"So, he's never made contact with you since then?" My gut was telling me she knew more.

"No, dear, I'm certain. You know I would have told you if he contacted me." She didn't make eye contact.

"Is there anything at all that could help, anything else you might know?" I asked.

"All I know, Samantha, is that Springfield was one of his favorite places to work. It is close to Branson and beautiful Table Rock Lake. He loved boating and the rolling hills with rock cliffs surrounding the lake. So gorgeous. Did I tell you John and I spent part of our honeymoon in Branson?" she asked. Changing the subject wasn't going to deter me.

"Yes, once or a hundred times." I was glad she had some pleasant memories with John. "But that doesn't help me find him."

"We didn't hear from him after that last phone call to you," she said matter-of-factly, glancing at me and then quickly looking away.

We? Why did she say we…am I being paranoid? Did she and Dad know something they are keeping from me and Kyle? Or did she mean "we" the family.

I said, "I've had strange dreams lately."

"Oh really, do tell," she said and leaned toward me.

I proceeded to explain the dreams, ending with the clue I'd been given. "It Began in The Isle of Palms."

Mom put her hand over her mouth and then sat back in her chair.

"Does that mean anything to you?" I asked.

"Well . . . not . . . really . . ."

She was choosing her words carefully. Stalling?

"Um . . . Your father and I visited The Isle of Palms the first time when he was on leave. Then we went back after he got out of the navy. He had an assignment or two near there. You know I used to travel with him early on. The Isle of Palms is a barrier island near Charleston. Haven't you heard of it?"

"No, actually I haven't," I said.

"It's a small town. On weekends John and I visited art galleries in the area. Afterwards, weather permitting, we'd go out to the Isle of Palms pier and enjoy the evening breeze and waves crashing on the shore. It was captivating being out over the water." She sighed.

"Wow, Mom, I've never heard you talk about that before," I said.

"It was before you kids came along. Things changed then." She shifted in the waiting room chair.

"I guess you couldn't travel much with him after that," I said.

"Yes, that's right, dear . . ." Tears filled her eyes.

"Oh, Mom. I didn't mean to make you cry." Now I'd done it. I knew Mom cried easily. Why did I end up ruining the conversation by bringing up John and painful memories. My mind started to spin. Was John here in South Carolina? Or did the clue refer to another island filled with palm trees? How could I possibly know or figure this out?

Mom dabbed her eyes and said, "We did have some nice times, Samantha. I may have pictures of the pier in my old photo boxes. I'll have to dig those out of the attic. It was a beautiful place with palm trees and sunrises over the ocean. Delightful! I know I still have them. Pictures are one thing I never throw out. It's just a matter of finding them. They are probably in the attic, which is cluttered with decades of junk, but I'll try."

"Oh, Mom, please do. And if you could locate John's social security number too, I'd appreciate it." I hoped that I had discovered the possible meaning of the first clue. But I was still not any closer to finding John.

"As far as his social security number goes, I came across that a few weeks ago when I was cleaning out old paperwork. I thought I'd thrown out most things related to John when we moved to the house. Let me see. I think I put it in my pocketbook, though I'm not sure what good it will do you." Mom rummaged through her handbag.

One by one she pulled out items and set them on the end table next to her chair. A small pack of tissues, cough drops, a nail file, tweezers, makeup, coupons, her wallet, an assortment of hair accessories, a small first aid kit, a small roll of duct tape, keys, change, and several index cards with notes mixed in with everything.

"Looks like you're prepared for that EMP we talked about," I said. "Not that my handbag is much different."

"You learned from the best. You never know what you'll need. Ah, here it is," she said triumphantly.

She handed me an index card with John's social security number on it. I'd have Spencer see what he could find.

"Thanks, Mom. You're the best. Do you think John is out there, still alive? Could my dreams contain real clues?" My questions tumbled out, my mind racing.

"I doubt it, honey. Your dreams are probably a product of your fantastic imagination. You've always had a gift for creating intriguing stories. Please don't get your hopes up based on a silly dream." She looked back down at her book.

Mom was probably right. She was trying to protect me

from getting my hopes dashed again. Over the years Mom and I had our differences, but I always knew she loved and wanted me. Unfortunately, that didn't balance the sting of John's half-hearted attempt at being there for me and Kyle, and his eventual disappearance. Did John figure he was off the hook because another man had taken over his responsibilities? Is it possible he faked the bloody scene on my twenty-first birthday? What an awful day to pull a stunt like that.

Mom and I alternated evenings with Dad. On the nights I stayed with Dad, she offered to watch the twins. It was a nice change for her. The twins were more than happy to engage Nana in board or card games. They knew Nana didn't play any of their video games.

The evenings at the hospital were quiet, too quiet. My mind often wandered to John. The gnawing feelings of abandonment drove my search on.

Chapter 14

Dream: Phillip Phony, Fred Fatalist, and Paul Passive

As I stood in front of the structure, I was captivated by its beauty. Three tiers of marble stairs, eight stately columns, and ornate carvings in the gable. It appeared to be a reproduction of the Parthenon.

Unfortunately, I hadn't seen the actual Parthenon when I travelled to Greece. Torrential rains and 110 kilometer winds hit the day my visit was scheduled, so the tour had been cancelled. But I'd seen a full-size replica in Centennial Park in Nashville, and this looked similar. The Parthenon in Nashville held an art gallery with spectacular paintings and a huge statue of a gold-gilded Athena, the Greek goddess of wisdom and warfare. An artistic and architectural treat, the Nashville Parthenon was the highlight of that trip.

A presence appeared next to me.

"Hello, Samantha!" Mr. Bidding greeted me cheerily.

"Hello, Mr. Bidding. I'm glad to finally be back to get more clues."

"Of course. We shall proceed without further delay."

"I've been researching the first clue. The Isle of Palms, South Carolina, has medical facilities nearby that may have hired John. Is there anything else you can tell me?"

"No. You must make the discoveries yourself, Sam. Trust me, in good time, Sam, all will be clear. Things are not always as they appear."

"So, you're a poet now?" I asked and chuckled.

"Unintentional, I assure you, Sam. Today you must visit the home of Phillip Phony, Fred Fatalist, and Paul Passive. Phillip owns the home. Fred and Paul, half-brothers, rent from him. They dwell in this lovely structure in front of you. Though you will be a little disappointed at the interior, but we'll discuss that later."

"Alright, I'm ready. Wish me luck!"

"Godspeed!" Mr. Bidding responded, and then he was gone.

I jumped. His sudden appearances and departures were hard to get used to. I turned toward the Parthenon-like structure and made my way up the marble path that extended from the cobblestone street. Over the far-left pillar was a monkey gargoyle, a playful looking fellow, almost cute if it weren't for the funky bat wings arched on its back. Over the far-right pillar was another monkey gargoyle, wings at its side, eyes closed, and lying on its back as if it were sleeping.

Over the two center pillars at the peak of the gable was a dragon gargoyle, fire flaming from its mouth. Wings much larger than the monkeys' extended from its shoulder blades as if it were trying to escape the edifice. Its face was twisted, and it looked . . . evil. A chill ran down my spine. The appeal of the architecture waned at the sight of this creature. I shook it off. No need to start my visit on a negative note.

I ascended the stairs leading to the portico. One, two, three, four, five. Back down one, and up. Six. Then six steps across the first platform to more stairs. I continued the pattern on the second and third set of stairs. Then ten steps across the third and largest platform. And finally, the last set of steps. Up one, two, three, four. A nice even number.

I stood before two massive bronze doors approximately twenty-five-feet tall and together about twelve-feet wide. Two smaller sets of bronze doors were on either side near the corners of the building. I didn't remember seeing the smaller doors or the gargoyles, for that matter, on the

Nashville replica. A door knocker with the same repulsive dragon greeted me as I approached the entrance. The twisted face became more contorted the closer I got. I refused to be dissuaded.

Steadying myself, I lifted the circular ring and let it drop onto the bronze door. The sound echoed inside as I imagined it would. The Parthenon replica was a glorious edifice, and I was thrilled to have the opportunity to see it again, even if only another reproduction.

A tall thin man about my age answered the door. "Can I help you?"

"Yes, I'm Samantha. Him Who Does His Bidding sent me," I said.

"Come in, Samantha. I'm Phillip Phony. We've been waiting for you."

Mr. Phony wore a white, flowing robe and a red and white kaffiyeh on his head. The turban was wrapped from an elegant woven scarf with the tail hanging to one side. His light brown skin and dark eyes were striking. Only a smidgeon of his dark hair was visible, and his beard and mustache were full, but neatly trimmed.

I stepped inside. Mr. Bidding was right. No fifty-foot ceilings. The home on the inside appeared to be upper-class, but conventional. Hallways extended to the left, right and center. Inside the entrance, the ceiling extended above the tall door for about fifteen feet in and then dropped sharply to about ten feet. No gleaming statue of Athena. No magnificent columns, though I hadn't seen the entire home. Yes, I was disappointed.

I quickly regained my bearings, reminding myself that I was not there to look at architecture or art. I was there to receive a clue and ultimately find John. "Focus," I told myself.

"Right this way," Phillip led me down the long center hallway. I glanced into each room as I followed.

On the left was a music room. A stunning white marble

grand piano was the central feature with several other instruments displayed on either side. On the right was a substantial library with a carved marble mantle fireplace that matched the exterior of the home and the grand piano. Next was an art studio on the right, with phenomenal impressionist style paintings of various sizes covering the walls and a blank canvas on the easel.

Paul stepped into the room across from the art studio. It was an elegant dining area. A large crystal chandelier hung over a long white marble, ball and claw foot pedestal table with fourteen matching high-back chairs. The chairs were upholstered with white leather, accented with brass nail heads bordering both sides of the back. This home and its furnishings indicated significant wealth.

Paul took his place at the head of the table with an air of sophistication. Seated on his left was a gaunt Asian man approximately twenty-five years old. As I approached, he stood. "Hi! I'm Fred Fatalist, and this is my younger half-brother, Paul Passive." He gestured toward the seat across from him.

Paul also looked Asian but was a substantial amount heavier than Fred.

Paul stood and bowed slightly, "Hello! So nice to meet you."

"Nice to meet you both," I responded glancing at the five empty chairs on either side of the table between me and them.

"Shall we get this over with?" Phillip asked as he waved his hand toward all the empty seats, suggesting I sit down—but nowhere in particular.

I planted myself next to Paul. I didn't want to invade their space, but certainly didn't want to awkwardly sit at the far end of that massive table.

After small talk about the fickle weather on the island, we moved on to their occupations. "What do you do for work, Phillip?"

"Glad you asked, Samantha. I've been the mayor of Harvest Island for twelve years. Before that I owned a shoe store. I'm one of the few to own a business on the island, and I do enjoy politics. All that hand shaking and baby kissing."

"That's interesting, Phillip. How about you, Fred?"

Phillip huffed. Was he upset that I had turned my attention away from him?

Fred ignored Phillip's displeasure and answered me. "I'm following in my dad's footsteps. He was the head honcho at the plant that shut down. I'm working in a similar factory, so I'm pretty sure I'll be plant foreman one day. It's my destiny. For now, I work on the assembly line making widgets."

"Ah, and do you enjoy your work?" I asked.

"No, not particularly, but what will be will be." He hung his head.

I hesitated, and then pressed the issue. "Have you ever tried to get another job?"

Fred gasped. "What? No, of course not. You can't fight fate."

"Of course. I didn't mean to pry. Paul, what do you do for work?"

"I started as a bus boy, then moved up to host and then kitchen help, and now I'm a waiter. Just following the path before me," Paul said.

Phillip rolled his eyes.

I was curious, so I dared to ask the same question. "And do you like your work, Paul?"

"Yeah, it's not bad. The tips are nice. I was offered an assistant manager's job, but I turned it down. It would be too much for me." Paul didn't offer any more explanation.

"Right. Management isn't for everyone," I said. Did he want to stay a waiter for the rest of his life?

"Phillip, what things have you done as mayor?"

He sat up straight and adjusted his kaffiyeh. "For starters, I lead all the big events. Introduce guests and that sort of thing. I'm a real people person. You know, I'm the face of this town. I love everyone on the island, especially Paul and Fred, and everyone loves me. I've implemented numerous changes for the betterment of my Harvest Island constituents."

"Ah, so what kinds of things have you done?" I asked.

"There are countless accomplishments. I stream a live weekly podcast about things that benefit the residents, help them financially, and promote social justice. You know that sort of thing."

"That's interesting, please tell me more about programs you've implemented."

"Well, uh, um . . . you know these folks on the island slow down a lot of my plans for improvement, but I keep pushing forward. They don't know what is good for them and stand in the way of real progress." His face twisted with contempt.

"I see." I said, but I didn't. There didn't appear to be any substance to this politician. I turned to questions about his hobbies, hoping his passions would help me dial in on who he was.

"Your home is magnificent, Phillip. I'm sure you enjoy playing that spectacular grand piano in the music room. Is it marble?" I asked.

"I don't play, and it's faux marble like the marble you see in the rest of my home," he said.

"Oh, then do you play the cello, violin, or one of the other instruments I saw?"

"No."

"Uh . . . oh . . . uh . . . you have a stellar art studio. The artwork is gorgeous. Do you spend much time painting?"

"No. None at all." He shifted uncomfortably and his face turned crimson.

I was striking out. "You must enjoy reading, right? Thousands of books lined the shelves in your library."

Phillip glared at me and took a deep breath. "No, but

please don't spread that outside these walls. I want people to believe I'm cultured and talented. I buy lesser-known paintings, and then frame and mat them over the signature. Visitors assume I painted them, and I don't enlighten them. If they ask me to play my instruments, I tell them I can't because I've sprained my wrist or some such excuse. But I can't lie to you, or I'll face the consequences. I'm sure Him Who Does His Bidding told you about the rules we must follow while speaking with you. If I lie, I suffer."

"Um . . . your next-door neighbors told me about that rule." I didn't know what else to say.

After an awkward moment of silence, I turned to Fred. I wasn't sure what I was looking for, so I threw out an open-ended question.

"Tell me more about yourself, Fred."

"Oh, not a lot to tell," he said and stared at the ceiling like he was trying to find the right words.

Maybe he didn't want to be exposed, like Phillip had been, so I didn't press.

He continued slowly, "My parents are from Singapore. My father passed when I was a baby. Mom remarried a year later, and then she and my stepdad moved to Tahiti when I was three. Paul was born shortly after we arrived in Tahiti."

If John had passed when I was a baby, would I feel better about myself? I thought I would.

Fred continued, "When the factory where I worked shut down, I moved in here with Paul. I've lived on Harvest Island for thirteen months now. Paul and I get along . . . like brothers," he said and then laughed at his own joke.

I politely laughed.

"I knew it was meant to be when Paul told me the former renter had moved out the week before. And then amazingly, a new factory opened on the big island. I was sure I'd get a job because of my previous experience. They hired me on the spot. Now I'm an assistant supervisor, and I'm only twenty-seven. Not bad, eh?"

"Wow. Congratulations!"

"Thanks. I believe I was meant to come to Harvest Island to live here with Paul and Phillip. I take the ferry across to the big island five days a week. The job pays my bills."

"I'm glad you enjoy living with Paul and Phillip. It certainly makes life easier," I said.

"Of course, life hasn't always been easy for me. As an early graduation gift, my stepdad gave me a fully restored 1969 garnet red Camaro convertible with a white stripe down the side and a white top . . . sweet ride. That car could move. But it was more than I could handle when I was driving drunk at seventeen. I suppose any car would have been more than I'd be able to manage in that shape. I hit another car . . . and totaled mine."

"Oh no. Were you hurt?" I asked.

"No, but the driver in the other car, Wally Works, suffered a broken back, and it took several years for him to recover. He still walks with a limp. But what will be, will be. He's leading a campaign against drunk driving now and does fund raising for a lot of charities including his own, Stop Drunk Driving. I know it was meant to be because he would never be doing all that charity work if I hadn't been driving drunk that day. I believe if something is meant to happen, it will. The universe will make sure of it," Fred said.

"Um . . . sure, that's one way to look at it," I said.

I was astonished at Fred's nonchalance toward his accident and the pain and suffering he'd caused Wally. It was a ridiculous excuse for irresponsibility, and I didn't want to hear any more.

Trying to calm myself, I turned to Paul, "Please tell me more about yourself."

"Fred told you about my birth in Tahiti. I've lived an average life. I had a happy childhood, with one older half-brother, Fred, of course. We're compatible housemates. He always stays calm, no matter what, because he believes that everything happens as it should. There's no reason for emotional upset."

"I see how that could be a good trait," I said.

"It is. That concept is also the foundation for my faith. But rather than an impersonal fate as Fred believes, I believe that The Maker is in control. He directs everything that happens in this world and the other one."

"What other one?" I asked.

"The spiritual world, of course!" Paul said.

"Oh, hmm. So, The Maker is in control of the spiritual world. Interesting."

"My philosophy is that we don't have to worry about anything. We don't have to do anything. The Maker is in control. He does it all. It makes life a lot easier," Paul said.

"That would, but how do you know that's true?"

"When I was young, my dad regularly read *The Book of Truth* to me. It tells the story of The Maker's creation. He has created everything on earth and in heaven. That's why we call him The Maker. He is all powerful, all knowing, and all present, so I'm not responsible for what happens. He is."

"That does sound appealing," I said. But did his logic make sense?

"Yes, I know my life is in His hands, so I take whatever comes my way," Paul cleared his throat. "When I was sixteen my next-door neighbor got a job at the local Italian restaurant, Angelo's, and told me they were looking for a busboy, so I applied, was hired, and have worked there ever since. They promoted me to waiter and give me raises every year."

"Earlier you said you didn't take the assistant manager's position they offered you. Why was that?"

"It would have required a lot of effort on my part to accept the position. I'd have to go to Angelo's corporate headquarters in Australia and train for eight weeks. Then I'd be on probation for three months until I proved myself. It was too much work and too much risk. If I wasn't successful,

I'd be without a job. I figured if The Maker wanted me to have that job, my company would provide on-the-job training with no probation. So, the job must not have been what The Maker had planned for me. It's not what I was created for."

"I see." I didn't want to be rude and say what I was thinking.

"I believe if it is The Maker's will everything falls into place easily," Paul replied matter-of-factly.

Paul appeared to be sweet and quite religious. His philosophy of life sounded lazy, but I genuinely liked him. Who was I to judge? I certainly didn't have time to figure out a creed to follow.

"How about your social life? Do you have a girlfriend?" The romantic in me couldn't resist asking the question. Spencer would have cringed at my question if he'd been there.

"I would love to be married and have a family of my own one day. It's what most men dream of, right? Having offspring to carry on the family name. Having a wonderful woman to grow old with. Having that loving companion and best friend at your side." Paul's eyes misted over, and then he continued, "But I know that when The Maker is ready for me to have a family, He'll bring one my way. I don't have to worry about that. I trust Him."

"I see. Is there anything else you can tell me about yourself?" I asked, hoping the interview would be over soon.

"That's pretty much my life. I'm content."

Paul's positive words were incongruous with his sad tone. He longed for a family but didn't pursue one. I chose to pry no further.

Glancing around the table, I was grateful that these three were not as frightening as Harry Hardhearted had been, but I felt sad. It seemed that life could be so much more for all of them, but they were stuck in their peculiar patterns. Looking at someone else and seeing their blind spots was a breeze for me. Looking at my own was daunting.

"Do you have something for me?" I asked. "I do appreciate your time and candor. Your stories were informative."

Phillip reached into his jacket pocket and pulled out an envelope about the size of the one I'd received from Harry. On the back were three seals similar to the gargoyles I'd seen as I entered. One fire-breathing dragon and two monkeys, one playing, one resting.

"Thank you," I clutched the new clue as if it were a million dollars.

"Come," Phillip instructed as he rose and gestured toward the back exit out of the dining room. Paul and Fred stayed seated.

"Oh, okay, goodbye, lovely meeting you." I rose and waved to Paul and Fred.

They nodded in return. I followed Phillip down the hall. We stepped into the back yard to the sound of power tools. "I am adding another wing to the home. There's never enough room for everything," Phillip said.

Odd. He didn't use most of the rooms, and yet wanted more to make additional false impressions. On the outside of the new extension were pillars, like the ones on the front facade. As we walked by, I reached out to touch one of them. I expected cold marble but instead felt warm plastic, the faux marble Phillip had mentioned.

Phillip turned to the back field of sapphire blue. "Here's our pride and joy," he said.

"It's gorgeous!" I was genuinely impressed with the bright sapphire blue crops.

As we strolled through the field, I discovered that from a distance the plants appeared real, but they were not. More false impressions. I reached out and touched one of them. They were, if I were to guess, blue silk with a reflective coating.

Suddenly I was at the north end of the island. How did

that happen? Then as quickly as I'd been transported, Mr. Bidding appeared in front of me. He was quite an impressive sight. I had been previously so preoccupied with his words, that I hadn't fully grasped his appearance. If I had to describe him in one word, it would be "radiant." His entire being exuded light. The second-best word would have to be "enormous." He was at least seven feet tall. His chiseled features reminded me of a young Arnold Schwarzenegger. Though he never claimed it, I assumed he was an angel. My guardian angel? Or are they only assigned to children?

"How was your meeting?" he asked, interrupting my stare.

"Productive, I hope. I'm anxious to open my next clue."

"Feel free, Samantha, but I'm not at liberty to comment."

"Perfect, an angel with 'no comment.' I guess I'll wait.'"

"As you please." Mr. Bidding was unfazed by my sarcasm. "Tell me what you learned about Phillip Phony, Fred Fatalist, and Paul Passive."

I had been preparing answers while I visited Phillip's home based on the previous conversation I had with Mr. Bidding about Daniel, George, and Harry. "I learned that Phillip is not as he desires to appear. From his home to his work and hobbies, and even how he treats other people. Everything about him is phony—his name fits. He wants to appear a successful, wealthy, proactive politician, and he wants people to believe he's a caring person, but it's all on the surface."

"Anything else?"

"Yes, as I watched the three residents' non-verbal cues, Phillip's words and affect were not consistent. He raved about those who shared his abode but scowled or rolled his eyes when they spoke."

Mr. Bidding nodded and added, "Indeed, Samantha. Prestige and power are most important to him. He fakes his way through life, focusing on the wrong things. Some are fooled, but many are not."

"That's so sad," I said and wondering if there was any personal resemblance.

"Now, tell me about Fred Fatalist," Mr. Bidding said.

"My first impression was that he was way too skinny, but he's a personable kid. I know a twenty-something isn't exactly a kid. But the older I get, the younger everyone else seems." I brushed back the hair the ocean breeze had blown into my eyes. "It seemed as if Fred is flying on autopilot, and he's left the cockpit. Attributing his drunk-driving accident to fate sounded psychotic. He has convinced himself that it was meant to be. How absurd is that?"

"Indeed," Mr. Bidding responded. "Fred takes no responsibility for his own choices. One's decisions become the building blocks of their life. Fate does not. Of course, there are things outside of one's control. Events may be due to Fred's actions, other people's actions, or The Thief's doing, but he believes whatever happens, it was meant to be. Fate's work."

"The Thief? Not to get off topic, but who is The Thief?" I asked.

"He is also known as Lucifer. He is The Deceiver, The Father of Lies, and the Ancient Serpent. He has several names, but one primary purpose on Earth. He wants to create trouble for mankind--to kill, steal and destroy."

"He doesn't sound like anyone I'd like to meet," I said.

"No, but he'll come to you when you least expect it, Samantha, so be on your guard. And tell me, what did you observe about Paul Passive?"

The thought of The Thief paying me a visit was unsettling. I failed to respond to Mr. Biddings question.

"Samantha?" Mr. Bidding prodded.

"Oh, um, Paul was more to my liking than Phillip and Fred. He seemed forlorn, even though he claimed to be content. He'd like to have a family, yet he waits at home for

The Maker to send the love of his life to him. I can see how that would take the pressure off Paul, but it certainly doesn't seem to bring any real happiness or quality of life. Not that I'm one to talk about romantic relationships," I said.

A big wave crashed on the shore, and I felt the salty spray on my legs. I looked down and saw I was wearing my favorite capris and sandals. The tide was coming in.

"Let's move toward the road, unless of course, you'd like to get wet," Mr. Bidding said.

"No, not today." I followed Mr. Bidding far enough away that we wouldn't be in the ocean's line of fire.

Mr. Bidding continued our conversation. "Paul is afraid of failure and therefore, takes no risks. If he doesn't try, he can't fail. He's convinced himself he is only a puppet in the Maker's play, not an active participant making his own choices."

"He did seem to have strong faith."

"It appears so. But The Maker has given gifts to all His children. It takes all the family actively participating to be healthy. When a member like Paul opts out of using his gifts and talents, everyone including himself misses out. The Maker promises eternal rewards for those who are faithful," Mr. Bidding said.

"But can't The Maker cause things to happen the way He wants them to?"

"He can and does at times intervene Himself or sends his Angels to assist, usually in answer to prayers, as in your case. But there is always something, be it ever so small, that His offspring can contribute."

"Uh huh . . ." My mind swirled as I tried to digest Mr. Bidding's insights.

"Enough about the inhabitants for today. We'll talk again soon. I'm sure you'd like to look at your clue, so please do so now," Mr. Bidding urged and then was gone.

Excited to see what else I might discover, I broke open the three seals on the sapphire blue envelope. I pulled out the card. In red ink the clue read *"In His New Life He Works No More."*

Thump. Thump.

I woke with a start. What was that noise? I lay awake for a long time but didn't hear anything else. It must have been in my dream. Was I really dreaming about Harvest Island again? Whatever did that clue mean? In his new life he works no more. Does that mean he's retired, or worse yet, dead? If retired, is he at the Isle of Palms that he and Mom loved so much early in their marriage. Or does it mean something entirely different?

Chapter 15

After getting the kids to bed, I began my search for John once again.

After a couple of hours my phone rang, startling me. Who could be calling this late?

It was a local number, so I answered, but when I heard a familiar voice on the other end of the line, my heart skipped a beat.

"Samantha, this is Doctor Graham."

The fact that he didn't say, "Doctor Gerald calling," like he did when calling about blood or other test results, scared me. I was on the edge of having a full-blown panic attack. I silently started counting my breaths to slow them, so I could focus on the bad news. One, two, three, four, one two--.

"Are you still there, Samantha?" Dr. Graham asked.

"Uh, yes, um, uh . . . is everything okay?" I asked, not wanting to know the answer.

"Yes, I'm sorry, Samantha. I didn't mean to alarm you. Nothing's wrong."

"Oh good. You said Doctor Graham instead of your usual Doctor Gerald. It made me think the worst."

"Ah, I see. I forgot who I was talking to. It's been a long day. But good news, Tom is much better this evening. His fever's finally going down, and his breathing is much clearer. There's still a little congestion in his lungs, but it's going in the right direction. If he's no worse in the morning, I'll be sending him back to Grand Haven tomorrow afternoon. Their staff is more than capable of taking over his care."

"That's the best news I've heard today, actually this week, or probably this month! Thank you so much for letting me know. I bet Mom was elated."

"Sure was. I haven't seen her smile that much in a long time. I told her I'd call you. She was going home to get some sleep."

"Thanks again, Doctor Gerald. I'll see you tomorrow."

"Have a good night, Samantha. Glad to occasionally be the bearer of good news."

Immediately after I disconnected, the phone rang again. I quickly picked it up thinking Doctor Graham had forgotten something. I didn't notice the caller ID.

"Hey, Doctor Gerald, what'd you forget?" I asked.

"Is this Samantha Anderson?" a robotic voice asked.

"Yes, who is this?" I said, startled to hear the mechanical voice again.

"Someone who is giving you fair warning. If you don't stop looking for your father, we'll do to you what we did to him."

"What did you do to him?" I demanded.

The phone went silent.

I took the phone away from my ear. They had hung up. I checked the recent calls list – "unavailable," like the other threatening calls I'd received. This is crazy. There was no doubt this message was intended for me. But I couldn't give up now that I was receiving clues. Even if they are clues from a bizarre dream world. Could I stop? Or a better question to ask myself was, should I stop? I certainly didn't want to endanger my family by continuing down this path, but I wasn't sure I'd be able to let it go. And I must be on to something if I was threatened.

Chapter 16

Dream: Ashley Ascetic, Lilly Legalist, and Wally Works

The crackling fire and smell of burning wood was soothing. I stared at the dancing flames for a long time and then glanced out a window. A wing of the home extended about a hundred feet south. I was in the log cabin of Ashley Ascetic, Lilly Legalist, and Wally Works. I didn't remember entering their home but had an uncanny awareness of where I was.

I've always loved log cabins. It's like the outside has come indoors, comfortably abiding in a natural setting, not a man-made abode. And this home was a grand example. An expansive stone fireplace graced the end wall with large glass windows flanking each side. A homey, braided jute rug lay in front of the fireplace.

Skylights added to the abundance of natural light flooding the home. Exposed wooden beams stretched across the twenty-five-foot cathedral ceilings. A staircase of split logs with a matching banister led to a quaint loft. Over the upper railing hung a brightly colored patchwork quilt. A wrought iron chandelier was suspended from a beam over the dining area. What appeared to be cedar lined the walls, while the floors were covered with wide knotted wood planks.

I was facing the blazing fire, sitting on a luxurious brown leather sofa with wooden accents. Antique distressed iron, bronze, and wood pieces filled this room. Woven tapestries on the walls completed the perfect woodsy ambiance. It reminded me of a home I'd seen on HGTV once, a home in which I'd love to live.

Not sure of what I was to do then, I spent a few minutes counting log beams, twelve—a nice even number. Sixteen stairs, phew another even number. I started counting the lights in the chandelier when a petite white woman in a gauze, tan dress entered the room. She wore wire rim glasses, no make-up or jewelry, and her graying hair was piled into a bun on the back of her head.

As she approached, she extended her hand.

"Hello, I'm Lilly Legalist. Thank you for coming."

I stood and shook her hand.

"Samantha Anderson. Pleased to meet you."

"Please be seated. I hope you find our home comfortable," she said.

"More than comfortable. Perfect! I love what you've done."

She took a seat in a rocking chair by the fire. "My goodness, I appreciate that. We've worked hard to get it right. The three of us have drastically different tastes, so we've each had to compromise."

After another quick glance around the room, I said, "It is not apparent. The décor blends beautifully creating a rustic, natural setting. You should be proud of what you have done here."

"Yes, I am. We tried to follow the builder's specifications to a T. I wouldn't let my brother, Wally Works, make any major changes to the basic plan. You know it's best to follow the letter of the law."

"Right." I had no idea what she was talking about.

"Against my wishes, Wally did add a few additional porches and a log outbuilding that were not on the original blueprints. He sits on the porches to whittle wood in the evenings, and he works in the outbuildings on weekends making furniture and toys to give away. He always has a project or two he's working on."

Because Lilly opened the door to talk about the inhabitants of this home, I jumped in and started my interview. "So, where's Wally now?"

"He's at work, of course. He procures capital for several charities in the Islands. If I do say so myself, he's one of the best fundraisers around, if not the best. Last year alone, he solicited over twenty-million dollars for other charities and five million for his own non-profit, 'Stop Drunk Driving.'"

I remembered Fred's story about Wally but didn't bring up the unfortunate and probably painful memory of the accident.

"When will Wally be home?" I asked.

"If he doesn't spend the night at his office, he'll arrive home at about eight, so if you're here in six hours, you'll see him," Lilly said.

"I'm not sure I'll be here then. What else can you tell me about Wally?"

"He's a wonderful brother. I don't know anyone who works as hard doing good for everyone. He doesn't care who you are or where you come from. If there's anything that needs to be done, he lends a helping hand.

"He sounds like a special person." I was impressed and wished I was more like that.

"Yes, and he is proud of his 'Local Hero' awards. He's received ten in the last twelve years. The plaques are displayed on his study wall. He believes if his good deeds outweigh his bad, he'll be in good standing with The Maker, so he continues to work, work, work."

"Tell me a little about your story, Lilly."

"For years I lived in Tahiti as a librarian at the university. I became disillusioned with the worldly culture all around, so I moved out here. I saved enough to build this log cabin."

Lilly stared at the flickering fire.

"Are you retired now?" I asked, trying to keep Lilly talking.

"You could say that. I'm proud to be a follower of The Maker. My life's mission is to keep my life holy. My understanding is that we shouldn't be doing anything that the world does. We are self-sufficient here at the log cabin, and I like it that way.

"We avoid things people in the world occupy themselves with. No televisions, radios, shopping, sports, or music. No extravagant clothes, furniture, or cars. No fancy hairdos, jewelry, or make-up like those students at the university flaunted. We lead a pure life. And Ashley makes sure we eat simply. She's a bit stricter than I am in that regard.

"Between us, we have lots of rules to follow, and I believe I'm a better person for it. Even though Wally doesn't always agree with our rules, he goes along with them because he's family, and honestly, he's too busy doing good deeds to care."

"Wow, that is, uh, interesting," I said. Was she judging my clothes and makeup? Residents of Harvest Island were more transparent about their motives and relationships than any people I'd ever met.

I heard a door close and a native American woman, about five feet tall, with long, braided brunette hair and a loose, calf-length, burlap dress and white tennis shoes entered the room. Her only adornment was a leather belt covered in beads creating a southwestern design with dozens of brown feathers dangling from it.

"Ashley, so glad you could join us. This is Samantha Anderson. She's here at the request of Him Who Does His Bidding, so she *must* be important. Samantha, this is Ashley," Lilly said.

"Hello, Ashley. No, I'm not anyone important. I'm just looking for answers, and Mr. Bidding promised the inhabitants of Harvest Island would help me in my search."

"Of course, Ms. Anderson. How can I be of assistance?" Ashley asked.

"Please call me Samantha. And if you don't mind, please tell me about yourself."

"That won't take long. I've dedicated my adult life to religious solitude and self-denial. I had wealthy parents who lived for the accumulation of things in life, but they were miserable, and their marriage ended in a bitter divorce. When I left home, I knew there had to be a better way, so I started the quest for true spirituality. I believe I have found it in my ascetic lifestyle. Therefore, I don't partake in the comforts that Lilly and Wally have built into this home. I prefer to stay in my room. Would you like to see it?"

"Yes, that would be nice. Thank you."

I followed Ashley down the narrow hall to her tiny room. It was about eight by ten feet with no windows. A faint scent of eucalyptus filled the air. A twin mattress was on the floor covered with a thin brown blanket. There was no pillow. Against the opposite wall was a plain wooden desk with a lit lantern and an open book on it. A straight back wood chair with no arms was pushed against the desk. The walls and floors were bare. This room stood in stark contrast to the homey living area. I didn't know what to say.

Ashley broke the silence. "It's okay. You don't have to compliment my room. I'm used to living this way. I spend hours in prayer, meditation, and reading *The Book of Truth*. My lifestyle affords few distractions. Without Lilly and Wally, I would probably neglect eating, but they never let me forget, unless, of course, I'm fasting, and then they know not to disturb me."

I blurted out, "But why?"

"That's simple. If I deny myself the indulgences of the world, I will not be tempted. No temptations allow me to live a holy life," she said.

"Of course, I didn't intend to be critical. I've just never

met anyone who lives like you."

I couldn't believe I was so rude as to question another person's choices for how they lived their life. Who was I to judge? She wasn't hurting anyone.

"You may be wondering about my elaborate belt. It probably appears to be a contradiction to my otherwise austere life."

"No, it's lovely," I said.

"It was a gift from my parents when I left home. It's a relic from my ancestors. I keep it as a reminder to pray to The Maker for my parents, that they would forsake their love of money and materialistic lifestyles."

"It's wonderful that you pray for your parents. I only pray if I am in trouble, and even then, not that often," I said.

"The Maker is eager for us to talk to him about anything and everything."

"How do you know that?" I asked.

"It's in *The Book of Truth*. You should read it, Samantha."

"I've heard about it. Is there anything else you'd like to share?"

"No, you have all you need from us today."

"Of course. Thank you for showing me your room. May I trouble you to show me the field behind your home?" I asked.

"Certainly, and before I forget, here's the clue you were promised." She handed me a taupe envelope.

I grasped the envelope and slipped it into my pocket for safe keeping.

Ashley walked me to a back door which opened to an expansive porch with cedar rocking chairs and a view of the taupe field.

"Take your time, Samantha."

"Thank you. It's been a pleasure meeting you, Ashley. Please say 'goodbye' to Lilly for me."

She nodded, turned, and closed the door.

I strolled down the dirt path to the crops and stopped short. Each plant looked like straw. I reached down to be certain. There was no question, it was dry and brittle, but shaped into a leafy lettuce-like plant. What was the lesson to learn from these inhabitants?

I glanced back at the picturesque log home and noticed carved wooden gargoyles in the ridges. A skeleton, a wolf, and a monk.

Instantly, I found myself at the north end of the island with Mr. Bidding.

"Greetings, Samantha. How was your visit?"

"Good, Mr. Bidding. I loved the living area of the log cabin. If I must move, I wouldn't mind a place like that."

Without addressing my comment, he said, "What did you learn about these inhabitants, Samantha?"

"Of these three, I related most to the person I didn't meet, Wally Works. He wasn't home because he was busy helping other people. I certainly don't come close to his achievements, but genuinely like to help when I can. I've never considered the ascetic lifestyles of Lilly and Ashley as a means to become holy or good. Is that what I'm missing in my life?"

"No. It's true, you resemble Wally more than Lilly or Ashley, but their simple lifestyle is not what you're missing. The Maker, on occasion, asks His children to deny themselves in order to accomplish His will. For example, missionaries often leave family, friends, and worldly wealth. They don't gain holiness for their sacrifice, but they give up much to accomplish The Maker's will.

"That's a lot to process," I said.

"It's okay, Samantha. You'll understand more when you study *The Book of Truth* or *The Good Book*, as some call it. And the Spirit of Truth can teach and guide you along the right path. Remember that your heart and spirit are the most important aspects of His will. The other areas will follow."

"I need to read that book."

"Yes, you do. Now back to the topic at hand. The inhabitants. Wally believes his charitable works earn him good standing with The Maker. His works are not being done to fulfill The Maker's will, though they sometimes do.

"In this regard, all three are trying to earn their standing, but that's not possible. Good standing with The Maker is only by His grace and mercy found through faith in The Maker's son and his finished work. It can't be earned," Mr. Bidding said.

"I'm confused. Paul Passive was not doing any works, and you said his faith may not be what it could be. Wally is doing lots of works, but he isn't earning good standing with The Maker?" I asked.

Mr. Bidding nodded and smiled. "Quite a paradox, isn't it? Faith is expressed through works, but works do not earn right standing."

"Hmm. Sounds complex."

"Not at all. The works may not be what you might think. When one comes to The Maker, He starts transforming them. Things like treating others the way you want to be treated, doing good in small or large ways like using your gifts and talents, time, or resources to help others when possible. Even offering someone a cold glass of water is regarded as a good work if done to bring honor to The Maker . . . you look confused, Samantha."

"I'm listening, go on," I said.

"The Maker calls some of his children to do spectacular works, like Billy Graham, but it takes all His children with their various talents and resources to accomplish His purposes. A kind word, a smile, a prayer, or a helping hand can be a good work if done with the right heart attitude."

"I certainly fall short frequently. I may be a lost cause when it comes to this faith thing."

"No, Samantha, all can come to faith. What I'm saying may appear contradictory, but it's not. Those who have been forgiven want to please The Maker and seek Him for help to do the right thing and make good choices. But they don't always do so. When they fail, and everyone does, the Spirit of Truth calls them to repent and turn back to Him."

"I'm familiar with failing. Good choices are not at the top of my resume," I said.

"The Maker wants the best for His children. They are not perfect, but perfectly forgiven. You are loved more than you can imagine, Samantha."

"That's reassuring. So, Paul and Wally do not have true faith?" I asked.

"I cannot say. Only The Maker knows their hearts. I leave that judgement to Him. What I can say is their focus is not on the full truth. They have selected certain parts of *The Book of Truth* and applied them to their lives without balancing those with other foundational aspects. The Maker continues to draw people to faith through the Spirit of Truth."

"Then Paul and Wally may be The Maker's children?"

"Oh, yes, Samantha. It's possible, for The Maker alone knows their hearts. But they are missing out on wonderful benefits. Wally could cease from trying to earn his salvation and rest in what The Maker's son has done for him. He may still be involved in good works, but not to earn good standing with The Maker."

"And Paul is missing out by being passive?" I asked.

"Yes. He has drifted through life following the path of least resistance. Those who diligently follow The Maker find much joy and fulfillment in their journey."

"I guess that makes sense," I said. My thoughts were racing to keep up. "What did you say before about The Maker's son and the Spirit of Truth?"

"Those are topics for another time, Samantha. For now . . . read your clue, and I'll see you soon."

I tore open the taupe envelope with three seals on it. A skeleton, a wolf, and a monk. What do these symbols mean? Not taking any more time to ponder such things, I read the next clue. *"Find your cue in the color blue."*

What in the world did that mean? Blue sky? Blue ocean? Blue house? A street named Blue? A town named Blue?

A doorbell rang in the distance. It rang again and again.

Finally, the cobwebs cleared. I sat up in bed, and then rushed to my closet, threw on a robe, and ran to the front door, hoping to catch whomever it was.

Chapter 17

I peeked through the peephole. It was Brandon, my half-brother, wearing his favorite Clemson Tigers baseball hat. I opened the door, and he stepped inside.

"Hey Brandon! What brings you to this neighborhood so early?"

"I was over at Grand Haven visiting Dad. I'm concerned about him, Sam. I've never seen him as weak as he is today. Do you have a few minutes to talk?"

"Sure, Brandon. I'll put on a pot of coffee."

Brandon and Brian were eight years younger than me, but we were still close. Until Dad got sick, he and Mom hosted game nights and Sunday lunches every week. I attended them as much as possible over the years, and our family had stayed close. Even after Dad started declining, Mom would hold family get togethers periodically. It had paid off. We had a family bond most would envy.

The twins bounded down the stairs. "Uncle Brandon!" Jayce and Jazmine squealed as they ran into his arms.

"How are my favorite twins? Still practicing the piano?" he asked.

"Of course, Mom makes us," Jayce said.

"How about a song for your best uncle?" Brandon asked.

Truth be told, they would probably agree he's the best uncle because he spent the most time with them.

They raced to the piano bench and plunked down.

"What do you want to hear?" Jaz asked and before he could answer added, "How about a Christmas carol? We learned a duet of 'Oh Come All Ye Faithful.'"

"That sounds perfect," Brandon said. "I love that song."

Jayce and Jazmine played the song with only a hiccup or two and Brandon cheered and applauded to their delight.

"That was awesome, but now it's time to get ready for school," I said.

I went into the kitchen with Brandon, made coffee, and started setting out breakfast for the twins. "Can I make you something for breakfast?" I asked him.

"No thanks, I've already eaten," Brandon said.

"Coffee and peanut butter cookies then?"

"Sure, sis. Sounds good."

I poured us each a cup of Low Country Coffee and put a plate of peanut butter cookies on the kitchen island in front of us. That would be enough for my breakfast. We talked about the weather and his business while the kids got ready.

The twins finished their school morning routines and were picked up by the carpool driver. Since the school bus accident, several parents in our neighborhood concluded that it would be safer for our children to travel in vehicles with seat belts. I wholeheartedly agreed and joined the carpool.

After the twins left, I refilled our coffees and carried a plate of the remaining cookies into the living room and set them on the coffee table. Brandon and I settled into more comfortable chairs.

"Are you okay?" I asked.

"Yes, I was just thinking about the great times we've had with Dad over the years. Do you remember our springtime trips to Washington D.C.?" Brandon asked. "That was the one place Dad loved going back to."

"Yes, they were so much fun. It was hard to fit everything in we wanted to do. And he always planned our visits there in the spring when the cherry blossoms were in bloom . . . so beautiful," I said.

"Dad wanted us to appreciate the majesty of creation and our country's heritage too." Brandon took a sip of coffee.

"True. I remember him commenting about how stunning nature is, but don't remember him talking about God and creation until recent years." I leaned back.

Brandon leaned forward and locked eyes, "You're right, Sam. Dad's only recently acknowledged how such incredible beauty in nature . . . the animals, trees, mountains, oceans, and sky must be the work of a divine artist, our creator."

"It doesn't seem likely it could all be random, does it?" I asked rhetorically and then changed the subject. "Do you remember our trip to Florida's Space Coast watching the rockets take off?"

"Yes, it was a blast!"

"Ha-ha. My favorite was our trip to Boston. I loved the cobblestones and old buildings and landmarks. That city has unmatched historic charm."

"I enjoyed Boston too, especially Old Ironsides with those big cannons. Dad always found places where we learned something while having fun. Most of my friends went on the exact same vacations year after year, but we were able to look forward to new and exciting trips." Brandon took a bite of his cookie.

"That's right, national parks, lighthouses, islands, and theme parks. He was always up for a fresh experience. Even when we went back to D.C., we went to different sites," I said. I broke my cookie into four pieces and arranged them on my plate.

As Brandon and I talked about these excursions, I realized how fortunate I was to be part of this family.

I considered asking Brandon about my dreams and the strange clues, but he would unlikely have any insight into John's life. He barely knew him. And I didn't know if my weird dreams meant anything or if it was my overactive imagination. I passed on filling him in, at least at that time. He might think I'd gone off the deep end.

"How's your handsome neighbor, Spencer?" Brandon asked and then winked.

"He's fine. And we are only friends. No matchmaking please," I said and smiled.

It was hard to consider Spencer as anything more than a friend because I'd met him when I was still married to Logan. He seemed like another brother. Could he ever be more than that? If I ever allowed myself the risk of a relationship again, it would be nice to have a man as supportive and fun as Spence. Was it time to expand my horizons?

Brandon and Spencer had hit it off with their mutual interest in tennis. Their skill level was similar, so it was challenging. And they both loved to win.

"Thanks so much for stopping by and going down memory lane with me, Brandon. I'm going over to Grand Haven in a while, so I'll keep you posted if there are any changes in Dad's condition," I said.

"I'll be back over there a little later this morning, after I catch up on work emails. God bless you, Sam. You're a wonderful sister." He got up to leave, and then hesitated and said, "You know Dad loves you as if you were his own. His relationship with God has grown over the last years, and I know he wants that for you too."

"Thank you, Brandon. I appreciate that." I knew how true that statement was.

Dad had talked to me about his newfound dedication to God before he got sick. At the time he was involved in volunteer work for charities, men's groups, and regularly attended the Seagrove Community Church. I usually cut him short when he talked about his faith. I didn't have the bandwidth to add any church involvement. But I allowed him to take Jayce and Jazmine to summer Vacation Bible School and to get involved in the kids' church holiday plays.

I wasn't against them learning about God. I knew Dad wished I was more open to joining him and Mom at church, but I honestly enjoyed sleeping in a little on Sunday morning. My life was already full.

Dad had succeeded in persuading Brandon to attend church with them for the last few years. The changes in Brandon's life were evident. He had a softer, sweeter demeanor and talked more about God and faith--it appeared genuine. I appreciated that he wanted me to find the peace that he and Dad had found. While I didn't embody that same peace, the change in Dad and Brandon made me feel closer to them than ever.

I wondered how my faith and works conversations with Mr. Bidding fit into Dad and Brandon's newfound religion. Did their new faith prompt my subconscious to create Mr. Bidding and Harvest Island? I wasn't sure.

Chapter 18

As I entered the Seagrove Public Library, the "old book" scent brought back memories of hours spent reading in the children's section while Mom worked on real estate deals. She utilized the library when her office was overflowing with other agents and their clients. Mom is now retired but has kept her real estate license active for friends and family. If she needs to meet them in person, they go to the Myers Mansion now.

I passed four small rooms Mom had frequented with clientele and strolled past the elevator that led to the research area upstairs. I glanced at the stacks of books piled on the circulation desk waiting to be returned to their assigned shelves. Malik Jones, the librarian, was peering over them. He'd worked tirelessly for decades serving our community. As I passed by, his broad smile warmed my cloudy disposition.

"Hi Samantha," he called. "Long time, no see. Can I help you find something?"

"Hey, Malik. No, I came to use one of your computers. They are still free for card carrying members?" I hadn't been in the library for several months. With access to so much information online and now reading mostly digital books, I didn't frequent the library as often as I used to.

"Oh, yours not working?" Malik asked.

"Something like that." I didn't want to tell him I was

afraid to use my own computer because of threats I'd received.

"You know where they are?"

"Sure do. Along the back wall, unless you've moved them since I've been in."

"Same place, Samantha. Take your time. Three hours till closing."

"Thanks, Malik."

As I sat down in front of the computer, I hoped I didn't need to enter my library card number to search old newspapers. I pulled down the research tab and went to "Magazines and Newspapers" and a long list of databases appeared. A statement at the top of the page read: "A valid library card is required to access these databases from outside the library."

I let out a long slow breath. I wouldn't have to enter my card number. I didn't know how my online searches were being tracked, but at least whoever it was wouldn't trace my activity today.

Seagrove Library subscribed to newspapers.com and the database contained thousands of digitized papers across the country. I typed in: "Springfield, Missouri, Springfield prison hospital, 1999-2011." Those were years I was sure John had assignments there. Numerous articles from The Springfield News-Leader popped up.

I skimmed the headlines for possible clues, and then read the more interesting articles.

John Gotti, head of New York's Gambino crime family, was sent to the federal hospital twice.

The Panamanian dictator Manuel Noriega and drug lord was held there.

Mob boss Vincent "the Chin" Gigante died there.

An inmate sued a nurse who stabbed him with a needle. It was a 'he said, she said' situation. The man stabbed by the nurse was undergoing dialysis.

Inmates were trained as hospice workers. This helped to

ease the burden of the paid hospital staff, like John. The article was mostly positive, but included a comment about one inmate with HIV who was "always threatening to bite people." So much for John having a safe work environment.

A prison riot broke out and a self-employed construction specialist with the Federal Bureau of Prisons was taken hostage by inmates for sixteen hours. To make matters worse, he was beat up by correctional officers from another prison trying to stop the riot. They mistook him for an inmate.

My jaw dropped when I saw the photo and article written during the last year John was at the prison hospital, the year he disappeared. The picture showed Giovanni Esposito, a.k.a. "The Mac Truck" of The Lorenzo crime family sitting in a wheelchair in front of the prison hospital. A frowning guard stood next to him, appearing uncomfortable being photographed with the notorious mobster. Behind Giovanni stood John with his hands on the back of the wheelchair. He was smiling and looking down at Giovanni.

Esposito had been convicted of numerous counts of bribery, extortion, gambling, witness tampering, and fraud. He'd also been accused of seven murders, but the prosecutor hadn't proven those beyond a reasonable doubt, so Giovanni avoided life in prison. He'd served twenty-five years of a fifty-five-year sentence when he was diagnosed with cancer. After ten years of treatment in prison facilities, he'd been granted a compassionate release from the Federal Bureau of Prisons. His doctors estimated he had three months or less to live.

John had never mentioned any of the potential risks of working at the federal prison hospital. Was he mixed up with the Lorenzo crime family or another mob or drug lord? Did he overhear something he shouldn't have? If so, he was likely buried in cement or at the bottom of a large body of water weighed down with cinder blocks. Or had he been too deep in one of their schemes and faked his own disappearance?

Chapter 19

Dream: Barb Beauty and Paige Pleasure

I'd never seen a performing arts theater painted hot pink like the one in front of me. In style it was closest to, but smaller than the Sydney Opera House. At the top peak a gargoyle with painted theater masks stared at me. On the peak below a lion gargoyle stood on its hind legs with its paws in the air. To the left I saw a small owl gargoyle. A field with fuchsia colored produce protruded on both sides from behind the enormous home.

I had started to feel the comfort of familiarity in Harvest Island. I wouldn't say I was looking forward to my next visit, but at least I knew the drill. I'd knock on the door, or find myself in the dwelling, talk to the residents about their lives, examine the crops in their backyard, and debrief with Mr. Bidding.

The inhabitants were odd at best. I'm all for individuality and forging one's own path, but these folks were downright quirky and some even terrifying. I was getting clues to John's whereabouts, though I hadn't cracked the key yet. Maybe the clues were like those crop circle designs that need to be seen from above to discern their pattern. This was my fourth visit, almost halfway to the final clue.

The sun warmed my face, and a light breeze blew through my hair as I approached the twenty-foot tall, glass double doors and rang the bell. A minute, then two passed. I rang again. After another minute, a stunning platinum blond with a gorgeous tan opened the door. Her high cheekbones, perfect eye makeup that highlighted large blue eyes, and snowy white teeth didn't hide her definite frown of disapproval.

"Hello? And who are you?" she asked.

"Oh, I'm Samantha Anderson . . . weren't you expecting me?"

"Not today, it is much too nice to be inside hosting guests. You disturbed me while I was outside lying by the pool. It is a perfect day to improve my tan."

"Oh, should I return later?" I asked, wondering if that was even possible.

"No, if you're here now, it is Him Who Does His Bidding's assignment, and I can't challenge that. Well, I could, but it would be pointless. Come in, and please try to make it quick."

I was taken back by her unpleasant personality, which stood in stark contrast to her beauty.

"Of course," I said. "Or we could sit by your pool if you'd prefer."

"Very well, follow me," she snapped.

We passed a sparkling, glass walled foyer that led to a magnificent theater. I estimated it would seat several hundred people. The soaring geometric patterned ceiling was dotted with spotlights. The ribbed walls held spectacular wooden box seat balconies on both sides. A massive, elevated platform filled the front.

After traversing a side aisle, we climbed the stairs. One, two, three, four, five. I stepped back one and then up, six. Crossing the stage, Barb wound her way around equipment and layered drapes as I trailed. Behind the last set of curtains, we followed a long hall with six closed doors on each side. Dressing rooms? At the end of the corridor, a blue exit sign lit the door. We stepped into a courtyard with turquoise tile around a shimmering hourglass shaped pool. Six white wicker patio chairs surrounded the pool, and Barb motioned for me to sit in the one across from her matching lounge chair.

"How can I help you?" She took a long sip of iced tea.

"Oh, um, what's your name and does anyone else live here with you?"

"I'm Barb Beauty, fitting, don't you think? And I live with Paige Pleasure. She's not here now. Out on one of her adventures. And my brother, Brad Brainiac spends time in the guest suite when he's writing. I expect him back in about a month."

"I see. Yes, your name does suit you. What else can you tell me about yourself?"

"I've lived on the islands my whole life. I'm an actress. From the time I was small I aspired to be on stage. It comes naturally for me to dramatize stories. I was used to being in the spotlight because I competed in pageants from the time I could walk. I receive so much praise for my appearance. They can't all be wrong, can they? Having a plastic surgeon as a father hasn't hurt either. He does marvelous work, don't you think?"

"Um, uh, yes, of course he does. What type of acting do you do?" I asked, wanting to change the subject of this strange conversation.

"Mostly love stories with a splash of drama. I can be incredibly entertaining if I do say so myself."

"What do you like to do when you're not on stage?"

"Everything I do is preparation for being in the spotlight. I spend hours on my makeup and hair each day, making sure everything is flawless. I don't show my face to anyone until that's done. And shopping for the most flattering clothes and accessories keeps me busy."

"Wow."

"And I tan, as I told you, but not too much, only enough to get my vitamin D."

"Your tan looks dark," I said.

"I've found wonderful sunless tanning products that keep me gorgeous. I swim, weight-lift, and do calisthenics, anything to keep me in shape and my muscles toned. I'm also on a strict diet, so I spend a lot of time planning meals and cooking things that help me maintain my youthful glow. Paige and I argue about our meals when she's home. She loves decadent desserts and high calorie foods. I indulge occasionally, but only a bite here and there. And of course, sleep is important for my life's work, so I make sure I get eight or nine hours every night."

"That sounds like an immense amount of work, except for the sleep part."

"It is, but it's worth it to get continual accolades. I'm valued and sought after for my beauty and grace. I wouldn't have it any other way," She tossed her hair back.

I was starting to see the unfortunate value Barb put on her appearance. Eventually, even the most skillful plastic surgeon can't hide all signs of aging without distorting the original beauty. The older she gets, the less she'll feel valued. How sad.

"Is there anything else you need from me," Barb asked impatiently.

"If I may briefly look at your field, that would be appreciated."

She pointed to one of the many exits. "Take that door. It will lead you to our produce."

I hurried to the field and admired the flamboyant fuchsia crops. I reached down and touched a plant. Was it plastic? Curious. I'd forgotten to ask about the other residents who weren't home. I turned back to the theater and jogged to the door I'd come through. Barb had relocated under the shade of a Canary Island Date Palm.

"Well, what now?" she asked.

"If you could spare a few more minutes. What can you tell me about Paige and your brother Brad?"

Barb huffed. "Not much to tell about Brad. He's the boring one in my family. Thinks he has the world figured out. He spends all his time reading and writing. Most people would call him a geek or a nerd. Science and engineering are his forte. That's about it, not terribly interesting. Oh, one more thing. When he's here, he helps me memorize my lines as payment. That's by far the best use of his time."

"Payment?" I asked.

"Of course, for staying in the guest suite. You don't think I let him stay here for free?"

"I, uh, guess not. What can you tell me about Paige?" I asked.

"Paige is a marvelous roommate, except for the food thing. She's a travel writer -- always off on some escapade, so I have the place to myself. She's content when she has an exciting new hobby, place, or person to explore. She tells me I'm missing out, but believe me, you wouldn't catch me dead doing most of the things Paige enjoys. If there is no new adventure, she becomes bored and irritable, so I help her find new places to visit or a thrilling activity to engage her senses. Come, I'll show you her room on your way out."

"Thank you, Barb."

We returned through the same door we had exited, and I followed Barb to the second door on the right.

"There it is, look around, but don't touch anything. You can take as long as you like. You know the way to the front door, don't you?"

"Yes, of course. I'll show myself out when I'm through here. Oh, before I forget, do you have something for me?"

She reached into her bikini top and pulled out a fuchsia envelope with three seals, the theater masks, a lion on its hind legs, and an owl just like the gargoyles on the front of the home.

"Wonderful, thank you so much, Barb. You've been extremely helpful."

As I stepped into Paige's room the sound of flutes and

stringed instruments filled the air. Then I noticed a strong scent of freshly baked chocolate chip cookies, but I didn't see any in the room. Just as well. I would have been tempted to snag one.

I glanced around Paige's room, approximately 20 by 30 feet with an ensuite bathroom and walk-in closet. At one end there was a massage chair about ten feet from a huge wall screen. Books lined one shelf under the screen. Large speakers flanked the screen and additional speakers sat in the opposite corners of the room, but they didn't seem to be the source of the music.

Bean bags of various materials and colors were scattered around with open magazines, books, and empty pizza boxes close by. A guitar stood in the corner of the room with wear marks on the frets and body, unlike Phillip Phony's pristine instruments.

A kayak, surfboard, canoe, and snow skis leaned against the back wall. Numerous pictures filled the rest of the back wall on either side of Paige's "toys." I assumed Paige was the person shown parasailing, surfing, skydiving, hot air ballooning, and white-water rafting, I moved to the other set of photos and saw the same person four-wheeling, mountain climbing, scuba diving, ziplining, and bungee jumping. Some were selfies, others were professional, probably taken by the company providing the service or thrill. Paige was alone in most of the shots, but in a few, she was accompanied by other thrill seekers.

Another wall contained pictures of Paige with a variety of people at theme parks, extravagant events, and beautiful locations like the Grand Canyon and Niagara Falls. In these posed photos, I noticed how lovely she was, not the striking beauty of Barb, but certainly attractive. She appeared to be a Hispanic woman in her mid-thirties with green eyes, shoulder length dark brown hair, most often worn with natural looking beachy waves. At a few of the events, she wore her hair in an updo with wavy strands escaping here and there. Paige was not as thin as Barb, but she was in good shape. If she did eat poorly as Barb suggested, she must burn off the calories with her active lifestyle.

Paige was rarely with the same person in any of the pictures. Did that mean she had a lot of friends to share her experiences with or were those all acquaintances she met briefly? In several shots her relationships looked romantic, but always with a different person. I wished I could ask her questions, but the room and photos were as close as I'd get to Paige.

In the middle of the room facing the long wall, was an elegant king size canopy bed with four carved wooden posts. The bed was covered with oversized blue and green pillows and what appeared to be a thick down comforter and a cashmere throw tossed across the bottom of the bed.

A door to the right of the bed led to a large walk-in closet, with a window looking out to a garden of multi-colored tulips and flowering cherry trees. The range of items in the closet was curious, from T-shirts, khakis, jeans, and sweats to frilly dresses and sparkling gowns. The variety of shoes was equally diverse, hiking, cowboy, and snow boots, a variety of tennis and boat shoes, sandals, flashy stilettos, and comfortable flats. Coats, jackets, shawls, and scarves for all occasions hung at the end wall of the closet next to shelves of colorful handbags and clutches.

A door to the left of the bed led to her bathroom. As I stepped in, I felt the heated tile floor through my thin-soled shoes. On the right was an enormous, enclosed glass shower with gold massage jets and an overhead rainfall shower head. The dark green tile in the shower was a beautiful contrast to the white floor tile.

A hot tub was adjacent to the shower. Two Sherpa lined long robes hung next to several plush Turkish cotton towels. Sweet-scented orchids adorned the marble vanity top. The soothing music that saturated the air created a spa-like ambiance in this spectacular bathroom.

In an instant, I was at the north end of the island where Mr. Bidding was waiting for me.

"Hello, Samantha!"

"Hi Mr. Bidding. How are you?"

"Fine, as always. And you?

"I'm doing alright. What an interesting home you sent me to."

"Ah yes, and what did you observe about these two?" Mr. Bidding got right down to business.

"Don't forget Brad Brainiac. I think I may be more like him than the other two. I love research and learning, though not great at technical stuff like Brad's engineering."

"You are different than Brad because he only trusts his intellect. Things that are provable through math or experiments," Mr. Bidding said.

"I guess I don't resemble him as much as I thought. I want to believe in love and trust and relationships. All abstracts, hardly empirically proved," I said.

"Science is Brad's religion. He believes it offers the meaning of life, unlike his cousin Barb. What did you learn about her?"

"She was as striking as any supermodel I've ever seen. From what she said, she's had a little or a lot of help with that. She appears happy with her life, although a little grumpy when I interrupted her time at the pool. Her focus is only on her appearance and acting, and she lives for the limelight. Her time is spent on taking care of herself, grooming for the moment she steps on stage."

"Yes, that's accurate," Mr. Bidding said. "And she only takes roles that depict beautiful characters. She wouldn't be seen without perfect makeup, hair, and clothing, although that varies greatly depending on what part she plays. Playing only gorgeous women has limited her options for being more widely known and appreciated for her superb acting skills."

"That's unfortunate. She seems to live for her performances."

"Yes, it is so," Mr. Bidding said. "Because she's consumed with the praises she receives for her appearance and acting skills, she's oblivious to her inner qualities, like being kind and hospitable. It's all about the exterior. Barb pays no attention to the condition of her heart."

"My parents always stressed inner beauty, but I fall short in that area. There's always too much to do and too little time to do it. Who has time to contemplate being a better person?" I asked more rhetorically than expecting an answer.

"You are too hard on yourself, Samantha. Your comments about yourself have been more negative than you deserve. They are not truth."

"Oh, uh, thank you."

"No need, truth will help your self-image to fully blossom," Mr. Bidding said.

"I'm trying to get there," I said.

"Yes, and you will see more clearly soon."

"I hope so." I thought about Barb's self-image. "Is it wrong to put effort into our appearance?"

"Of course not, Samantha. The Maker has created a gorgeous world. He values beauty. But physical beauty will fade in this life. Spiritual beauty is the opposite. It grows more splendid as it's nurtured. We make time for the things that are important to us. It's a matter of priorities. Barb only makes time for one thing."

"It looks like I have work to do in this area," I said. *I might be a lost cause.*

As if reading my mind, Mr. Bidding said, "You are not a lost cause, Samantha. As long as you have life, you have choices. The Maker initiates heart changes in anyone who seeks Him. It is never too late."

"I appreciate that."

"What was your impression of Paige Pleasure?"

"Without having met her, I'd say she is going after all that life has to offer. She lives each day to the fullest, having all kinds of experiences that most of us only dream about. I get the appeal. Though I didn't meet her, I grasped a glimmer of who she was from the photos and her delightful suite. It appealed to my senses, all of them."

"Indeed, Paige does live for all kinds of enjoyment and unique experiences. But she is shallow in her inner life. Her friendships and romantic relationships are short-lived because she's chasing the next thrill. And she makes friends easily, so she moves on to the next person without looking back. She believes this life is the only life, so she goes after it with gusto," Mr. Bidding said.

"This is our only life, isn't it?" I asked.

"Samantha, this life is only a shadow of real life. It fades by comparison. Highs, and lows for that matter, are fleeting. We'll talk more about this later," he said. "Now it's time for you to open your clue, Samantha."

I took out the fuchsia envelope and broke the seals. I pulled out the card and read the words **"From the Mountains to the Valley."**

"Mom, Mom, wake up!"

The words were distant, but when I heard them a second time, I opened my eyes.

Chapter 20

"Mom," **Jayce** **whispered.** "Mom, are you awake? I heard a noise."

Frantically trying to wake up, I saw Jayce's sweet face leaning close to mine.

"What kind of noise?" I whispered as I rolled out of bed onto my feet.

"I'm not sure, but it sounded like someone was downstairs."

I froze listening and could only hear my heart thumping. I took a deep breath, in one, two, three, four; out one, two, three, four.

"Okay, let me check it out." I went to the closet and pulled out a baseball bat. It was the bat that Dad used years ago when he played on the Seagrove Police Team, The Pelicans. I always loved going to his games but was surprised when he gave the bat to me instead of one of my brothers. He told me it was good for protection as well as playing. He'd shown me how to wheel it to do the most damage if I ever needed to.

"Jayce, go into Jazminc's room and lock the door, but don't wake her up. Okay?"

"Sure, Mom," Jayce said.

If Jaz woke up, she'd be terrified and might start screaming or crying which would tip off any intruder. I'd lose the element of surprise. And, of course, I didn't want to upset her either.

I crept down the stairs, one hand holding the bat in strike position, the other hand inching along the banister, so I wouldn't stumble. My heart throbbed so loud in my ears, I was sure everyone in the house could hear it. Why didn't I get that alarm system Spencer had recommended? Should I call him? No, it was 2:00 a.m., I didn't want to wake him for a false alarm. The racoon in the garbage again? Surely that was it.

As I stepped onto the carpet at the bottom of the stairs, I heard the back patio door close. That was a sound I was sure of, that familiar whoosh. A racoon couldn't do that. Turning around, I retreated to my bedroom, closed and locked the door, and then called Spence.

Out of breath, I whispered, "Spence, someone was in my house or still is. I don't know for sure. Jayce heard a noise and woke me up. I snuck downstairs and heard the patio door close. I'm back in my bedroom, and I locked the door. Jayce locked himself in Jazmine's room. Can you check it out?"

"On my way." I pictured him grabbing his gun and carefully approaching, taking necessary precautions. He'd been on the police force for about seven years. He and my dad were both detectives for the Seagrove Police Department, though Dad had retired several years ago. Maybe that's why I was so comfortable around Spence.

Spence tapped on my bedroom door quietly identifying himself. I opened it, he came in, and I locked it behind him.

"I checked out the yard and didn't find anyone or evidence of anyone having been there. Then I went to your back patio door. It was unlocked. I drew my pistol, just in case. But I didn't find anyone on the lower level, so I checked out the guest bath and spare bedroom up here. No intruder is in the house now, Sam."

I opened the door, and we went to Jazmine's room. I tapped on the door. "It's okay, Jayce. Spence is here now, but he didn't find anyone in the house or out in the yard."

Jayce opened the door. "Hi, Spence."

"Hey, buddy." Spence tousled Jayce's hair.

"Why don't you go back to your room and try to get some sleep. It was probably just that racoon again." I lied.

"Are you sure, Mom? It sounded like someone was in the house."

"Yes, sweetie. It's all right. I'm glad you let me know you heard something. Better safe than sorry."

I hadn't told Spence or the kids about the threatening calls I'd received over the last couple of weeks. I'd planned on telling Spence but hadn't found the right time.

After Jayce went back to bed, I went downstairs with Spence and turned on my electric kettle.

"How about a cup of mint tea, Spence?"

"Sure, that won't keep me awake. But knowing someone broke into your house may."

"I know. I'd really like coffee, but my nerves are frayed enough without adding caffeine," I said.

"Let's take a quick look around to see if anything is missing. I'll go with you," Spence said.

After checking out the lower level, we made our way back to the kitchen. Nothing appeared to be missing. I poured our tea, and we sat down at the kitchen table.

"I know you probably don't want to, but you should call the station about this break in, Sam," Spence said.

"I'll report it in the morning, after Jayce and Jazmine have left for school. Whoever it was is gone now. It doesn't appear anything is missing."

"At least let me call the station and have them send a patrol officer by. I'll tell them no flashing lights or sirens," he said.

"That's fine. I don't want to upset Jayce any more tonight. I doubt he'd go back to sleep if he knows I've called the police, so please emphasize the need for a quiet arrival," I said.

"Technically you already called the police when you

called me." He winked at me.

"You know what I mean!" I swatted his arm.

He chuckled and then pulled out his cell phone to make the call to station eleven, Spence's post. When he finished instructing the officers to make as stealth an arrival as possible, he hung up.

I took the opportunity before the officer arrived to tell Spence about the threatening phone calls I'd received.

"I didn't write them down, but I remember most of what they said. The first one warned me to, 'stop digging, or else.' I hoped it was a sick prank or even a wrong number. But I'd been on my computer searching for John when that call came. Another message said, 'If you find him, you'll be sorry.' Another 'We will do to you what we did to him.' They were all short messages, Spence. And one time they asked if I was Samantha Anderson, so I'm sure the threats were meant for me."

As I was repeating the threatening messages out loud, my throat constricted, and my palms became sweaty. It was real. I was being threatened, and a stranger had entered my home that night.

"Samantha, did you report them?" Spence asked.

"No. I knew the police would have wanted to try to trace them, but I doubt there was enough time, and the calls all showed 'unavailable' on caller ID. I didn't think it would help. And with everything going on with Dad, I didn't want another drama in my life.

"Was it a man or a woman who called?" Spence asked.

"All the messages sounded like they were put through a voice altering software or mechanism, so I can't tell you what the person sounds like – young, old, male or female. It was sort of robotic, like a machine instead of a person."

Spence didn't chide me for failing to report those calls. His furrowed brow revealed the grave concern he felt. I was convicted without a word, and the compassion in his eyes made me look away.

Two officers in uniform arrived. We went out to the back patio to be sure we were out of Jayce and Jazmine's hearing. As I went over the events of the evening, Spence excused himself and went inside, but quickly returned looking alarmed.

"Uh, I hate to interrupt, but there's something you all need to see," Spence

whispered.

We followed him to the half bath on the first floor. I was stunned as I read the red writing on the mirror. It resembled blood but was likely paint or lipstick.

I CAN GET TO YOU AND YOUR KIDS - STOP LOOKING NOW.

Spence said, "I glanced in here earlier to be sure it was empty but didn't turn the light on. And when we looked around together for missing items, we didn't even go in there. I didn't imagine anything in a half bath was valuable enough to steal."

All four of us looked around the rest of the first floor again to see if we'd missed anything else. Nothing appeared out of order, so we retreated to the back patio and finished the police report.

Spence offered to sleep on the sofa. I took him up on it.

Chapter 21

Dream: Mary Mystic and Ellie Ecstasy

I was flying again. All felt right in the world. Drifting over sparkling aqua water, rising on the wind, gliding gently through the wispy clouds. I was lost in the experience of willing myself up, down, gently curving to the left, then to the right, so easily coasting along with no fear, no heaviness, no concerns.

On the horizon, I saw land, so I drifted slowly toward the mass. The colorful sphere of land drew me toward it. It was Harvest Island. The homes, the fields, the residents came tumbling back to my consciousness or subconsciousness, whatever the actual case was right then.

I descended in front of a grand gothic stone cathedral, much like the old churches I'd visited in New York City. This building most resembled St. Patrick's Cathedral, my favorite. I stood in awe at the enormous structure with three massive pointed arched doors with additional smaller pointed arches above each, two soaring spires, stained glass windows, and ornate patterns that reminded me of designs I made with a Spirograph set I owned as a child.

Seeing such an awe-inspiring cathedral on Harvest Island left me speechless. No one was around, so I stood gazing at the magnificent building. After a few minutes, a black raven flew by croaking as it went. It circled around one, two, three times, and then stopped on the landing atop the stairs leading to the massive, bronze double-doors. I wished it would circle around an even number of times . . . ah, it happened. It flew back up over my head and around again. I started counting where I'd left off, four, five, six, and it landed, this time on the top stair. Good enough. Six, a nice even number.

As I stared at the grand structure, the corbels caught my attention. Protruding from the left was a white stone Angel Gargoyle complete with wings and halo but with a terrified expression on its face and on the right corbel was a black Bat Gargoyle with beady orange eyes. The gargoyles cast long dark shadows on the cathedral's exquisite exterior.

The wind picked up as I contemplated the gargoyles, and a particularly cold gust prompted me to ascend the stairs leading to the splendid building. The temperature was rapidly dropping, clouds moved over the island, and a few snowflakes floated around my head. I shivered and picked up my pace. I felt smaller and smaller as I approached the massive structure, like Gulliver in Brobdingnag. Up the stairs - one, two three, four, five, six.

The door swung open, revealing a tall woman with a turban on her head. She wore a long, flowing, earth-toned robe covered in embroidered stars and crescent moons. Her smooth brown skin and dark eyes were reminiscent of Middle Eastern or Indian descent. Without saying a word, she waved a wand motioning for me to enter. I hesitated but was curious and cold enough to let my guard down. I stepped inside.

Viewing the interior, I was speechless. Spectacular ornate beams, pointed arches, stained glass windows, but unlike St. Patrick's cathedral, the hundred-foot ceiling was painted with flying angels and what appeared to be biblical characters.

"Take your time. It's worth it," she said.

"Wow!" I finally said. "It's incredible."

"Yes, my home has that effect on most people."

"I imagine. It's . . . it's breathtaking. I'm Samantha."

"Yes, Samantha. I have been expecting you. I am Mary Mystic."

"So nice to meet you."

"Likewise. Come let us go into the sitting room." Mary turned and walked through the center of this massive room.

She led me to a side room with walls covered in renaissance paintings like the ones in the sanctuary. Two red tufted wingback armchairs accented with brass nail heads sat on either side of an antique wooden table.

"Please have a seat." She motioned to the chair on the left.

"Thank you. And thank you for allowing me time to absorb the wonders of your home. I can't imagine living in such a fantastic place. Do you live here by yourself?" I asked.

"No, my second cousin lives with me. Or is she a third cousin? Not sure. But she's a wonderful housemate . . . although a little dramatic at times. Her name is Ellie Ecstasy. Our abilities are . . . complementary. We've lived here for about ten years . . ."

Her comment about cousins reminded me of my own confusion regarding relatives I'd found through my DNA search. Mental rabbit trail. Focus.

Mary was still speaking. ". . . and then about sixteen years ago, I had a vision of this place, so when I saw it, I knew it was where I was meant to be. I'd cast a spell for prosperity, and wouldn't you know it, the next day I saw an ad for a caretaker of the Harvest Island Cathedral. Ellie was looking for a place to live at that time, so we applied as a team and won the opportunity to be here. Not only do we get to enjoy this heavenly home, but we are compensated to look after it. The magnificence never dims."

"Thanks for sharing. It's a remarkable story. Is Ellie here now?"

"No, she's gone to the market this afternoon, but if

you're here long enough, you'll get to meet her."

"I'd like that. Mary, tell me about your visions. Do you have them often?"

"Almost daily. I ask my spirit guide for direction, and he does not disappoint. I see all kinds of visions, like departed spirits, the past and the future or at least a potential version of the future."

"I'd love to know what's coming next in my life. Your gift is amazing."

"Most of the time, it is. But since it hasn't happened yet, it isn't set. That's why my visions don't always come to pass exactly as I predicted, but sometimes they do."

'That makes sense," I said.

"And interpreting what I see is not black and white either. It's more of an art than a science. During seances, I go into a trance to channel spirits of the dead, so that others can be comforted in their loss or find direction for their future. Other tools I use for predicting the future are tarot cards, tea leaves, and Ouija boards."

My breath hitched as alarm bells started going off in my head. I remembered a terrifying experience I'd had as a child playing with a Ouija board with friends. We had seen something shoot across the room and heard a shriek. It was the most terrifying thing I've ever experienced. I'd never told anyone what happened and never went near anything like that again.

"Samantha?"

"Uh, oh, um." I needed to say something. Anything. "My, that's an interesting list." I swallowed hard hoping she didn't detect my fear.

"You know there is more to this world than meets the eye. I see angels, demons, and glimpses of the afterlife. Pursuing the supernatural makes me feel alive and gives me hope for a better world," Mary said.

"Yes, I do believe we all need hope." I was unsure what I believed about spiritual things. "So, you're a psychic and caretaker?" I wanted to uphold my side of the arrangement with Mr. Bidding but wasn't interested in hearing any more about demons or seances.

"Yes, some would call me that, but I prefer the title Spiritualist. I've even been called a witch, but I'm not a fan of that label either. People come to me from around the world to communicate with the other side. They bring an article from a loved one, or some holy artifact. It's amazing what people will pay to contact a departed friend or family member. And often wealthy clients come to me with requests about direction for their future, their love life, or which investments to make, and such things."

"And you always succeed in contacting the spirit world?" I asked. "To be honest, and I currently have no choice but to tell you the truth, I do not *always* succeed. My clients don't know that. If I don't contact a spirit, I make up lies and speak in generalities. I sprinkle magic dust and pronounce blessings or curses, pretend to be in a trance, and predict the future in vague terms. Ellie dances and sings or chants, often in a trance whirling about while I'm attempting to channel my spirit guide or deceased spirits. Our seances are quite a good show, even when I am not truly successful."

"How does The Maker fit into all of this?" I ignorantly asked.

Her countenance darkened. "You are joking, are you not?" She paused, and then realizing I was serious, continued, "He is not involved. The Maker forbids such things in *The Book of Truth*. But He cannot stop me. I have free will. And I have power. Power from the Angel of Light. His power is as strong as The Makers, and I'm learning how to harness it. Everyone envies my power."

"I see," I mumbled hoping I'd heard enough to satisfy Mr. Bidding and gain another clue.

Then I heard ethereal singing coming closer. It made the hair on the back of my neck stand up. I wanted to run but my feet were not cooperating. Mary jumped up and swung the door open. A woman floated into the room. Yes, she floated like a ghost, but was not transparent as one would imagine.

"Ellie, so glad you could join us," Mary said.

"I see you have 'borrowed' my wand again, Mary." Ellie snatched it from Mary's hand.

Then she saw me. "Ah, this must be Samantha. You are a special one, you know?"

"Oh, uh, . . . I don't think so." I was riveted by her amazing appearance.

She was floating about a foot off the floor and her eyes were a piercing amber color. Her hair was piled in a bun of braids, and she was dressed as I'd imagine a witch doctor would be in a robe of woven colors with a necklace of bones and feathers with matching earrings. A colorful mask resembling a skull covered most of her face with large holes revealing those penetrating eyes.

"Yes, you are special. Him Who Does His Bidding has made that clear. We are not to harm you, and we can only speak truth to you, which is tortuous. Normally we lie to achieve our goals whenever necessary. It's only the end result that matters."

"Hmm, I see." I didn't agree but wasn't going to argue with this frightening character. I asked the open-ended question I'd grown accustomed to, "Tell me about your life here, Ellie."

"Of course, what choice do I have? While Mary believes her work here is helping humanity find a better existence and direction in the world. I live to transcend to the highest cosmic path, finding my ultimate spiritual experience. My greatest desire is to achieve ascension, which I believe starts with tapping into the divine spark in each of us. I am most fulfilled when I'm in the heights of ecstasy through trances, mantras, and incantations. I lose myself as I'm transported to another dimension. Certainly, we were created to reach higher levels of consciousness.

That's where we're meant to dwell. Those who fully transcend become one and divine."

More than a little confused, I changed the subject, "Uh, okay. And your ability to . . . uh, levitate? Where does that come from?"

"From the Angel of Light, of course," she said. "He is The Ruler of earth and rules above all the ascended masters. Our Master shares his divine powers with his followers."

I never heard of the Angel of Light or ascended masters. A question for Mr. Bidding later. I didn't want to be there longer than necessary, and that information didn't help me understand Mary and Ellie, at least at the time. Both Mary and Ellie emitted a heavy darkness, so I quickly moved on to another question.

"Um, what would you call your occupation?" I asked Ellie.

"We are caretakers of this phenomenal building and grounds, but my primary occupation is what you would call a wizardess or a witch. I'm a healer. A white witch. So, in that regard, I do help others find relief from physical suffering. It's a step toward total enlightenment. Yesterday, after Him Who Does His Bidding told us of your upcoming visit, Mary investigated your life. She may not have told you about her crystal ball because it scares people. She divined that you suffer from migraines, Samantha. Would you like me to perform a healing ritual over you?" Ellie asked.

"Uh—"

"You would sit inside an inverted pentagram surrounded by candles. I'll kill a black cat and sprinkle its blood on you while you repeat a healing incantation: 'Healing Power Black as Night, Bring Your Child to the Light, Heal My Body, Heal My Sight, Make Your Power Shine, oh so Bright.' During the ritual, I'll wave my wand over you twelve times. That would align the cosmic energy to complete the healing, but afterwards you would need to wear an amulet to stay healthy. I'd recommend a clear quartz crystal. It is a simple process for your healing."

"Uh--"

"Shall I retrieve a black cat for sacrifice?" Ellie sneered seeing my repulsed expression.

"Uh, um, no, no, tha, thank you. I'm fa, fine, I'm, I'm good," I stammered.

"No need to get upset, Samantha. It was a simple offer."

I took a deep breath and exhaled slowly. "Yes, I do appreciate the offer. Maybe another time." I lied. Fortunately, I was able to fib without any of the consequences that befell the inhabitants of Harvest Island. No pain.

Ellie said, "Very well then, may I show you our work area?"

"No need but thank you." I scanned the room for exits.

I hoped I didn't need to see their work area to complete my assignment. I realized my palms were sweaty as I gripped the arms of the chair.

"Are you sure? It is . . . mesmerizing," Mary said.

"Yes, I'm sure. But I would like to see your fields . . . if that's possible."

"Yes, you may. This way," Mary said.

Mary and Ellie escorted me out the back entrance of the cathedral and down a gravel path to their amber field.

Ellie, with a beguiling smile, extended her wand in a sweeping motion over the field. "Mother earth has provided us this sacred field. Please do not damage or disturb it."

Mary reached into her flowing robe and pulled out an amber colored envelope with a glimmering angel seal next to a scary bat seal. Once again, the images resembled the gargoyles who sat watch over the front of the building.

"This is for you," she said.

"Thank you both. Have a good day." I wasn't sure what to say.

"The signs are all around, Samantha, don't ignore them," Mary said.

"Yes, you are special. The all-powerful Angel of Light would like your allegiance," Ellie said. She effortlessly turned and floated back up the path to their glorious home. Mary followed without another word.

The smell of sulfur permeated the air. I walked to the back of the field in case I inadvertently did any damage. It would be less obvious. The last thing I wanted to do was to make Mary or Ellie angry. Leaning down, I gently touched the glowing amber crops with my index finger and immediately pulled it back. The leaf was hot, not warm, but burning hot.

I raced back towards the road. Little flames shot up from the leaves and followed me as I passed by one row after another. The wind picked up and snowflakes began to fall once again. This time it was more than flurries, but not a blizzard.

"Ahoy there," said a handsome gentleman jogging by. He slowed his pace and his beautiful golden retriever started wagging its tail.

"Ahoy? Nice dog," I said. Ahoy was a strange greeting on land. I reached down to let the dog sniff my hand and then petted his wet head as snowflakes blanketed the ground.

"I'm a little unconventional in my greetings. A mutual dog lover, I see."

"Uh-huh, did Mr. Bidding send you?"

"Oh no, I'm Mr. T. How was your visit?"

"So nice to meet you, Mr. T. The building is amazing. I loved the grand architecture and stained glass. The edifice truly inspires awe."

"It certainly does. I understand Mary and Ellie explained the source of their powers and the splendid deal on their living arrangement."

"They did. They said the Angel of Light provides them with powers and the owner of the cathedral lets them stay there in exchange for looking after the place."

"Yes, Angel of Light. Such a lovely title, isn't it?"

"I guess."

"Did they tell you the owner is The Angel of Light?"

"No, they didn't tell me that."

"The Angel of Light is not stingy, and I'd know, for I am one and the same. The Angel of Light, Mr. T. . . . I have numerous names."

"I see. I didn't realize--"

"Yes, I am The Angel of Light and provide those little *gifts and perks* to anyone who follows me. I don't ask for much in return. Perhaps a bit of allegiance."

Surely not. The Angel of Light? He looked like a young athlete dressed in running attire, not like an angel.

"Ah, I don't look like an angel, is that it?"

"Um . . . no offence, but yes, that's exactly what I was thinking."

"No problem, I appear in different forms. It's possible next time we meet you'll see a different side of me. Samantha, think about my offer. Imagine how magnificent it would be to have powers like Mary and Ellie, know the future, talk to those who have passed, give comfort to their families, and perhaps even live in a spectacular home like theirs?"

"I uh, I, I don't know."

"I'll come back again after you have time to consider it. It's a once in a lifetime offer. Alas, the proposition won't stand forever, so you must decide quickly. And know that I don't make deals with just anyone. You are special, Samantha."

I shivered in the falling snow, and then abruptly found myself with Mr. Bidding at the north end of the island, the sun shining and a light breeze blowing.

"Greetings, Samantha!" he called out as he approached.

"Greetings, Mr. Bidding! Thank you for getting me out of there."

"Oh, that was not my doing, Samantha. It was all you."

"If you say so."

"I do. When you fly over Harvest Island, you will yourself up, down, left, or right. Correct?"

"Yes."

"Likewise, while on Harvest Island you may choose to remove yourself out of any situation you find yourself in. You have free will, Samantha."

"That is good news. I had no idea that I was able to free myself from the grip of the inhabitants and owners of the homes on Harvest Island by simply making that choice . . . phew." I sighed, genuinely relieved.

"Yes, Samantha. Free will is free choice. It is one of mankind's greatest gifts, but it also allowed the curse on humanity . . . but for you, I believe it will become a gift more than a curse, my dear."

"On another topic," he said, "how did your visit with Mary and Ellie go?"

"Before I answer that, I wanted to ask you about the Angel of Light. Mary said he is as powerful as The Maker. Ellie called him deity. Do you know anything about him?"

"I do."

"What can you tell me?"

His brow furrowed, "He is not deity or as powerful as The Maker, but in his pride, deceives himself and his followers. Mary and Ellie were telling you what they believe to be true."

"I see."

"Remember The Thief you asked about? The Angel of Light is one and the same. And he is anything but light. He is The Deceiver, also known as the Devil, Satan, Lucifer, and Beelzebub. His is a woeful story. He was once a beautiful angel, high ranking in The Maker's host of angels. But pride infiltrated his heart. He believed he should be equal to The Maker."

"Mr. T. Ah! The Thief!"

"Mr. T?"

"Yes, I saw him a few minutes ago in front of the

cathedral. He was confident of his powers and abilities and wanted to share those *gifts* with me. He introduced himself as Mr. T. and then told me he was also called The Angel of Light."

"Ah, I'm not surprised that he approached you. He lost his heavenly authority and was cast down to earth by The Maker but is allowed to deceive and draw mankind away from The Maker through countless ways."

"Like offering them supernatural powers if they follow him?" I asked.

"Exactly. He also instigates pride and sins of the flesh. The Thief has caused much suffering in the world, created false religions, and even convinced some of a warped view of mankind's purpose, like Ellie's understanding that man was created to reach a spiritual ascension and become divine. Wherever he sees an opening, The Angel of Light or Deceiver, which is a much better name to describe him, will insert a lie or half-truth to gain entrance."

"That is a lot to process. Don't tell me, that information is found in *The Book of Truth*?"

"It is."

"I'll have to start reading it."

"Please do. *The Book of Truth* is full of information about The Angel of Light and also about The Maker and His son. Do your research, Samantha, but also be on guard against The Deceiver's tactics. He attacks when least expected."

Mr. Bidding continued, "So back to my original question, Samantha. What did you learn from Mary and Ellie?"

"They both seem sincere in their belief they are on a path that will lead to betterment of themselves or others. I was intrigued and repulsed by them at the same time. Ellie was a lot scarier than Mary, and I believe she was more aware of how her methods defy truth. She realized that her healing ritual sickened me but enjoyed offering it anyway. A little sadistic . . . or did she want to show off her powers? Mary and Ellie both claim their abilities are from the Angel of Light and believe they are on the path to a more spiritual existence. I understand how that could be tempting for the right individuals. I'm too scared to even dip my toe into any of their practices. I wasn't enticed by Mr. T's offer."

"I'm glad you're not interested in The Thief's offer of power, but beware, he has other tactics."

"Oh, I almost forgot. I have an envelope with another clue."

"Please, Samantha, open it."

I carefully broke the seals and found another clue in blood red ink.

"The Light is Flickering"

What? Another nonsensical clue. Flickering? Candles for incantations or a séance? These inhabitants would certainly be familiar with those things, but I wasn't about to go back and ask for their help. Or could it be something completely different? John's antique collection of lamps?

Chapter 22

I woke to the smell of coffee and bacon drifting up the stairs. Startled at first, I quickly remembered Spence had slept on the sofa. He was once again taking care of me and the kids. What a guy. He'll be a fantastic husband someday. I hope he finds a gal worthy of him.

Not wanting to look like I'd just climbed out of bed, I went into the bathroom and ran a comb through my hair which usually sticks out in weird places in the morning. Then I did a quick teeth brush and mouth wash swirl. I wouldn't want to repulse my kind protector. I threw on a pair of jeans and a T-shirt, glanced in the mirror, straightened my bangs and went downstairs.

"Good morning, Spence. So nice of you to make coffee and breakfast."

"Mornin', Sam. It's the least I could do after the scare you had last night. Hope I didn't wake you. I took the liberty of cleaning up where the officer smeared fingerprint dust on the door handles and in the half bath last night after you went to bed. And I cleaned off the message from the mirror too. I didn't want the kids to see it. Unfortunately, no fingerprints were found."

"You didn't have to do that. But thank you. The person who broke in must have worn gloves, not surprising. Who would want to threaten me and the kids?" I poured myself a cup of coffee.

"I'd say it is the same person or people who are calling

and threatening you." He grinned.

"You know that is not what I meant." I chuckled.

"The obvious answer is that it must have to do with John. I called the station and asked Officer Mitchell to run his name in our system this morning. She found that he was reported missing fifteen years ago, a few weeks after you got that call on your twenty-first birthday.

"By whom?" I started setting the table.

"It was a Bobby Baxter from Wilmington, North Carolina. Know him?" Spence flipped over a pancake.

"He was one of John's fishing buddies. I remember him from when I was a kid. I didn't know they were still in touch then. They were in the Navy together. I heard that Bobby passed away in a car accident about a year after John disappeared."

"Possibly, Mitchell said John and Bobby planned to meet for a fishing trip, but John was a no show. Bobby tried to call for several days, but got no response, so he reported him missing. The New Hanover County officer told him they couldn't open an investigation since John didn't have a permanent residence there." Spencer brought a stack of pancakes and a plate of crispy bacon to the table.

I stared at the plate trying to process this new information.

"Please, Sam, try to eat," Spencer said.

"Sorry. Just thinking. So, they didn't do anything?" I put two pancakes and two pieces of bacon on my plate.

"They contacted Horry County and found out about the bloody scene at John's apartment. They informed Bobby but that was the end of it. It was out of their jurisdiction."

I poured hot maple syrup on my pancakes, "I wish I'd contacted Bobby back then. He may have had insight or known what was happening in John's life. If only . . ." I sighed.

"I understand, but the 'what if's' and 'if only's' will get you nowhere, Sam. You can't go back and change the past.

It's done. But I get the need for answers. I'll take a look at the hard copy file when I get into the office. If Bobby was interviewed, I may find more information. The threatening message told *you* to stop looking but didn't say anything about me investigating."

"Thanks, Spence. You're a dear. Please be careful." I smiled, and he held my gaze for a second longer than was comfortable for both of us.

"No problem, Sam. I'll use other resources to see what else I can find out. It would be a good idea for you to back off for a while. I'm not sure what nerve you touched, but your search triggered something, and I'm worried about you, Sam."

"I know, I would never forgive myself if the twins were hurt." I sucked in a breath, suppressing a sob.

"And you have parents and siblings who love and need you . . . and a lot of other people who care about you too." He shot me a comforting smile.

"I know you're right," I said. "John's disappearance has been such a mystery. I'd love to have closure. But not at the expense of my sweet Jayce and Jazmine's safety."

"Or yours, Sam. You are greatly valued."

"Thank you, Spence. You're a good friend." I avoided locking eyes again.

Over coffee, pancakes, and bacon, we moved on to other topics. Spence had researched John's social security number and had no additional leads. It hadn't been used in fifteen years.

I debated about telling Spence my most recent dream but decided against it. He'd probably credit my dreams to my wacky imagination like Mom had, and he'd probably be right.

Chapter 23

After Spence left and the twins were off to school, I double checked every window and door lock in the house and then sat down at the kitchen table with paper and pen. Unless the intruder planted a camera in the house, the person or people threatening us would not see what I was about to do.

On the lined yellow legal pad, I wrote the first clue from my dreams.

1. It began in the Isle of Palms

Harry made the additional comment "Here you'll find light." So far, I'd discovered that John and Mom used to visit The Isle of Palms early in their marriage. John worked in the area and bought antiques and art from dealers there. Was he mixed up in something illegal? The light Harry mentioned might have referred to his collection of antique lights. Or was it a sunny island in the south Pacific with a lot of palm trees? I knew that Harvest Island was not a real place, but in my dream, I was told it was in the South Pacific. Was the location of Harvest Island a clue in itself?

I jotted down Antique dealers in the Isle of Palms, Antique Lights, South Pacific, and then on another line wrote the second clue:

2. In His New Life He Works No More

A new life. New family? New Name? What was he running from? He works no more. He's no longer working, retired. That makes sense since he would be almost seventy now. It's probably been a waste to search for current employment. Not that I dared to after the warnings. I wrote "Retired."

Then I wrote the third clue.

3. Find your cue in the color blue

If I combined this with the Isle of Palms clue, it might be referring to the ocean. The photo of Mom and John was on the pier surrounded by blue water. In my dreams the blue water surrounding Harvest Island was brilliant. Is John in the South Pacific?

Or was it Blue Mountains? John had a few assignments there and loved the area. When I searched Blue Mountains on the internet, I was surprised to find numerous Blue Mountains – Australia, Jamaica, and the Pacific Northwest. I realized the place where John worked was The Blue *Ridge* Mountains in North Carolina which also extended into seven other states. Too many options to eliminate.

Was there a town named Blue? I searched online and found five US towns called Blue: West Virginia, Texas, Oklahoma, Indiana, and Arizona. Who knew? In addition, there were other towns with Blue in the name--The Blue Mountains, Ontario; Blue Hill, Maine; Blue River, Colorado, Blue Mountain, Mississippi, and Blue Springs, Missouri. Again, too many options to narrow down.

I certainly couldn't travel to all of the places the Blue clue yielded. Maybe the meaning would become more evident with additional clues.

I wrote, "Blue – location or a thing like the ocean?"

4. From the Mountains to the Valley

If I combined this with the previous clues, I could eliminate the blue regions, blue towns, and blue water. Did he get into trouble in the Blue Ridge Mountains and go to a town in a valley close by. If so, that's a needle in a haystack. And doesn't fit with The Isle of Palms clue. I didn't write anything under that clue.

5. The Light is Flickering

This clue took me back to John's collection of lights. He owned antique oil lanterns that would produce a flickering flame. John also boasted about an antique candlelit chandelier. It was a gorgeous two-tiered French bronze piece with an intricate gothic design holding about ten candles. Those certainly would flicker. Or did it refer to something else entirely? A dark basement with flickering fluorescent lights? My imagination was running wild. It was time to move on and see if anything else made more sense when I received new clues. Clue number 5, useless at this point.

How else could I find out what happened to John? I'd back off on my digging into the Isle of Palms' art and antique shops. After Mom told me about their visits early in their marriage, I'd called several local galleries hoping to get a forwarding address for John if he was still in contact with them. That could easily have been monitored if any of the people I spoke with knew John or the people threatening me.

I also resolved to stop calling and doing internet searches of traveling nurse agencies. Something triggered the threats, and I didn't want to put my family in danger.

If my DNA search sparked the warnings, there was nothing I could do about that. My DNA was out there, and I couldn't take it back. I wasn't sure if it was possible to block anyone from seeing it. I didn't remember what was in the fine print and may have already signed away that right. I hoped one of John's relatives would reach out to me.

I needed to find another approach.

Chapter 24

After making little sense of the dream clues, I called Mom.

"Hey, Mom. Do you have any other information about John? I know it's been a while since Kyle and I made our massive effort to find out what happened. But I'd be grateful if you remember anything else that might help."

"Good timing, Sam. I was cleaning out my downstairs closet and found a shoebox full of miscellaneous things from John. I flipped through them and didn't see anything important, but I didn't spend much time looking at everything. I've got a mess to clean up before Kristin and Bev come over for book club later. Are you interested in taking a look?"

"Yes, that would be fantastic." Hope was renewed. "I'll stop by and pick up the box if that works."

"Sure, dear."

A few hours later I laid the large shoebox on my kitchen table. In addition to old photos, I found letters John sent Mom after their divorce. After skimming several, I slowed my pace and read every word of one dated September 10, 2005.

Dear Georgia,
    A quick note to say I'm fine. I was in an area that didn't flood – one of the few. About 80% of New

Orleans is under water. We still don't know the final number of deaths, but it is in the hundreds. I've been helping the rescue effort with a FEMA Disaster Medical Team. One of the 'rescues' has been keeping me awake at night, and I wanted to give you and the kids a heads up.

A leader of the Devil's Saints Motorcycle Club was injured in a collapsed home. At the time I didn't know who he was. But his leg became badly infected and the doctor recommended amputation. The man begged our team doctor not to amputate. The doc delayed, but when the man was no longer responsive, and it was a matter of his leg or his life, we amputated. After he regained consciousness, the man vowed to find the doc, me, and our families and "return the favor." Georgia, there is no question it was a veiled threat. It's unlikely he'll ever deliver on his promise, but I wanted you to be aware. The man's name is Theodore M. Raven. The gang he leads has been linked to drug trafficking and numerous homicides. This gang has chapters of the club up and down the east coast. Please be vigilant and tell the kids to watch their backs.

I hope you, Tom, and all the kids are well.

Take care,

John

Would a person wait for close to twenty years to seek revenge for a lost leg? It was unlikely, but worth following up on. I now had Detective Spencer McKenna on speed dial.

"Hey Spence, it's Samantha. Please call when you get this message. Thanks!"

A couple of hours later Spencer returned my call. "Hi Sam. What's up?"

"Can you check out the status of a Theodore M. Raven?

He was associated with the Devil's Saints Motorcycle Club."

"And what's the relevance?"

"Nothing much, only that John helped to amputate his leg in 2005 after Katrina. Theo pledged to return the favor to John and his family."

"Ah, is that all? I'll see what I can find out. It's been a long time since Katrina hit, but I should be able to track him. The justice department' agencies surveil all the one-percenters. You'd make a good detective, Sam, if you ever get tired of teaching."

"Ha-ha. I wouldn't attempt to keep up with you, Mr. Ninety Percent Solve Rate. So, what's a one-percenter?"

"It's an outlaw designation for criminal biker clubs. They wear it proudly. And the Devil's Saints are no doubt criminals. I'll be relieved when we solve this one, Sam. I worry about you."

"Thanks, Spence. You're one of a kind."

Chapter 25

Dream: Ryan Rich

The weather felt perfect, about seventy-five degrees with a slight breeze and low humidity. I was standing over the water on a southern pier of Harvest Island looking toward the sandy white beach speckled with seagulls and pelicans basking in the warm sun. A few found refuge from the heat in the shade of the swaying palm trees. Occasionally a large blue heron or white egret would disturb the resting birds and force them to relocate farther down the beach.

I glanced back towards the west. The only home on the island that sat on the beachside of the cobblestone road encircling the island resembled a fairy tale castle. But it didn't have a moat, so it would likely be considered a palace. The mostly emerald-green structure had a smooth exterior that reflected the blinding sunlight. I squinted to gaze at the sparkling gems covering the towers, turrets, and roofs. Emeralds and diamonds? This terraced building contained both conical roof towers and turrets with crenelations like the rook pieces in a chess game. Directly across the wide cobblestone street, lay the field of gold that surely belonged to this palatial home. I instinctively knew this was my next assignment.

I strolled down the beach toward the castle without a moat, sandals in hand, kicking the sand and sending the gulls to flight as I went. I didn't hurry because I wasn't sure who

I'd encounter in this beautiful home. Most inhabitants of Harvest Island were cordial enough, but some were sinister, and their homes didn't always reflect their disposition. But if I wanted to capture another clue, I'd have to proceed. As I neared the building, I saw a massive arched entrance to a courtyard flanked by golden king gargoyles. I heard opera music streaming from inside.

As I passed through the thirty-foot deep entrance, I was enchanted by the magical sight in front of me. Flowers and trees, a plethora of color and species, along with gold statues of animals, wild and tame, filled the enclosure. A cobblestone path wound its way throughout the exquisite yard.

I followed the trail to the right where an assortment of lilies grew. Bright yellow daylilies, peach Asiatic lilies, and bright orange with black speckled tiger lilies. Red, yellow, and white rose bushes and magenta peonies were sprinkled throughout the area creating a captivating display.

"Hello, Samantha!" a cheery voice called.

"Uh, hello! Where are you?" I looked around but didn't see anyone.

"Right here, how are you, Samantha? I am Duke Ryan Rich." A tall, lanky, dark-skinned gentleman emerged from behind a small grove of rubber trees. His palm tree print polo shirt, khaki cargo shorts, and leather sandals created a relaxed impression. He had round wire spectacles, a short flattop hair style, and an unlit cigar protruding from his mouth.

"Oh, hi there, Duke Rich," I said. He didn't look scary at all. He was kind of familiar, but I couldn't place him.

"Please, call me Duke Ryan. I see you have finally found your way to the absolute best real estate on the island," he said.

"Yes, how wonderful. Right on the beach. That's always been a dream of mine. And your garden isn't too shabby either!"

"Thank you. Him Who Does His Bidding tells me you are on a quest, and we, the inhabitants of this island, are part of your solution. How delightful!"

"Yes, delightful," I responded. He seemed harmless enough. Certainly, he was more "normal" than several of the other inhabitants I'd encountered.

"Follow me. I'll show you in, so we can get out of the sun."

"That would be lovely."

"This wing of the palace leads to the main living area."

I followed him through a long stone corridor into an expansive living space appointed with gorgeous modern furnishings and accessories. The unique stacked stone and glass fireplace in the center of the open concept room was visible from all four sides. I stood still absorbing the incredible design details and perfectly paired layers of texture and color.

"Please don't gawk. It is not becoming for a young lady," Duke Ryan said.

His rapid change in his manner surprised me. "Sorry . . . I've never been in such a glamorous home."

"I understand, but now let's get down to business. You know, time is money."

"Yes certainly. I don't want to keep you from your work."

"So, Samantha, how can I help? What do you need to know?"

"I need to know about your life here on Harvest Island. How long have you been here, what you do, who else lives here with you, those sort of things . . . if you don't mind."

"Whether I mind or not, is irrelevant. I must provide any information you request per direction of Him Who Does His Bidding."

"I see. If you could briefly tell me about yourself, it would be helpful."

"I have lived on Harvest Island for a few decades. I'm

an attorney. Duchess Rita, my ex-wife, lived with me for about twelve years. She was a CPA but is no longer working and no longer living here. The north wing of the castle is the business suite where we both worked and where I still work. She helped in embezzlement cases when I needed an expert witness."

"How long ago did you divorce?"

"It was about fifteen years ago now. We have one daughter Ashley and when she was ten, we went our separate ways. We had drifted apart and couldn't agree on anything. Ashley was in boarding school by then, so she didn't see the worst of our final days together."

"I'm sorry to hear that. I've had a similar divorce. Do go on."

"We raised our daughter Ashley with the best of everything – nannies, education, travel, clothes, jewels, hobbies -- anything her heart desired. But she was a terribly rebellious teenager and rejected our way of life and now lives an impoverished existence on the other side of the island. I still love her deeply and wish she would put aside her disapproval of my lifestyle long enough to visit on occasion, but alas, she has made her choice and we, my ex and I, are no longer a part of her life. I have tried to see her, but she refuses."

"I'm sorry to hear that. I met Ashley, and if it is any consolation, she seems content. But I do hope you are able to reconcile someday."

"As do I. But for now, we live our separate lives minutes away from each other." He paused. I thought I saw a glimmer of regret in his eyes. "As for other residents in the castle, it's only me and the hired help. I have a full-time staff of fourteen including groundskeepers, cooks, maids, a business manager for the household, and my personal butler. They are all top-notch employees, but that is all they are, workers. I do my best to keep them at arm's length, so they know their place."

"Um, uh, I see. Tell me about being a lawyer on Harvest Island."

"It's a lucrative position. I take on clients from all the surrounding islands, and consequently make more money than anyone else on the island. I can afford any luxury that I desire. I own a magnificent yacht, several sports cars, a chateau in the Swiss Alps, a condo in New York overlooking Central Park, a cottage and 600-acre vineyard in France, and this lovely domicile."

"That's impressive."

"Most days I work twelve or fourteen hours, but it's worth it. I have the best legal team working for me. Therefore, we get all the high-profile cases in the region. I rarely lose a case, which helps to increase my net worth. If it's a settlement case, we take 49 percent after expenses. My attorneys bill $600 an hour for the firm, and they work 70-90 hours a week. After all, the bottom line is what matters most, right?"

"Some think so."

"But you don't?"

"I uh . . . um . . . having money helps for sure, but for me, loving my job and making a difference is more important."

"Indeed, I do love my job because it helps me to relish the time when I'm not working. I take a month off here and there to enjoy my four estates and magnificent yacht. When I'm away from here, you'll find me floating under the sparkling stars, skiing the Alps, or sampling the fruit of my vast vineyard. I have an elite staff around the world, so everything is the absolute best. Exactly how I like it."

"That sounds incredible. But I couldn't work all those hours and keep up with my kids and the rest of my family and friends."

"Indeed, there are sacrifices. My marriage and family life have suffered. Duchess Rita said I was married to the job, and she was right, but I never admitted that to her. She wanted to have all the nice things in the world and loved to travel as much as I do. I believed I could do it all and have it all. I was wrong, but I still cherish having anything and everything I want. There are always more desirable properties to acquire, more places to travel to, and more unique experiences to have. That is only done by procuring *more* money. I would not do anything differently if given another chance. The sacrifices are worth it."

"So, money really is the bottom line for you."

"Yes, indeed, I would say."

"Tell me about Duchess Rita."

He sighed as if he'd hoped the interview was over.

He rattled off a description of his ex-wife. "She is a wonderful woman of Asian descent. Bright and beautiful, with long, luxurious black hair and striking blue eyes. Duchess Rita always wore the most fashionable clothes and jewelry. She insisted on the highest quality gemstones, and I'm sure that hasn't changed. We made a corner of our panic room from floor to ceiling into a jewelry safe. As if the panic room wasn't safe enough."

"I've never seen a panic room." It was off topic, but hoped he'd offer to show me more of the home. He didn't.

"She made sure we shared our wealth with the less fortunate by setting up charities for kids with cancer and muscular dystrophy." Duke Rich's face turned bright red.

It was obvious he didn't want to "share" their wealth. I concluded he was both selfish and stingy.

"When we divorced, she continued the charities on her own. Good riddance. No more 'stealing' my hard-earned money. Shortly after our divorce she inherited a couple hundred million from an aunt, so she continues her extravagant lifestyle. No more fighting over money. No more giving away or squandering that for which I have worked so diligently."

"It sounds like you are happier now," I said.

"Indeed, indeed. Is there anything else? I must be

getting back to work."

"If I could bother you to take a look at your field, I would appreciate it."

"Certainly. I'll show you across the street."

I tried to keep up as he bolted out the way we'd entered. He paused until I caught up and then hurried me across the cobblestone road to the produce.

"This field is the pinnacle of my pride and joy. The more I work and bill my clients, the larger the produce grows. It is exquisite!" We arrived at the edge of the shimmering gold plot that appeared to be dancing in the sun.

"It is stunning. Thank you for your time, Duke Ryan. I know you're busy."

"Indeed. I'll leave you here then. I hope I've done enough to fulfill Him Who Does His Biddings requirements. I don't want to waste my time with you needing to come back for a second visit. Remain here as long as you like. I'll be heading to work now." He handed me an emerald-green envelope with two gold seals with a king's crown embossed on each of them. He spun around and dashed back to the palace.

"Thanks again, Duke Ryan," I called as he retreated.

I turned back toward the hypnotizing gold field. I reached down and touched the plant at my feet. To my amazement, this crop was hard, cold, and smooth . . . actual gold? The mesmerizing produce stretched as far as I could see in three directions. This was by far the largest of the fields I'd seen. But I didn't understand how it could be harvested for eating or nourishment. It must be sold for its actual gold content at market. Certainly not for eating. King Midas came to mind.

I looked from the crops to my hand which held the beautiful emerald color envelope. I quickly broke the gold seals and read the next clue.

"The Answer is in His Name"

His name, John Garcia. What does that tell me? His full

name was John Alvin Garcia. He never used his middle name or even initial. He didn't want to be teased about being a chipmunk. I had searched all the John Garcia's and John A. Garcia's in the locations he loved. I only recently started John Alvin Garcia searches. Was it possible, he was using his middle name, and that held the key to finding him?

I looked up and was at the north end of the island. How did that happen? Mr. Bidding said I can control where I am, but I don't remember willing myself here.

"Hello, Mr. Bidding!"

"Greetings, Samantha! A lovely day, isn't it?"

"Yes, it certainly is."

"How was your visit to Duke Ryan Rich's palace?"

"Quite pleasant. I loved his courtyard with cobblestone paths, beautiful flowers, trees, and the statues were incredibly lifelike, except for being gold, of course. But that's probably not what you're asking."

"That's fine. Any observations are welcome."

"In that case, I wish he'd invited me to see the entire home. I've never seen furnishings so upscale and glamorous. The other homes in Harvest Island have been extraordinary, each in their own way, but none measure up to the chic interior of the palace."

"No doubt, he does have the most stylish decor on the island. And what about Duke Ryan?"

"He's an attractive man . . . I was drawn to him -- especially at first. His appearance was warm and inviting. His smile was charming. He exuded confidence in knowing what he wants and how to get it. It is sad that his obsession with work and having the finest of everything cost him his family . . . at least his wife. I hope he will one day have a relationship with his daughter, Ashley."

"It's unfortunate, but not surprising that Duchess Rita and Ashley went their own way. Duchess Rita was correct in believing that Duke Ryan's first love was his work because it provides for his opulent lifestyle," Mr. Bidding said.

"I understand why he loves his possessions. The little I saw was spectacular, but how could he desire wealth above his family?" I asked.

"It's a trap that's easy to fall into, Samantha. The Maker warned that you cannot serve both him and be enslaved to money."

"Is it wrong to have wealth and nice things?"

"Oh goodness, no. The Maker has created beauty and riches to be enjoyed by his children. Multitudes of his children have abundant wealth to enjoy and use their riches for good. The warning is against putting money in place of The Maker. Earthly treasures can snuff out the devotion and desire for The Maker if not clearly viewed."

"What is that scripture I've heard? Money is the root of all evil or something like that."

Mr. Bidding chuckled. "That's a common misquote from *The Book of Truth*. It actually says, 'the love of money is the root of all kinds of evil.' When wealth becomes the driving force in one's life, its accumulation guides them. It becomes their source instead of The Maker. The evils of greed, selfishness, dishonesty, status, or pride can prevail."

"I observed selfishness in Duke Ryan's attitude toward Duchess Rita and her charities. He also appeared to be a snob when he spoke about his staff who lived in the palace."

"A good thing is able to turn into something unhealthy if not kept in check, Samantha."

"I understand how that can happen."

"Money is one of The Thief's primary tools for drawing people away from The Maker who has created the whole world and everything in it. It's important to remember that wealth and possessions are temporary, but The Maker, His Word, and His children are eternal."

"That certainly puts things into perspective. Thanks for your sage advice, Mr. Bidding. You've given me a lot to ponder."

"Just fulfilling my assignment," Mr. Bidding said and

disappeared.

I turned and headed down the cobblestone street toward the palace and that magnificent golden field. I wanted one more look.

"Hello, miss." A lovely middle-aged Asian woman adorned with diamonds sporting a Gucci gown greeted me as I reached the golden field."

The inhabitants of the island were not much for convention. I shouldn't have been surprised.

"Oh, hello! I came to take another look at that stunning palace, and the golden field is hypnotizing."

"Of course, it's grand. I used to live in the palace. So glad you came to take another look." She pushed her long jet-black hair back over her shoulder.

"Duchess Rita Rich?"

"Yes, please call me Duchess Rita. I now own my own island, but I like to come back and see how the field is growing now and then. It is captivating, and I still own shares, so its growth interests me."

"Do you miss Harvest Island?" I asked.

"Oh no. Not at all. I do miss my daughter, Ashley, though."

"I'm sure that's difficult."

"I still don't understand why she's chosen to go on a path of self-denial, when we lavished her with so much." Duchess Rita shook her head.

"I guess we each need to find our own way," I said.

"Let me help you find your way, Samantha. I'll offer you a splendid deal. For a small price, you'll own half of my shares in this field. I currently own half, so that would be about a quarter of this field."

"And what is the price?" I asked.

"You would need to make the golden field a top priority in your life, to grow your portion, whatever it takes. I believe you'd have enormous potential to multiply your stakes. You would love to enhance your lifestyle, wouldn't you? Lovely clothing, jewels, a home on the coast or perhaps your own island. And you could even start a charity in your own name, like I have. You could help the less fortunate. Wouldn't that be worth a little time and effort?"

A step up in my lifestyle wouldn't be the worst thing to ever happen to me. And I do love to make a difference. "What do you get out of this arrangement?" I asked.

"First as your share grows, my share grows, so eventually, I would have more with less effort. But primarily, Mr. T. has promised to double the size of my golden field on my island. All I have to do is persuade you to comply with this simple request. What do you say?"

"Mr. T. has put you up to this?"

"Yes, he said if you returned to take another look, he'd like me to make the offer. He detected a spark of interest in your first visit."

It was true I hadn't returned to any of the other homes. This one was different. "How did he see my interest? I didn't see him when I visited the palace."

"Of course not. He has exceptional talents, not the least is to see us when we don't see him. He said he was busy and didn't have time to materialize to make you the offer in person."

"But he had time to make you an offer? Why not cut out the middleman so to speak?"

"An offer coming from another human makes it more enticing because Mr. T's presence scares some people. And he generously wanted me to benefit from the arrangement too. We've known each other for a long time. And he mentioned you hadn't responded to his previous offer of supernatural abilities, so he wanted to make an offer that may be more interesting to you."

Remembering my conversation with Mr. Bidding, I realized I'd walked into a trap of my own making. "Thanks, Duchess Rita, but no thanks, I need to leave now."

"If you change your mind, here's my card." She thrust

a card toward me, but I refused it.

I spun around and ran, tripping and falling . . . .

I awoke with a start, my heart racing. The dreams were getting more personal.

Chapter 26

Spencer stopped by my home to give me an update. We stood by the kitchen island sipping coffee and eating peanut butter chocolate chip cookies while he told me what he'd found.

He'd looked into the biker gang that John had crossed paths with and found that most of the top leaders of the Devil's Saints were incarcerated or dead. The club was now a mere shadow of its former corrupt enterprise. Theodore M. Raven was among the dead, so unless a family member had decided to take revenge, it was unlikely the reason for John's disappearance or my recent threats. Theodore has two sons in the business now, but neither was a likely suspect according to Spencer.

After that rabbit trail led nowhere, I hesitated, but shared with Spencer my most recent dream clues along with the possible meanings I'd come up with. "Have I lost it?"

"No, Samantha. It might be your subconscious working while you're asleep. I'm not sure about blue or flickering lights, but you knew John's middle name before you had the latest dream, right?"

"I did."

"Then, I'd say your subconscious is doing its job, trying to remember anything that might help you discover what happened." He reached over and placed his hand on my shoulder.

I was relieved to know he was with me in my search.

"Good. I hoped you'd help. I'm scared to do any research from my home computer." I sighed.

"No worries, Sam. We'll figure this out, however long it takes."

A couple of days after sharing John's middle name with Spence, he asked me to stop by the station.

I found him drinking coffee at a table in the detective's lounge.

"Hey, Spence."

"Glad you could make it, Sam. Have a seat."

"So, what'd you discover?" I asked.

"On a hunch, I called all the storage facilities in and around Seagrove, and asked if any were rented to a John Garcia, John A. Garcia, or an Alvin Garcia. Many owners wouldn't give out information without a subpoena, but a few companies' rental agreements stated they could legally provide requested information to authorities concerning their lessees. I found a nearby storage unit rented to an Alvin Garcia."

"That's great."

Spencer nodded. "Samantha, it's possible Alvin Garcia's unit may belong to your father. It was paid for with cash twenty-five years in advance. The owner said each renter has a unique code to enter the gated property. No one has signed in with your dad's code for the last fifteen years. The first month after it was rented the code was used four times. Nothing after that. The timeframe lines up with your dad's disappearance. It's quite a coincidence if it's not his."

"Yes, I'd have to agree. And it's not a big deal, Spence, but I don't like to call John my dad. That title belongs to Tom. John's my biological father. He never earned the 'dad' title in my life. And believe it or not, he told me and Kyle that he thought we should call Tom "Dad.""

"Sorry, Sam. I understand. John it is."

"No worries. How much does a unit like that go for?"

"The unit's a climate controlled twelve by twenty that

currently costs $310 a month. The owner, Dexter Gordon, said it would have gone for around $150 a month fifteen years ago. He calculated a twenty-five-year rental would have been around $45,000."

"He didn't know exactly how much he charged Alvin Garcia?"

"The current owner bought the facility ten years ago, and that particular unit's record only specified the date rented, paid with cash, and the end date, no amount. He said the previous owner probably cut Alvin Garcia a deal for the multiple year cash payment and didn't want record of it. Or maybe he was trying to avoid taxes."

"Or did he overcharge him promising to ask no questions? Who knows? The reason he didn't record the amount of the transaction isn't important." I shifted in the hard chair. "The most interesting thing is that he paid for twenty-five years at once. He must have planned on disappearing. What did John get himself into?"

"Not sure, Sam. I looked into his financials, and nothing indicated criminal activity. One odd thing though. There's been a hundred dollars deposited into his savings account every six months or so. That's probably kept the account from going dormant and turned over to the state as unclaimed property."

"Spence, you know what that means?" I reached out and touched his arm.

He put his hand over mine. "If I were to guess, it means John's still alive. But I don't want to jump to conclusions. Somone else could be making the deposits."

"Why would anyone else do that? He has to be alive." I pulled my hand back.

"I hope so, Sam. Prior to the one-hundred-dollar deposits, he'd been depositing paychecks and had typical expenses. Nothing out of the ordinary. His savings account is a modest fifty thousand. It's still collecting interest. He has a 401K with no recent withdrawals and sporadic small deposits. It's over two million dollars."

"Wow. He must have started putting money into his retirement account early. That's quite a nest egg."

"Way more than I've been able to invest in my retirement." Spencer said. "Those are the only accounts I was able to locate, but it's possible he has offshore accounts too."

"Thanks, Spence. Is it possible to get into Alvin Garcia's unit?" I asked.

"Already on it, Sam. I called Judge Gavin Norsk to try to get a warrant. Since John's been considered a missing person for fifteen years, and after your break-in and threats, he granted the warrant. I need to go by the courthouse and pick it up later. He's going to sign it when he arrives at court today."

Spence's phone rang.

"Thanks, Judge Norsk. I'll be by in twenty." Spence smiled and hung up. "We're finally making a little headway. Hopefully it won't be another dead end. Sorry, Sam, poor choice of words."

Chapter 27

Soft flute and string music filled the waiting room with the occasional sound of a bubbling brook breaking through. I closed my eyes and breathed in the sandalwood incense. I was almost asleep when a door opening startled me. A friend from group therapy emerged from Dr. Lakesha Davenport's office.

"Hi, Sam!" she greeted.

"Oh hi, Julie!" I said. "How are you?"

"How much time do you have?" She laughed. "Probably about two minutes, while Dr. Davenport updates her notes." I hoped Julie still wasn't in the abusive relationship with her boyfriend.

"I'm doing okay with the good doctor's help, keeping my boundaries in place," Julie said. "How are you, Samantha?"

"I'll tell you after I talk to her. I kinda think I'm losing it."

"Oh, no worries, girl. We all do from time to time. I sure hope your visit helps. But right now, I gotta run. Picking up my kids from soccer practice, among other things."

"I know the drill. Good to see you, Julie. Take care of yourself."

"You too, Sam. It's bound to be better after you see Lakesha. I love her insights."

"Me too. She always helps. But you'd better get going. I don't want to be the reason you're late getting your kiddos."

I understood her struggles. We'd been part of a single parent support group for a year before several of the gals ended up not so single anymore. The group was cancelled. It was good while it lasted. Under the guidance and encouragement of Dr. Davenport, we'd all learned from each other.

Within two minutes of Julie's departure, Dr. Lakesha Davenport appeared in the doorway and beckoned me into her office. She was always punctual. My kind of gal.

"Sam, it's been a minute. What's going on?"

"Other than losing my mind, nothing much." I smiled.

"Do tell." She returned my smile, her dark skin and eyes glowing with warmth.

For the next forty minutes I recounted the recent events and dreams while Lakesha scribbled notes, nodded, and asked an occasional question.

What were you thinking about before you went to bed?

How did that make you feel?

What do you think that means?

They were all good questions. I had few answers.

"Am I losing my mind?" I asked when I finished recounting the final clues I had received in my dreams.

"No, you're not losing your mind, Sam. The fact that you are asking that question shows you know the difference between your conscious reality and the unconscious symbolism you've experienced. Your dreams are most remarkable, unlike any I've ever heard. And the fact that you remember them with such clarity is amazing. The universe is speaking to you, Sam."

"I've never had dreams with such vivid, enduring images. Could it be God speaking?" I asked timidly, not knowing where she stood on such things.

"In the past, we've only talked about coping mechanisms for your emotions and compulsions which have hindered your daily life, Sam. But your dreams, they are on another level, an expression of the universal psyche."

"What's that?" I felt uncomfortable with the phrase.

"The mind is a magnificent thing, Sam. It contains the collective unconscious—a wealth of wisdom and archetypes that can manifest in dreams. When we're awake, we rely strongly on what we see and our conscious awareness. We repress instincts and memories we've inherited. The collective unconscious is a universal dimension that spans all time and humanity."

"Hmm. That's a new concept for me. I've never heard of the collective unconscious. And why am I tapping into that now?" I wanted to be open to her ideas about my dreams but had a nagging feeling something was off. She'd been instrumental in helping me with my compulsions, so I could live a mostly normal life. She deserved to be heard.

"Your deep longings for acceptance from your father have brought these to the surface in your dreams. With the stress of your stepdad's illness, the old feelings of abandonment have added to the tension in your life. You realize this may be close to the end for your stepdad. To balance the conscious crisis you're experiencing, the unconscious knowledge and instinct are being displayed in your dreams."

"That's a lot of psychology. But kinda makes sense."

"They are concepts from the works of Carl Jung. You may want to read his writings. They're quite enlightening."

I dared to ask again, "So, you don't believe it's God speaking to me?"

"I believe the universe is speaking to you, Sam. I only ask the probing questions. You'll find the answers within. There's a deeper truth for you to discover than the archetypal characters in your dreams. I'm sure of it."

Chapter 28

Under the dim yellow light, six-foot-high piles of boxes, crates, and covered furniture lined both sides of the storage unit. A narrow path down the center divided the contents in half with little space to access items along the outer edges without rearranging.

I deduced most pieces were antiques from the segments showing under the loosely thrown protectors--ornate carvings, turned legs, and aged wood. Scattered throughout the unit, tall, thin crates housed pieces of artwork that John had collected. A thick layer of dust had settled on most of the boxes, but one box by the front left corner appeared to have been wiped recently.

"Achoo, excuse me!" The musty smell and dust tickled my nose.

"Bless you!" Spence and Abigail said in unison.

"Jinx! You owe me a Coke!" Spence laughed.

Abigail looked at Spencer warmly and started asking about another case they were working together. They appeared comfortable with each other.

"All right guys, enough goofing off," I said.

"Ah, humph, who's the one goofing off, Anderson?" Spence asked.

"Hey, I'm hard at work supervising," I said.

Spence glanced up and nodded. "Right."

I returned the nod and sat up a little straighter in my padded camping chair. He went back to the task at hand.

Abigail pushed her glasses up on her nose and shot a quick look at Spencer and then me. Her golden blond hair was in a French braid and her delicate features were accentuated with freckles across her nose and cheeks. She looked like the stereotypical all-American girl next door. Did Spencer find her attractive? I glanced at her left hand. A wedding band and large diamond ring. *Sam, what are you doing? Focus.*

Detective Spencer McKenna and Officer Abigail Mitchell had begun the search at 7:00 a.m., while I observed from outside the unit. Abigail took pictures of everything and catalogued what Spence set aside to take back to the station. Spence opened boxes and hunted for anything that would explain John's disappearance and the threats I'd been receiving. The unit was full, so they couldn't remove everything. Spencer was being selective. The warrant included any property and electronically stored information found in the storage unit. Spence hoped to find a computer or paperwork containing information about suspicious activity if there was any.

About a half hour into the search Spencer announced, "No question. This is John's storage unit, Sam. All the paperwork I've found says either John Garcia or John A. Garcia. He must have rented the unit under Alvin Garcia to hide it from anyone who was looking for him or this unit's contents."

"You've really come through for me, I could kiss you," I said and then immediately regretted it.

His head jerked up. I wasn't sure what I was reading in his expression. Empathy? Compassion? Amusement?

"Uh, um, figure of speech," I said.

"I figured. Get it?"

"Ha-ha. I meant I appreciate all you've done for me."

"Just doin' my job, Ms. Anderson."

"Certainly, Detective McKenna." I said with a weak smile. His broad grin said volumes. He was more than just doing his job. He was doing his job for me.

"Now to find evidence that leads us somewhere," he said.

"Yes, let's," Abigail said.

The clue from my dream was starting to pay off. Now what about the other clues? What did they mean? Deliberations for another time.

"I had no idea John owned so much stuff. He told me he'd taken most of his collections to an aunt and uncle's farm in Mississippi when he leased the small apartment in Seagrove. He said he didn't have room for them anymore," I said.

Spencer raised his eyebrows. "Really? Did you ever meet them?"

I shook my head. "As far as I remember, I never did -- Aunt Mable and Uncle Jerry. Mable was John's mother's sister and suffered from a crippling disease, so she and his Uncle Jerry rarely travelled. If we ever visited them when I was young, I don't remember. I'll have to ask Kyle if he remembers them."

"Do you know where they lived or hopefully still live?" Spencer asked.

I shifted in my chair trying to find a comfortable spot. "Mom tried to find them after John disappeared but had no luck. Could you perform your magic and locate them? That is, if they're still alive."

"I'll give it a shot when I get back to the precinct," he said.

I brought a cooler full of water bottles which I handed out as requested, but after two and a half hours of searching and cataloguing Spence and Abigail needed more fuel for their flagging energy. I asked, "Hey guys, are you ready for a break? I'm going to run out for coffee."

"Yeah, sounds good. After two bottles of water and a large coffee this morning, I need to find a restroom." Spencer exited the unit.

"Me too. There were some up by the front office," Abigail said.

"What kind of coffee do you like? They have espressos, cappuccinos, Frappuccino's, whatever you like," I said.

"The strongest black coffee they have," Spence said as he headed toward the office.

"French Vanilla Cappuccino for me. Thanks, Samantha." Abigail stepped out of the unit. "Ah fresh air. I forgot what it smelled like."

"I feel a little guilty sitting outside watching you guys do all the work," I said.

"No worries, Samantha. We couldn't allow you inside if we wanted to. All items need a chain of custody within the department. At least for now. They may release some of it later. So, what are you going to order?" she asked.

"My favorite, Mocha Frappuccino," I said. "And a surprise for all of us."

I planned to bring back Beach Blueberry Cream Cheese Muffins and Coastal Chocolate Croissants. Whoever came up with the latter was my hero, combining two of my favorite foods.

"I'm always up for a culinary surprise. By the way, did you have the gate code to get into the facility?" Abigail asked.

"No, I followed someone else in. Glad you thought of that. What is it?"

"Oh, you'll never guess. Something real creative. One, two, three, four, five," she rattled off.

"It may be difficult, but I should be able to remember that. Spectacular security." I shook my head.

Abigail pulled the unit door closed and put on a new lock for safe keeping.

As we walked toward the office, she said, "We had to cut the locks off. There were two. John was certainly serious about safeguarding his stuff. And rightfully so. Looks like it could be worth some real money."

"John had an eye for phenomenal deals, and as a traveling nurse he had most of his expenses paid. That provided him with substantial discretionary income to invest. He also contributed a sizeable child support payment for me and my brother, Kyle. It's based on income, at least it is now," I said.

"Yes, that's right. My mom collected child support too. I'll see you back here in a few. Thanks again for grabbing coffees for us." Abigail cocked her head to the side and added, "Spencer is lucky to have a good friend like you." She winked and went inside the office.

When I returned, the duo was back inside the unit hard at work.

"Carb reinforcements have arrived!" I called as I approached.

"Mitchell, let's take a break. Something smells good." Spencer's voice was weary.

"Sounds good to me." Abigail also sounded drained from their monumental task.

They joined me outside the unit. Spencer took the tray of drinks and bag of baked goods from my outstretched hands.

"I'll get the chairs from my Jeep," I said.

I hastily retrieved and unfolded two camping chairs and set them facing the one I'd been putting to good use. Then I moved the large cooler on wheels into the middle, so we could use it as a table.

When I reached for the bag of goodies from Spence, his hand lingered on mine for a moment longer than necessary. Was that my imagination? I didn't dare look at him while we each selected our treat.

Spence applied a pat of butter to his warm, blueberry cream cheese muffin, while Abigail and I each relished a chocolate croissant. It was silent for a few minutes while we finished our delicacies.

"So, anything of interest yet?" I inquired after passing around napkins and wiping the remnants of chocolate cream cheese filling off my fingers. I wanted to lick them but didn't want to appear uncouth.

Spence had told me had authority to discuss the case with me as a consultant because I possessed inside information about John's personal history. He hoped I could help shed light on the threats I'd received by connecting something suspicious in the unit.

"I found two four-drawer filing cabinets in the back of the unit after moving a lot of boxes out of the way. They contain tons of paperwork, but I haven't seen anything yet that would be an explanation for his horrific disappearance or the recent threats you've received. Nothing from a surface investigation at least."

"Will you take those back to the station with you?" I asked.

"We'll take the files but leave the filing cabinets--too cumbersome. I'll put them in file boxes back at the station. We will examine everything eventually. But for now, I'm setting aside financial files, especially large purchases for antiques and artwork to look at first. Something may pop when we take a deeper look." His voice was stronger.

"I've got a bunch of pictures I'll share with you back at the station, Samantha," Abigail said. "Your father had an amazing collection of antiques and artwork."

"He did. Outside of work those were his passions." Women and partying also qualified as John's passions, but no need to mention those. "I had no idea his collection was as substantial as it appears to be."

"Did he have usual sources for the items he collected?" Abigail asked.

"Yes, I recently called one in Sullivan Island. The Sand Dollar Gallery. My mom mentioned he bought numerous paintings from them. If John had visited there before his disappearance, I thought the gallery might have a lead."

"And had he?" She reached for another croissant.

I followed her lead and grabbed another one. "They wouldn't give out any information. You know, customer's privacy and all."

"Of course. We'll have the paperwork, but sometimes items are exchanged without a paper trail. Do you know of other places he patronized?" Spence asked.

"Yes, I know there were art and antique dealers in New Orleans that received frequent shipments from overseas. John visited there every time he was in the area. He showed me lamps and clocks he picked up there. One of the shops was a family name . . . something Antiques. Nile, Nell . . . or Neil, that sounds right, Neil Antiques. My mom may remember names of other places. I'll look online too and see if anything jogs my memory."

"That would be helpful. If he changed his buying habits right before he disappeared, that may be a clue about what got him into trouble." Spence stood and stretched looking back at the full unit.

"I'll see what we come up with." I assumed by 'trouble' Spence was referring to was criminal enterprises, like selling goods on the black market, but he used the euphemism to spare my feelings. I hoped that if John had been involved in criminal activity, it was unwittingly.

"We'll contact any places you and your mom find. They may be leads. We have an art expert in Charleston who consults with us from time to time. We'll fill him in on some of your father's pieces, and he'll do a little digging for us too," Abigail said.

"The carbs did the trick." Spence winked and shot me one of his charming smiles.

"Good! I've done my part – pulling my own weight which is probably more after those two croissants." I smiled at Spence. He smiled back, but I didn't hold his gaze too long. I didn't need to be distracted by anything else. The threats and my dad's health were weighing heavy enough on my mind.

"If you are heavier after those, I'm right there with you. I couldn't resist a second croissant either. They were delectable. Were they from the Seacoast Café?" Abigail quizzed.

"Yes, my Aunt Karen owns the place. It's my favorite spot for coffee and yummy treats," I answered. Had Spence asked the question, I would have made a snarky comment since the bag clearly displayed the name Seacoast Café and Bakery with their dolphin logo. Spence and I had been teasing each other a lot lately. What does that mean?

"Thanks for the tasty muffins, Sam. Those blueberry ones are my favorite. I didn't want you gals to feel bad, so I had two as well. But at least I'll be working it off unlike some people." Spence smiled at me and winked again as he headed toward the unit.

Those dimples made my heart race. *Sam, watch yourself.*

As Spence returned to the spot where he'd been working, he shouted, "Mitchell, can you get that battery operated spotlight and fan out of the car? I've worked myself into a stuffy dark corner back here."

"Sure thing, McKenna," She retrieved it and set up the light to illuminate his work area.

Spence resumed his search while Abby cataloged and took pictures, occasionally thumbing through a box when she was caught up. I settled into my camping chair and connected Jaz's iPad to the free wi-fi, looking for an explanation for John's disappearance. I was using her iPad and had made a fake Facebook account to avoid any detection from whomever was threatening me. I waded through a plethora of John Garcia's Facebook pages hoping to find him there. No luck.

After two more hours, Spence howled, "Woohoo, I found it!" He held up an old computer. "This may yield helpful information. Let's call it for lunch and come back

later. Where do you gals want to eat? It's on me." He shot
me a warm smile.

Chapter 29

Dream: Anna Angst & Felicia Fear; Visitors Uncle Unforgiveness and Aunt Anger

I stared at the eggplant-colored field surrounding the next *home* I was about to visit. The crop was small and sickly, barely hanging on, like my poinsettias three months after Christmas. I bent down and touched the plant in front of me. Ouch, I pulled my hand back in pain. Thorns covered this crop and weeds had infiltrated the field strangling the plants. Wow, this was at the top of my list as the least desirable field on the island. Harvesting these plants would be unpleasant. And why bother?

I turned my attention from the grounds to the dwelling. It was the only structure on the island with the field surrounding it, a two-story concrete square approximately one hundred feet across. A twenty-foot-high barbed wire fence bordered the dwelling. This home resembled a prison, except there was no guard tower.

Four gargoyles sat on the roof. On the left was a tiger on its hind legs, paws raised, ready to pounce. On the right was a snake coiled, with its head up, in strike position. In the middle was a mouse with its tail facing the front looking over its shoulder next to a pufferfish. A strange assortment.

How could I get in? I'd have to wade through the weeds and prickly plants to get to the gate, but then what?

Mr. Bidding appeared with his usual cheery greeting, "Good to see you again, Samantha!"

"Greetings, Mr. Bidding!" He must be telepathic.

"I see you're in a bit of a pickle here."

"Yes, you could call it that."

"Let me give you some assistance, Samantha."

In an instant I was inside the building at the end of a long dimly lit corridor with rows of small cells lining each side. Steel bars enclosed each cell on three sides with a solid concrete block back wall. This was definitely a prison. I heard strange sounds in the distance -- whack, thump, boom. Construction?

I started down the corridor where signs hung over each cell door. The first one was "Family," then "Security," "Disasters," and "Finance." Across from these were "Friends," "Health," "Employment," and "Death."

The cells appeared empty until I noticed movement in the cell that read "Employment." A small woman cowered in the corner of the cell.

"Hello, I'm Samantha. What is your name?" I asked.

"I'm Anna, Anna Angst." Her eyes darted back and forth.

"It's okay, Anna. I'm not going to hurt you," I said in my most soothing voice—the tone I use with Jayce and Jazmine when they're scared.

"You promise? There's . . . so much evil in the world. I don't trust anyone." Her lips quivered.

"I promise, I won't hurt you. Didn't Mr. Bidding tell you I was coming?"

"He did."

"Yes, he did." A second voice came from a cell further down the aisle.

"Oh hello. I didn't know anyone else was here." I walked toward the voice.

"I'm Felicia Fear." Her voice was shrill.

"Anna and Felicia, so glad to meet you both."

Each chamber had a cot with a blanket, a pillow, and a folding chair. Books lined the small shelves along each back wall. All the cells held either a television or a computer. When I reached Felicia, she was standing with her back against the wall. Her television was playing a muted news channel with closed captions on. The sign on her door read "Crime." It was across from the cell that read "Germs" and next to the one with the "Failure" sign.

I said, "Felicia, tell me about your life here."

"Okay. Anna is my mother. I've grown up in this home. We don't go out of our dwelling because as mother said, it is an evil world out there."

"But don't you believe there's good, too?" I asked.

"Yes, there is, but we don't know who we can trust, so we stay here."

"How do you survive?"

"Mother and I both have jobs that we do online. We pay our friends to bring us supplies each month."

"I'm glad that you have friends that help out."

"And relatives too. Uncle Unforgiveness and Aunt Anger come to visit us frequently. It's their friends from a church they used to attend who bring us the necessities, you know, food, clothes, and toilet paper. They never forget the toilet paper, though mother constantly worries we'll run out."

"Since Covid struck, I certainly understand that concern. I couldn't find any toilet paper for a month, so now I have a stock of it in my attic for future emergencies." I hoped sharing my similar fears may help her to be comfortable disclosing even more.

"Did you say that your aunt and uncle don't attend that church anymore?" I asked.

"No, they had a falling out. Uncle Unforgiveness said they were treated unfairly, so they left. Aunt Anger won't even talk about whatever happened."

"But their previous church friends continue to bring you

supplies?"

"Yes, they said The Maker has asked them to help take care of us until we are ready to leave. But I doubt we'll ever leave. There is so much to fear beyond these walls, and sometimes even within. Mother is anxious about losing our jobs one day and not having money for food, which in turn makes me fear that we will starve to death and die."

"Is it likely you'll lose your jobs?" I asked. "Bad things happen when you least expect them. As you mentioned, Covid-19 hit the entire world. Losing our jobs is surely a possibility."

I wasn't sure where to go from there, so I changed the subject. "It looks like there are several empty 'rooms' here. Are there any other inhabitants in this home?"

I heard Anna laughing at my question, so I walked back to her cell.

"Oh no, it's usually just the two of us." Anna said, "These rooms all belong to me and Felicia. When we tire of one, we can go to another, see?" She clicked open the lock that was on the inside of the cell, stepped out and crossed over to the "Disasters" cell, stepped inside, and locked it behind her. As she passed by, I saw her beautiful brown eyes more clearly and admired her long wavy dark hair. She appeared Hispanic.

"You know there are earthquakes, floods, and even volcanic eruptions that are happening all over the world. You never know when one could hit Harvest Island," Anna said.

"True, those things are possible. Have there been recent predictions that any of those are likely?" I asked.

"Uh, well, not that I know of, but as Felicia said, bad things happen when you least expect them. People bomb, shoot, and stab each other. It's a wicked world we live in."

I nodded. She was right. The Thief proved that--evil personified. A change of subject was in order. "Tell me more about your life here, Anna."

"I love that my daughter lives with me. As long as she's

under my roof, I know she's safe. That is unless a tornado, volcano, or tsunami hits, then we're trouble."

"That's nice you have each other. What else can you tell me?"

"When we're not working, we like to read or watch television. It helps us to understand the world without taking any of the risks."

"True, but . . ." I stopped. No need to offend Anna. "When was the last time you and Felicia left your home?"

"Oh, let me think. It has been a long, long time. Felicia was about nine, so that would be sixteen years ago. I had the bright idea of going out in the yard and weeding the fields. It was a mess. I got all scratched up, and Felicia ended up with a rash, poison ivy or some such thing."

"That's horrible. I did notice the thorns on the leaves and an assortment of weeds growing." I started to itch. The amazing power of suggestion.

"Yes, it's safer to let them continue to grow on their own untouched, no matter how ugly it gets out there."

Without more to learn on that topic, I moved on. "How often do your uncle and aunt visit, Anna?"

"About once or twice a month. We have set aside space for them since they visit so frequently."

Felicia chimed in, "The second story of our home is for Uncle Unforgiveness and Aunt Anger. Their rooms are much larger than ours. Would you like to see them?"

"Sure."

"Follow me," Felicia unlocked her cell and slowly crept up the stairs at the end of the hall. As I followed, the banging noises in the distance grew louder. She quietly opened the door at the top of the stairs and glanced around like she was making sure no danger was lurking. I stepped into the hall behind her.

"Yes, these areas are huge." I resisted calling them cells.

Each "room" had three concrete walls and bars on the front. The loud scraping and thumping continued with no apparent origin. I stepped further into the center passageway. The signs on these cells read, "Bitterness," "Rage," "Irritability," "Resentment," and "Entitlement." The chambers were at least four times the size of Anna and Felicia's. On the walls in each cell were white boards with hand-written sentences. I moved closer to read the items in the "Resentment" cell.

Great Uncle Joe bought the boat I wanted and brags about it whenever I see him.

Darrell, Jack's dad, was asked to lead the scouts instead of me.

Lowly HR worker Susie embarrassed me when she publicly asked about my qualifications for a promotion I was applying for.

My boss, Bobbi, was out of line when she gave the promotion to John instead of me.

John rubs my nose in the promotion he received every chance he gets.

Interesting that they have posted these as unpleasant reminders. I walked down the hall toward the cell with the "Rage" sign. The noises grew louder as I approached.

"What's that clanging?" I asked.

Felicia said, "That's the rage of Aunt Anger. Be careful not to get too close. You could get hurt. Her anger lingers even after she's gone."

I inched closer to the "Rage" cell, keeping to the other side of the corridor. The cot, chair, and white board were tossed around the room with no visible force, banging and scraping the walls, bars, and commode. I stifled a scream as the white board slammed against the bars. Several complaints were posted on it.

Inflation is so high, and no one is doing anything about it.

Politicians are ruining our country with their crazy policies.

A guy in a pickup cut me off when I was minding my own business.

My mother left more of her estate to my brother than me.

The kids take us for granted and only call when they are in trouble or need money.

I hurried back to Felicia and the stairwell door. "Why do your aunt and uncle record all these bad experiences?' I asked.

"I don't know. But they add new items and erase some of the old ones every month when they visit. Maybe they're trying to prepare for future problems? Uncle Unforgiveness and Aunt Anger are family, so we try to be nice to them, but to tell you the truth, they terrify me sometimes, especially Aunt Anger," Felicia said.

"I can imagine." I didn't know what else to say.

"I'd better get back down to mother. She frets when I am not close by."

"Thanks for the tour. I appreciate you showing me their rooms."

Felicia pulled an envelope out of her pocket and handed it to me. "This is for you, Samantha. I hope it helps."

Thoughts of John's disappearance and my dad's illness came flooding back. What am I doing here? I need to be searching for John or attending to my dad.

Instantly I was outside standing on the cobblestone road in front of the eggplant-colored field. The wind started swirling around so violently that my hair was whipping into my eyes and mouth. Snow started falling and a flash of lightning was followed by an explosive clap of thunder. A white-out blizzard moved in, and the *home* I had just visited was completely obscured.

I assumed I had all I needed to debrief with Mr. Bidding.

As I walked north, the storm raged, but I wasn't cold. Strange. I looked down and discovered I was wearing snow boots and a parka. I reached back and a hood with faux fur trim was attached. I pulled it up over my head and sinched the tie under my chin. In the coat pockets I found gloves, nice warm fur line leather gloves. Other than the snow pelting my eyes and face, I was comfortable.

I jumped when Mr. Bidding tapped me on the shoulder.

"Oh, I didn't see you there," I shouted over the wind and waves.

"Step this way," he shouted back.

I trailed him relaxing in the peace I felt in his presence. After a few steps, I was standing in the sun with only a light breeze against my face. The snowstorm had disappeared.

"What happened?" I asked as I peeled off the parka and gloves.

"Your worries and fears came with you from Anna Angst and Felicia Fear's home. When you turned your focus away from fear, the storm ceased."

"That's uncanny."

"So, it may seem. How was your visit?"

"Um, not sure, still trying to wrap my brain around the blizzard turned to sunshine." It took me a minute to regroup.

Mr. Bidding waited a beat and then broke the silence. "I'm sure a lot of what you have experienced here on Harvest Island is confusing for you,".

"That's a definite understatement."

"Whenever you're ready to talk about your recent visit is fine, Samantha. I don't have anywhere else I need to be."

"I'm good now. Let's talk about the prison. That's what it was, right?"

"You're partially correct."

"How so?"

"Prisons are created to keep the prisoners in. The inhabitants of this prison keep themselves captive. You noticed the locks were on the inside, not the outside of the cells?"

"Yes, I did."

"The inhabitants of this home are enslaved by worries and fears. They no longer live freely."

"True. Anna said they hadn't been outside, never mind off the property in over sixteen years. It is a sad existence," I said.

"As a child, Anna was free from worries and anxieties. When she became an adult, she had a few bad experiences and began to focus on the 'what if's' building walls around herself for protection. Her constant worries modeled fear for her daughter. Now Felicia also believes that the world isn't safe outside their home. She hasn't known any other life. Her mother's walls have been passed down and now enslave her too."

"And those walls keep Anna and Felicia from really living. They are consumed with worst case scenarios. I can sort of relate to that," I said.

"Yes, you can, Samantha."

"And you believe I brought my own fears and worries with me when I left their home?"

"You did. Your anxieties created unnecessary distress."

"I wasn't consciously distressed."

"When one frequently worries, it becomes a comfortable companion. They don't realize it keeps them from experiencing an abundant life. Over the years, you've chosen to dwell in this abode more often than any of the other homes you've visited."

"But aren't worries and fears good? Like when you see a poisonous snake in the grass, you stay far away. You don't pick it up and get bitten."

Mr. Bidding chuckled. "Yes, Samantha, fear is an emotion that is helpful at times. It can keep us from harm and help us to face true threats. But when we fret about things that we have no control over or that haven't yet happened, it's unhealthy. We create a prison of our own making."

"That makes sense." I knew I had a lot of work to do in that area.

"Although you didn't meet Uncle Unforgiveness and Aunt Anger, what did you learn about them?"

"They kept a list of offenses on white boards. That was strange."

"Strange, but not unusual. People who have been offended often keep a mental checklist of the ways they've been mistreated or slighted. It creates a host of bad emotions that keep them locked up. They rehearse those things over and over, justifying to themselves their anger, bitterness, and unforgiveness. In time it grows larger and larger until the anger or unforgiveness turns to bitterness. Bitterness is a harsh taskmaster and steals much from the one holding on to it. The Maker has said that 'love keeps no record of wrongs.'"

"How can we not think about the bad or unjust things that have happened to us?"

"It's not so much a matter of not thinking about them, it's a matter of not holding it against the person or offender. It's letting it go, forgiving. And at times it's forgiving over and over until it no longer has power over your life. It releases you from the prison."

"That's a pretty tall order." I thought about John's neglect of me and Kyle. His disappearance may not have been by choice, but even before that, he wasn't there for us much.

"In one's own strength, it's difficult, but with The Maker's help and example, you can learn to forgive and move on."

"I assume this is all in *The Book of Truth*?"

"It is, Samantha."

The stream of light coming in around the wooden blinds in my bedroom woke me from the dream of this enigmatic, but intriguing place. Oh no. I never read the clue that Felicia handed me. Was I really putting stock in my bizarre imagination?

Chapter 30

Dad was sleeping in his chair when I arrived at his Grand Haven room. I touched his shoulder, and he awoke with a start. His face lit up when he saw me.

"Hey there," he said. "So good to see you."

It appeared he hadn't been sedated. "It's good to see you sitting up in your chair, Dad."

"Yes." He nodded.

"How are you feeling? Do you want to go to the activities room?"

He shrugged. "I supposed that would be okay."

I wheeled him to the shared living area at Grand Haven.

"Do you want to paint or work on puzzles?" I asked.

"No. Just sit with me." He took several deep breaths and coughed.

"That's fine. We can just sit here," I said.

I made small talk about the weather and the kids but wasn't sure anything registered. He never called me by name and rarely made eye contact. After a couple of hours, he started rambling again.

"No, Georgia . . . we should tell . . . kids about . . . John . . . please, it's right." His voice grew louder.

"What are you saying, Dad?" I hoped the staff wouldn't think he was causing a disturbance and sedate him.

"No, no, we can't. Truth . . . . it's important." Dad shouted and began to breathe heavily.

A nurse approached. "I think your dad needs to rest

now. I'll take him back to his room and bring him dinner in a while. It's best if you conclude your visit now."

"Of course." I leaned over and kissed Dad on the cheek. "I'll see you soon. Get some rest."

He weakly raised his arm and touched my cheek. "Thank you."

"I love you, Dad."

"You too, dear."

The nurse wheeled him back to his room.

I walked across the flower speckled grounds of Grand Haven to the parking lot at the far end of the building. Residents in wheelchairs or with walkers waved as I passed. Walking trails and fountains lined the front and other end of the building.

I reached the parking lot and a large white envelope had been placed under the windshield wiper on my vehicle. I grabbed it, unlocked the door, and scanned the parking lot. Not seeing anyone, I climbed into the vehicle, pushed the ignition button, and turned the air on full blast to combat the muggy day.

On the front of the envelope was SAMANTHA handwritten in block letters. I turned it over, ripped open the seal, and pulled out two pictures. One was of Jayce climbing on the monkey-bars at the school playground. He had on the clothes he had worn last Friday. The other was of Jazmine playing jump rope with friends in our neighborhood. In the photo she was wearing the outfit from yesterday. Her hair was in a French braid like it had been. I sat stunned staring at the pictures.

A hand touched my shoulder. I flinched and started to scream, but before any sound erupted, the barrel of a revolver was jammed against my temple, and a gloved hand was placed over my mouth.

"Quiet and don't turn around. Stop investigating John Garcia's disappearance, or you and your kids might disappear too. You've been warned."

I nodded in agreement. Without turning my head, I glanced at the rearview mirror, but it had been turned away, so I couldn't see my intruder.

He continued, "Take off your PI hat and go back to teaching English. And don't contact the authorities. We know every move you make. Now sit here for five minutes. Don't leave, don't call anyone, and don't turn around. My partner is watching and is a very good shot. He's a trained sniper. If you start your search again, you'll regret it.

With that threat, he took his hand from my mouth, the barrel of the gun from my head, and exited the vehicle disappearing behind my line of sight. I sat trembling but didn't dare leave, call for help, or turn around.

Watching the clock on my dash click through five minutes felt like five hours. I waited an extra minute until six minutes passed, a nice even number, to be sure I wouldn't be in violation of the intruder's directions and then, still trembling, put the vehicle in reverse, backed out, and headed for home.

When my panic subsided, I asked Siri to call Spence but got his voicemail. "Uh Spence, I uh, need to talk to you, It's important. Please call as soon as you can."

I debated about calling the police or FBI but decided to wait until I spoke with Spence. He'd know the best way to handle this.

Chapter 31

"But Spence, I can't tell you anything about the person other than they had a deeper voice, a male, I assume. He was careful not to let me see him by sitting behind me. I only saw his gloves – black leather. I couldn't see him at all." My voice was shaky in spite of my best effort to sound calm as I talked to Spence on my cellphone.

"How about an accent or a smell or tattoo on an arm?"

"No accent. I don't remember any smell. I was so scared that if there was one, I didn't notice. And certainly, I didn't see any tattoos. He wore long sleeves. A black shirt buttoned at the wrist."

"And you couldn't see anything in the rearview mirror?"

"No, it was turned toward the passenger side and flipped down. He must have turned it when he first got in the Jeep."

"Where is the envelope with the pictures in it?" Spence asked, an edge in his voice.

"I have them here at the house. When can you come by?"

"Glad he didn't take them back. I'm on my way. Sit tight and keep the doors locked."

"Already done. Thanks, Spence."

When he arrived, we sat at my white painted farmhouse kitchen table. I showed Spence the photos and went over what happened again. Nothing new came to mind.

"Samantha, I'm concerned about you. That was a close

call. He could have hurt you or worse. I'm going to have an unmarked car stationed on the street, but not directly in front of your home. If the guy who was in your car or his partner is watching your house, I don't want to tip them off."

"Are Jayce and Jaz still carpooling to school?"

"Yes. They love riding with the neighborhood kids. And I have peace of mind they're in seatbelts."

"It would be a good idea to pull them from the carpool and drive them yourself, or I can when I'm free. And keep them in the house when they're not in school for a few days, until we're sure there's no threat to them," Spencer said.

"Of course. I'll drive them and pick them up and work my visits with Dad around their schedule. When I'm not available, Mom will come over and watch the twins for me. She's always saying she wants more time with them because, 'they grow up too fast.'

"But keeping them inside for a few days will be more difficult. They love playing in the backyard on the trampoline and in the woods back there. What should I tell them?"

"Pray for rain. Then you won't have to tell them anything."

"Right." I smiled at Spencer's attempt to lighten the mood.

"Seriously, just tell them that I told you it would be a good idea. Remind them that I'm a police detective. Let them know I have my reasons and will protect them, so they don't need to be concerned. I'll talk to them after my shift. They love Uncle Spencer, right?"

"Yes, of course, they love you, Spence, *like* an uncle. You've been incredible with them. I don't want to scare them. I'm panicked enough for all three of us."

"No need to panic, Sam. I'll be creative in my explanation. I have a few hours to come up with something. Please, try not to worry." Spence placed his warm protective hand over mine. "I won't let anything happen to you or the kids."

I appreciated his encouragement, though I didn't know how not to be afraid. The fact that he was going to station someone on the street was comforting.

"I know you'll try." I sighed.

"Hey, where's the confidence in your favorite detective?" He smiled.

"You win. You will protect me. That better?"

"Yes, much. I'll be back after my shift and sleep on the sofa again, Sam. No need to take any chances, even with the car on the street, a person coming from the back of your home through the woods at night might slip through on foot undetected."

"Thanks for planting that thought."

"Sorry, just planning for any contingency. Don't worry. I'll have the detective keep an eye on the backyard as much as possible. Detective Luke Pierce has a retired police dog, Book'em Danno, Danno for short. I'll ask him to walk the block with Danno every hour while an officer stays in the vehicle."

"That sounds good. Thanks for everything, Spence. I keep looking at these photos . . . photos taken by a stranger . . . photos of my kids. It all seems surreal."

"It's going to be okay, Sam. Pierce and Danno are experts. I'll have him check in every hour until I get here tonight. I'll see if another detective with a dog can help handle the overnight shift. We'll set the schedule for a week to start with, and then we'll see where we are with the investigation. I'll drop Riggs by, and he can stay with you too. He and Lucy will have to make nice."

Riggs and Lucy typically made a wide berth around each other but having Riggs in the house would be an added layer of protection. Lucy would have to deal with it.

Chapter 32

"Yes, ma'am, I can hold." Epps Gallery was on speakerphone while Spence sat across from me in his living room. I was using his home phone, trying to avoid detection.

Elevator music played while we waited for information that I hoped would reveal the reason for John's disappearance. I tapped my pen in an even rhythm, one, two, three, four, pause, one two, three, four, pause . . .

Spence leaned toward me. "These unidentified items may be clues, or they could be nothing. Let's try to not get our hopes up," Spence said.

Abigail had emailed me a list of items with photos that she and Spencer had documented in the storage unit. In addition, Spence had brought home a notebook full of receipts, notes, and invoices. A few pieces were suspiciously absent of paperwork. One, a Pharoah Ramses bust, had a card taped to the wrapping.

"Are you still there?" A cheery male voice came on the line.

"Yes, I'm here."

"This is Gary Carver, assistant curator at the gallery. How may I help you?"

"Did your coworker show you the pictures I emailed her?"

"Yes, she showed me. Are they from a private collection?"

"That's right."

"And do you have any paperwork – invoices, receipts, or appraisals?"

"No, nothing like that," I said.

"Were there other artifacts in the collection?"

"Yes, it's quite an extensive group of antiquities-- paintings, lamps, and other relics," I answered, not seeing the relevance. "Do you recognize the photos?"

"Two of the three items you sent appear to be pieces that were exhibited but withdrawn after a short time when they didn't sell. We can't be sure unless we examine them, but they were both brought to us from the same person, so they are likely the same items we had displayed."

"I see. Is it possible to get the name of the owner?"

"No, we don't give out clients' names. We act as the third party for sales, so owners can remain anonymous."

Spencer raised his eyebrows but didn't comment.

"Which of the three did you display?"

"The lamp and the painting, but not the Ramses bust. But there was an artifact stolen from the gallery about fifteen years ago—one similar to the Ramses statue in your photo. It belonged to a different party than the two other artifacts you sent. Did you say you have it in your possession?"

"Uh, yes, and it has a business card with your gallery's name taped to the wrapping, but nothing official. Curator Carl Johnson's name is on the card. Does he still work there?"

"Yes, he does, but he won't be in until Wednesday."

"Oh, I see. Is it possible there's more than one of these Egyptian Pharaoh Ramses sculptures?"

"Yes, there are many and, unfortunately, a lot of forgeries too. We'd need to see the piece to know if it's the stolen item. It belonged to a client, rather than the gallery. We extensively document everything entrusted to our care, but don't publish all the details of each piece, you know nicks, cracks, or unusual markings. Without knowing these details, it's more difficult for a forger to attempt to replicate it.”

“You can’t tell from the photo if it matches?”

“It is similar, but we’d need to examine it to verify it’s the same piece. And that holds true for the other two pieces. If you want to be sure they’re the ones we had in our gallery, we’d need to see them.”

“I need to bring them to the gallery?”

“Yes, or you could ship them to us, but there is always a risk of damage if you do that. Do you live close by?”

“Not too far. We are in northeast South Carolina.” A trip to the Isle of Palms would be a welcome break. I’d have to check out the pier Mom mentioned if it was still there. I’d ask Spence to go with me.

“Where did you say you located it?” Mr. Carver asked.

“Uh, um, it was in a storage unit that has been unattended.”

“Do you know whose unit it is?”

“I’d rather not say right now.”

“Understood. It’s kind of you to track down its rightful owner.”

“Uh, okay. We thought the paperwork had been lost and you could provide copies or something. You’re sure you never sold a similar piece?”

“Quite. We have no record of selling a Ramses artifact like that, but if it’s the stolen antiquity from our gallery, there might be a reward. We would need to talk to the client and their insurance company to know exactly how to proceed. Sometimes when stolen paintings or artifacts are recovered, the client repays the insurance company and gives a finder’s fee to the person who returned it. A lot depends on how much they prized the piece.”

I glanced at Spence, and he nodded as if he knew what I was thinking.

“I’ll do my best to bring it by Wednesday. Mr. Johnson may remember something. I hope it isn’t the stolen statue.” I sighed.

"We look forward to seeing what you have, and if it is not the same figure, but authentic, we may find a buyer for it."

"Okay. We'll see you then." I set the receiver back on its base.

"Seems shady," Spence said.

"How so?" I asked.

"From my limited understanding of gallery sales, sellers are allowed to be anonymous until an item is sold, and then buyers have access to that information, so they can be sure what they purchased is not a fake. And if John's Pharoah head is not the stolen piece, Mr. Carver was willing to sell it without knowing you're the legal owner. We need to be cautious, Sam."

"Noted." My stomach sank. Was John a thief? Had he displayed the other items to get access to the gallery? That wasn't like the John I knew.

Chapter 33

Dream: Clue 7

As I drifted off to sleep, my thoughts swirled. The unsettled feeling that Mom and Dad knew more about John's disappearance lay on me like a wet blanket on a frigid night. I'll talk to Mom tomorrow.

"Hello Samantha, good to see you again." Mr. Bidding was in his usual good spirits.

"Hi, Mr. Bidding. It looks like another lovely day on Harvest Island." The warmth of the sun on my face and the slight cool breeze were a perfect pair.

"Every day is a good day in the Maker's kingdom."

"Oh, is Harvest Island The Maker's kingdom?"

He chuckled. "No Samantha. Being in The Maker's kingdom is being in His service, knowing Him, following Him. Some of the residents here on Harvest Island may be in His kingdom, but not all that live here have made that commitment. Today his kingdom on earth is a spiritual kingdom. One day it will be a literal physical kingdom too."

"More information from *The Book of Truth*?"

"Yes, my dear."

"I keep meaning to make time to read it, but something is always more pressing."

"I understand." His brow furrowed and then he continued. "The thief will do whatever he can to keep humanity from exploring the depths of The Maker and His plans."

"The thief? Not him again. I'm beginning to really dislike the way he operates."

"Yes, he's cunning and deceitful. If he came to you and said, 'Sam, I don't want you to understand The Maker or his plans for your life, so don't read *The Book of Truth,*' you'd send him on his way. But when he comes and says, 'The laundry needs doing, the project for work can't wait, you need to make that phone call, you can read *The Book of Truth* another time." You believe his lies and never understand the book's treasures for your soul."

"You're right. If I'm ever going to understand my dad and Brandon's faith, I need to make that a priority."

"Yes, Sam. Reading *The Book of Truth* can transform your life."

"Thanks for the encouragement." In my gut, I believed him.

The gray envelope from Felicia when I last visited Harvest Island was in my hand. Four seals matching the gargoyles on the 'home' kept the clue secure, a mouse, a pufferfish, a tiger, and a serpent. I broke the seals and pulled out the clue.

"Three, three, zero, four, five"

Another ambiguous clue. What does this one mean? An address, a zip code, a security code? I'll be glad when I have all the clues and can put this jigsaw puzzle together.

Chapter 34

A few days later Spence and I drove to the Epps Gallery at the northern tip of the Isle of Palms. On the way Spencer filled me in on what he'd found out about Aunt Mable and Uncle Jerry who had kept some of John's belongings. They both passed away in a car wreck fifteen years ago. They had no children, so all their possessions were sold at auction and given to the charity they'd assigned in their wills. The auction home said there were no valuable antiques or paintings among their items, so John must have heard about the accident and retrieved his property before the rest of their assets were sold.

Spence and I chatted non-stop all the way to the Isle of Palms. I was lucky to have such a supportive friend. When we pulled onto the island, I was impressed by the wide streets lined with walking trails, palmetto palm trees, and mossy live oaks. No high-rise buildings populated the beachfront like they did in the Seagrove area of South Carolina.

"What a spectacular place," I said.

"Yeah, a great place to visit, but an expensive place to live." Spence laughed.

A small parking lot adjoined the gallery. We parked and walked the cobblestone path toward the brick stairs that led to a sprawling veranda. One, two, three, four. I was relieved that there was an even number. Spencer was aware of my OCD tendencies but hadn't observed a few of my quirkier habits.

The two-story Victorian beach house had been converted into a stunning gallery. Teal shutters and porch rails complemented the pale-yellow wood siding. An elegant dark wood door with a transom window and side lights created a welcoming entrance. A gilded gallery sign hung next to the entrance.

I felt faint and reached for Spence's arm.

"Whoa, you okay there?"

"I'll be fine, just jitters, I think."

"I understand. It's going to be fine, Sam. I've got you."

"Thanks, Spence. It's the moment of truth. I hope John was not dealing in stolen antiquities. Is it possible he thought the person he bought the Ramses head from came by it legitimately?" I asked.

"Sam, I don't want to burst your bubble, but you know how knowledgeable John was. He had an extensive collection. We found invoices or histories for most of his pieces. I don't want to sound harsh, but it's unlikely he got duped, though not impossible. Forgers and scam artists are extremely creative. And we don't know for sure that it is the stolen statue." Spence's voice was gentle as he delivered the truth. If it was stolen, John was likely aware.

"You're right. I hate to think he was mixed up in something illegal. I know John was unfaithful to Mom, but he was always above board and ethical in his business dealings, nothing ever criminal." But how much did I really know about the man?

"I hope and pray you're right, Sam. Let's go inside and see what we find out." He held the door for me and placed his hand on my lower back sending a tingle up my spine.

The gallery was huge. Room after room of elegant sculptures and breath-taking paintings. Ancient artifacts from Egypt and Rome were encased in glass, protected from thieves and curious touchers. John had taught me that much about antiquities. Always handle with care and as little as possible so artifacts won't be damaged or devalued by fingerprints, oils, or dirt.

A middle-aged, tall, slender woman, in a floral maxi dress approached us. "Are you finding anything of interest? Everything you see is for sale." She tucked a stray hair back into her perfect updo.

"Oh, thank you. But we are here to speak with Curator Carl Johnson," I said.

"Of course, may I tell him your name?"

"Samantha Anderson, and this is my friend Spencer McKenna."

A stocky, balding man about my same five-foot, five-inch height stepped out from a restricted area. The sign on the door read "Staff Only."

Mr. Johnson's round wire spectacles sat halfway down his nose. He peered over them as he extended his right hand to each of us. "Hello Miss Anderson, Mr. McKenna. Mr. Carver told me to expect you today. He's out of the gallery, but he emailed me the photos you sent, and the Ramses head *is* similar to the piece that was stolen. You brought it with you?"

"Yes, we did." I opened the large shoulder bag and withdrew the artifact. I carefully passed it to the curator.

He peeled back the cover and nodded as he took a cursory look. "Excellent, let's go back to my work bench. At first glance it appears to be authentic and in pristine condition."

Surely John was not a thief.

My heart pounded as we tailed Mr. Johnson through two hallways, each only accessible with his card key. Then he placed his right hand on a biometric scanner, and the door to his workroom clicked open.

"As you can see, we have robust security here. Normally it would've been impossible for a thief to steal the artifact, but the security system was offline at the time, so we have no video footage or record of who accessed the room where the Pharaoh Ramses bust was stored. Oddly, it was the only thing taken."

"It wasn't on display at the time?"

"No, it wasn't, and because of that, we considered the possibility of an inside job. All our employees were questioned, and the Charleston Police didn't find any evidence of their involvement. The Forensic Unit's digital specialist was able to determine that we were hacked and taken offline, but he couldn't trace it."

As we reached Mr. Johnson's table at the far end of the long narrow room, he spread a thick padding across its surface. I opened the bag, and Mr. Johnson reached in and gently took the Pharoah Ramses out and laid it on the table, unwrapping it slowly.

"Now to find the file for the stolen artifact." He typed a file number into the laptop on the edge of the table and a picture of a Pharaoh Ramses statue appeared.

I gasped, unable to take my eyes off the photo. It looked exactly like the piece we brought.

Spence touched my arm. "Let's not jump to conclusions, Sam. It may not be the stolen artifact."

"You are correct, Mr. McKenna. Many similar busts exist. The characteristics of the stolen piece are listed here, so please step to the side while I scroll through the details. The specifics are not public information."

"Of course," I said. Spence and I stepped aside, so we couldn't see the screen.

I wrung my hands as Mr. Johnson did an extensive examination of our Pharoah Ramses head.

"Hmm. Uh huh. Hmm. Oh." He jotted notes and took measurements, inspected it with a lighted magnifying glass, and compared its colors to those on a color guide.

When he finally finished logging information, he said, "I've seen this piece before."

"The stolen item?" I asked, the dizziness returning.

"No, no. It was brought in for an appraisal a long time ago. Let me check my records. I remember the three-tone coloring on the bottom. That's not typical, but I believe this relic is authentic. A true piece of history you have here. Our stolen artifact had distinct markings that were absent on this piece and the measurements are not exact, close, but not the same piece."

I squeezed Spencer's arm, and he nodded and smiled back.

Mr. Johnson was scrolling through old files when he stopped. "Yes, here it is. February 2008. My notes say the owner acquired it while he was in the military and brought it home from Egypt in 1983 along with a few other pieces. I offered to purchase it, but he declined. I'll make you the same offer if you're interested."

Spence shook his head, and I politely declined the curator's offer.

I turned to Spence. "I forgot about John's military service in Egypt and Italy. He was part of a Naval Medical Research Unit. He hardly ever talked about it."

"He might have brought all three items back from Egypt. Odd that he waited so long to get them appraised. And then where are the appraisals?" Spence asked.

Chapter 35

"The kids are doing fine. I'll bring them by the next time I visit." I sat in the old leather love seat in Dad's apartment at Grand Haven. He knew who I was that day.

"That would be nice, Sam. I uh, . . . um, need to tell you something about your father." He paused to catch his breath and stared out the window at the palm trees swaying in the wind.

My heart raced. "What about him?"

"Your father, Sam. Georgia doesn't want to tell you. She's so stubborn. But I love her. I love her so."

"Mom is keeping secrets?" My hands grew clammy.

"No, no, not at all. I want you to know that he loves you. He disappeared and then ran away."

"What do you mean ran away?"

"Oh, you know from home. When I was eight years old, I ran away from home. I got in trouble at school. I was afraid to go home and face my father. He could be mean. I went to the park and hid there. Back in the palm shrubs by the lake."

"Yes, I remember that story." Dad was confused and rambling. But he said Mom didn't want to tell me. What didn't she want to tell me? Could that be a glimpse of light breaking through the shadows clouding his mind? I'd press Mom again next time we talked.

"I know you're looking for John, Sam. He walked away. . . . He left. He didn't say goodbye. So sorry . . . So unhappy. But Sam, your father, he loves you . . . I know he does."

"Do you know what happened to John, Dad?"

"I know . . . but I don't know. I should tell Sam and Kyle . . . but I can't. It's not right, it's not fair . . .Why? Because we know." Dad was becoming more agitated, talking to himself, only vaguely aware of my presence.

"It's okay, Dad. I'm fine. I have fantastic relationships with the twins, you and Mom, Kyle, Brandon, and Brian. That's more than most people could hope for." And I have a special friend in Spencer but didn't say it out loud.

Dad quieted down. "And you have God, Sam . . . He loves you so much. Your heavenly father loves you so much more . . . than any earthly father ever could."

"Sure, Dad. I understand." But I didn't. "I'll let you rest now. I love you, Dad."

I hugged Dad and kissed him on the cheek. promising to return soon. He returned my hug which was something he didn't always do since he'd been sick. I waved as I exited his small apartment at Grand Haven and was grateful that he'd remembered my name, even if he hadn't made any sense about John.

Determined to get answers, I stopped by the five-acre Myers Mansion Mom and Dad had shared for the last twenty-five years. The colonial home was a gift from Tom's parents after they won a twenty-million-dollar lottery.

The house was much larger than Dad and Mom ever needed, five-thousand square feet. This stately two-story, red brick, black shuttered home possessed four gigantic white columns across the massive front stone porch. Three dormers adorned the four-car, side garage which housed an upstairs apartment that was reserved as a guest suite complete with a full bath and kitchenette.

After Brian and Brandon graduated, I assumed Mom and Dad would move to a smaller home, but they had planted trees and gardens and had renovated the entire house. Each year they chose a room to remodel. After they finished refurbishing every nook and cranny to suit their taste, they started over on the most used rooms. That stopped when Dad got sick.

"Good morning, Mom." I tried to sound upbeat, though I was anything but.

"Good morning, dear. What brings you by so early?"

"Just checking in. I thought you may be lonely in the Myers Mansion."

"It's not a mansion, but it is pretty big for little ol' me." She touched the cross-necklace Dad had given her.

"It's been almost a year since Dad moved to Grand Haven. Isn't it time to find something smaller?"

"Maybe, but my best memories are here. I couldn't stand moving somewhere we've never had a family Thanksgiving or Christmas. You, your brothers, and the grandkids can all come here for more holidays," she said.

My heart softened. Mom and Tom had hosted wonderful family get togethers. "Sure, but it's a lot to care for. And we're all local, so we don't need bedrooms to stay in anymore."

"You're right, Sam. I should probably sell, but I wouldn't be as happy anywhere else. Here I get to tend the rose bushes, lilies, and my gorgeous pink crape myrtles. I sit under our live oaks with the Spanish moss and watch the palms swaying. It's like therapy for me washing my troubles away. I'm sure my doctor would give me a prescription if I asked," she said.

I recognized that twinkle in her eyes. "I get the point, Mom, you love it here, and I understand, but wouldn't it be easier on you to have a house smaller than a six bedroom, five bath on five acres?"

"I have a gardener to take care of the outside. And I don't go into most of the bedrooms or bathrooms, except to occasionally dust and vacuum. You know, Kyle's old bedroom is set up as a craft room, so when I get bored, I have lots of space to work on my projects. His old room has that wall of built-ins, so it works nicely for all my paraphernalia."

I nodded in agreement. "I know it makes a darling craft room. But couldn't you recreate that kind of room with storage in a smaller place?"

Her eyes darted to the kitchen, dining room, and up the stairs. "It may be irrational, but I feel your dad here." Her voice cracked. "I hated to take him to Grand Haven, but I just couldn't physically manage anymore." She sighed.

My heart melted. The confrontation I planned was going to have to wait. "No one blames you, Mom. Dad was over two hundred pounds at that time. You can't be more than a hundred and ten pounds. Right?"

Mom nodded.

"No one expected you to care for him after he wasn't mobile anymore."

"I know, but I still feel guilty. It was an agonizing thing to do, but at least I know he has around the clock care now."

"Exactly, and with him being such a social butterfly, we know there's always someone there for him to talk to when he feels like it. He usually seems content." I hoped he was.

"Yes, I'd have to agree. Enough about me. How are you doing?" Mom asked.

"I'm okay. Seeing Dad's deterioration is hard. I'm not sure why, but Dad's failing health has increased the urgency to find John."

I needed to fill the imminent loss with a sensational find – my biological father whom I hoped was still alive. I hadn't told Mom about the phone threats or gun to my head incident. She'd be beside herself with worry if she knew.

"You're not still pursuing those silly clues from your dreams, are you?"

"A little. I did have an interesting one the other night. The numbers three, three, zero, four, and five . . ." I paused when I saw her surprised expression. "Mom, does that mean something to you?"

"Now dear, don't be ridiculous." Mom's voice went up an octave. "Those clues don't provide any real information.

It's your imagination running wild. You're wasting your time and energy following those rabbit trails."

"I'm not so sure. I found out the zip code 33045 is for Key West, Florida. John really loved being there, but do you think it was enough for him to relocate? It's warm year-round, the sand is a gorgeous white, and they have swaying palm trees too." I forced a smile.

"Sam, you're sounding ridiculous. This isn't like you. Forget about the whacky clues you're getting in your sleep. They're only your mind playing tricks on you."

"You may be right . . . I don't know . . . it's . . . um, there is one other thing, Mom." I took the plunge. "When I was talking to Dad, he implied that you both knew more about John. But he was rambling, so I'm not sure."

"Of course not. We don't know where John is."

"But you do know something?"

She glanced away. "He could be anywhere. And what's the point now, Sam? You have your life, your kids, and a respectable job. It won't do you any good to find the man who has only disappointed you time after time."

"I know you're right, but I can't seem to let it go."

"You'll need to if you don't want to lose your mind."

"Too late for that." I smiled.

"Look, sweetie. When Tom and I were married, John was fine with you and Kyle calling Tom 'Dad.' And wasn't Tom always there for you?"

"Yes, of course, Mom. He's been better than ninety-nine, point nine percent of dads." I knew in my head that should be enough, but in my heart, I still longed for that approval from my 'real' father.

I remembered the conversation with John. It was upsetting, even at six-years old.

He was matter-of-fact. "It's your decision. I'll understand if you want to call Tom, Dad. After all, you're living under the same roof with him, and you see him a lot more than me. You know, with my job, I'm not here much.

It's not that I don't want to be. I'd love to spend every day with you guys. But I can't." His words sounded like they were rehearsed. It felt like my father was disowning me and my nine-year-old brother. How could a father relinquish the 'dad' title without a fight?

That day feelings of rejection and abandonment took root in my young heart. Each subsequent disappointment added layer upon layer of hurt.

"Penny for your thoughts," Mom said.

"Mom, I know that Tom has been generous, sometimes to a fault, and more than willing to fill in the gap that John chose not to, or he didn't have the ability to—I don't know which for sure. But I wish my real father would have loved me the way Tom has. And if he's out there, I want a second chance."

Mom's face turned red. She stood and stomped into the kitchen. I sighed and followed her, bracing for a lecture.

She slapped her hand on the counter. "Now you listen to me, Samantha Joy Anderson. You know better than that! Let all this go. It does no good to dig up the past. Me and Tom have tried to be the best parents we could. We're not perfect, but certainly have done everything we could. You're being childish and selfish." Her voice shook with emotion.

Her words hurt. "But, Mom, I know the clues have meaning. I can feel it." I didn't want to tell her about the threats that were not a creation of my imagination. She'd freak out.

She gained her composure. "Samantha, it's all well and good if you want to run down rabbit trails, but you've involved Spencer McKenna in your fantasy. I saw him at Grand Haven a few days ago, and he mentioned he's been helping you to find out what happened to John. I can't believe you got him involved." Her voice was raised. "That man does not need to be involved." She enunciated every word.

"He offered, Mom. That's more than what you're

willing to do. And my gut tells me you and Dad know more than you're telling." I lashed out, angry at her criticism.

Mom's eyes filled with tears. "That's it, Sam. Please leave. I don't want to hear any more of this nonsense." She pointed toward the front door.

"Fine, if that's how you want to treat your only daughter. I'll leave, and don't expect me to come back anytime soon," I said.

"Fine!" she shouted.

"Fine!" I yelled and stormed out, slamming the door behind me.

Chapter 36

Spence sounded serious when he asked if he could come over. I paced while I waited. One, two, three, four. About face. One, two, three, four. About face. He was coming from the station, so it would be a few more minutes before he arrived. Maybe a cup of tea would help to settle my nerves. I stopped pacing and headed for the kitchen when Jayce came tromping down the stairs.

"Hi, Jayce. Is your homework all done?"

"Yes, Mom. I've been reading a book about astronomy for extra credit." He beamed.

"Good for you." He made me so proud. My little science geek.

"Ready to have a snack before bed? How about a banana?"

"Sounds good, Mom. I'll go see if Jaz wants one too." He turned and bounded up the stairs.

"Thanks, sweetie." I turned on the electric kettle and pulled a mint teabag from the pantry.

A couple of minutes later Jayce trotted down the stairs with Jazmine in her pink unicorn print pajamas close behind.

"Look at you – getting ready for bed without me having to tell you," I said.

"I'm tired Mom. We ran the track at school, and Coach Foster told us to run as many laps as we could. I kept going until I couldn't run anymore, and I came in third for most laps. Tommy and June came in first and second." She grabbed the banana I'd put on the island, flopped into a chair at the end of the table, and began to peel her banana.

"Jaz, I'm proud of you." I poured the boiling water over the teabag.

"Thanks, Mom. And before you ask, yes, I finished my homework."

"You know me--" The doorbell rang.

"That must be Spence. After you eat the rest of your bananas, finish getting ready for bed. I'll be up in a while to say goodnight."

As I opened the door, I saw deep creases in Spencer's brow. "What's wrong?"

"Let's go into the living room, out of earshot of the twins," he whispered.

"Sure." I led the way, and Spence sat down on the recliner, and I on the sofa.

"So, what's up?" I asked but wasn't sure I wanted to know the answer.

"As I was going through more of John's files, I found these." He opened the folder he'd set on the coffee table. On the top was a photo of John and a woman inside a large auditorium, a selfie taken at a concert from the back stadium seating. The floor below the stage and both sides were full of fans listening to a band. Several spotlights shone down on the stage, but the picture was too blurry to make out who the musicians were.

"What a unique auditorium," I said. The ceiling was curved with wooden beams that reached the top of the seating. Symmetrical arches over windows were displayed between each beam.

Spencer turned the photo over. "John wrote on the back. It's the Shrine Mosque in Springfield, Missouri."

I looked at the familiar handwriting. "Shrine Mosque, Springfield, MO, Me and Natalie. March 15, 2009."

"That was the last day I spoke to John. He told me he had a date and was going to the Shrine Mosque. I remember thinking it was odd to hold a concert at a mosque."

"It's not a Muslim religious mosque, but is used by the Shriners, a Masonic society. This photo was taken two months before John disappeared. I did a facial recognition search and found out his date's name was Natalie Torres. Paperclipped to the photo were these two notes." He handed them to me.

"You're a dead man, Garcia. Stop messing with my girl." And "You didn't listen, so watch your back. I'm coming when you least expect it."

Spence shifted in his seat. "We lifted fingerprints. They belonged to Patrick Jackson. He has a lengthy rap sheet and has been in and out of prison. Assault, robbery, drug dealing, you name it, he's dabbled in it. But never murder charges."

"At least there's that. Any connection between him and John or Natalie?" I asked.

"Natalie was a nurse and Patrick a maintenance worker at the federal prison hospital where John worked. I determined from old social media posts that Patrick and Natalie dated for a while before the photo with John. I'm trying to track her down, but evidently, she's moved out of the area."

"Do you believe Patrick was jealous and didn't want to see her with someone else?" I asked.

"Yes, she posted this exact photo on her social media page the day after the concert. Patrick may have seen it. There were no other pictures of her with John, and she hasn't posted, at least on that account for about fifteen years. It's possible she got married and has a new name. I'll try to find out more about her tomorrow."

"Thanks, Spence. What's Patrick doing now?" I asked.

"He was released from prison about six months ago. He's in Miami, Florida, still on parole. Oh, and one more thing, Sam." He leaned toward me and placed his hand on mine.

"What?" I braced myself.

"Sam, on the way from the station, I received a threatening call like the ones you've received. I don't know how they connected me to you and your search for John, but they have. The voice was distorted by a modulator, just like your calls."

"Oh no, Spence. That's horrible. What'd they say?" My heart started beating faster.

"The caller said to let the past stay in the past and warned me to stop searching for John. The person told me to warn you too. But that is not the worst of it."

"That's pretty bad, what else?"

"I stopped by my house trying to calm myself before I came over, and there was a package on my front porch. When I opened it, there was a mask of a devil crawling with live tarantulas."

I put my hand over my mouth and sucked in a breath. "Oh no, Spence. I didn't mean to get you involved in this. Why are they doing this?"

"I'm not sure, but I believe something's going on that needs to be uncovered, and I don't plan on stopping until I find out what it is."

My mind began to spin, and I started shaking.

"Hey kiddo, it's going to be ok." Spence moved from the recliner to the sofa. He reached for my hand, and I let him take it. His arm went around my shoulder and pulled me close.

"I'm sorry, Spence. I didn't want to put you in danger." I suppressed a sob.

"You didn't Sam. I'm looking out for you and the twins, not to mention doing my job. I couldn't bear it if anything happened to you, Jayce, or Jaz. On that note, I brought you a gift."

"Oh?"

Spence got up and retrieved a small hard-shell case he'd set by the door. He came back and sat on the sofa next to me. "Now Sam, I know you don't own any guns and with the kids in the house I completely understand. You can keep it locked in the gun case when you're at home and take it with you when you go out."

He took a key out of his pocket and opened the case. Inside was a gun in a cloth pouch and a box of bullets.

I swallowed hard. "Oh, uh, um, Spence, I um, I uh, don't know."

"Please take it, Sam. It's a Taurus Ultra-Lite, 38 special. Light weight and easy to use. It was sitting in my closet, not doing much good there."

"I have no idea how to use a gun," I said.

"We'll get you a concealed weapons permit, so you can put it in your purse. I'll take you to the range to learn how to use it. I would feel better knowing you can protect yourself when you're out alone."

Jaz leaned over the banister at the top of the stairs. ""Hi, Spencer. We are ready for bed now, Mom."

I was glad for the excuse to continue this conversation later. "I'll be right up."

Chapter 37

I awoke to the sound of sirens and the smell of smoke. As the piercing noise grew louder, I began to panic. What's happening? I glanced at the clock, 2:00 a.m.

I sat up, threw my legs over the side of the bed, and slipped on my house shoes. I grabbed my robe from the footboard post, threw it around my shoulders, and hurried to the window. Flashing lights reflected off the trees in the backyard, but I didn't see a fire. No neighboring homes were visible from my window. At least the woods weren't burning.

I padded down the stairs as quickly as possible, and then heard one of the twin's bedroom doors creak open. I ran back up to see Jaz standing in the hallway, looking half asleep.

"Mom, what are all the sirens?"

"Not sure, honey. I was going downstairs to check it out. Put your shoes on and come with me." I grabbed a couple of spare throw blankets from her closet while she put on her pink glitter Crocs.

"I smell smoke. Should we wake Jayce?" Jaz asked, her pitch higher than normal.

"Not yet. Let's see what's going on. No need for him to lose sleep."

Out the front picture window, we saw flames shooting from Spencer's roof and around the perimeter—his junipers, yellow irises, and swamp lilies, all engulfed in an insatiable fire. Jaz let out a squeal. "Oh no! It's Spencer's house,

Mom."

My breath hitched. *Breathe.* I exhaled slowly trying to calm myself. I needed to be strong for my daughter. "He's a police officer. I'm sure he's fine," I said, trying to convince myself and Jaz that he was not in trouble.

I closed my eyes and focused on breathing to slow my racing heart. Breathe in. Breathe out. Breathe in. Breathe out.

"Mom? What should we do?" Jaz's voice was shrill.

I opened my eyes. Jaz was staring at me, eyes wild with panic.

"Honey, go wake up Jayce and make sure he puts something on his feet. We need to go outside and see how bad the fire is." If the wind carried any embers, it might ignite our home.

A minute later a sleepy, tousled hair Jayce followed his sister down the stairs looking confused and irritated.

"What's going on? I was having a lit dream about being at the beach. Now I'll never know if I get to go for a ride on that dope sailboat," he moaned.

He was his mother's child when it came to imagination and strange dreams.

"Sorry, sweetie, but there's a fire at Spencer's home," I said, my voice quivering.

"Mom, it will be okay. Spencer's a police officer. He knows what to do in an emergency," Jayce said. My heart melted. This ten-year old was worried about his mom's wellbeing.

"That's right Jayce. I told Jaz the same thing." I wrapped a blanket around each of the twins, and we stepped outside into the cool night air.

Two police cars, an ambulance, two firetrucks and several neighbors lined the street. Firemen with hoses gushing water were trying to put out the fire on the bushes and a few trees that had flared up between our properties. I spied a police officer in front of Spencer's home and ran over to her while tightly holding the twins' hands. It was Abigail

Mitchell.

"Hey, Abigail. Where's Spencer?"

"We're not sure. I was filling in for a friend on the night shift when the call came in."

"Was Spencer the one who called 9-1-1?" I asked.

"No, it was your neighbor across the street, Cassidy Nelson. Three firemen are in there now trying to locate him. They took a backboard and a water hose to help clear a path. More trucks are on the way."

I turned back to his home, and my legs started to buckle. Flames were shooting out the front picture window and upstairs bedrooms.

"Oh God, if you're there, help Spence. Keep him safe," I said under my breath. I collapsed to my knees between the twins.

"God is real, Mom. We learned about him in Kid's Class at Grandpa Tom and Uncle Brandon's church," Jayce said.

The faith of an innocent child. I needed some of that right now. "Of course, he is, sweetie." I wrapped my arms around the twins and pulled them close.

The minutes ticked by, feeling like hours. One fireman came out carrying Riggs. We ran to him as the fireman laid him on a gurney.

"Is he going to be okay?" I asked, looking at the motionless dog lying in front of us.

"No burns, but he may have smoke inhalation," he said and nodded at the EMT who put an oxygen mask over Riggs' nose and mouth.

A tear slid down Jaz's cheek, and her shoulders rose in silent sobs. She gently stroked the dog's head.

"Riggs will be fine when they get him to the vet. He's in good hands, Jaz. Don't worry, honey." I tried to comfort her, hoping my words were true.

"The veterinary hospital is three minutes away. He'll be fine. His pulse is a little slow but still strong," the EMT said and gave Jaz a reassuring nod. He lifted the stretcher into the back of the emergency vehicle and closed the doors. Another ambulance pulled in as the one carrying our canine hero, Riggs, departed for the animal hospital. We went back and stood beside Abigail. I held onto Jayce and Jazmine's hands hoping to help them feel safe.

"How about Spencer? Where is he, Mom?" Jaz asked sounding frantic.

"They'll get him out. That's what firemen are trained to do—to save people." The tremor in my voice had returned.

"But, Mom, the fire's so big," Jaz wailed.

Two firemen carrying a man on a board rushed from the engulfed home.

I glanced at Abigail, and she nodded. "Go ahead, Samantha, I'll watch them."

"Jayce and Jaz, you stay here with Officer Mitchell. I'm going to check on Spencer."

Abigail took their hands as I bolted toward the backboard carrying firemen. When a safe distance from the house, they set the board on the ground. The EMT's were waiting with oxygen and placed the mask over the man's face. It was Spence.

"His pulse is weak, but he's still breathing," One EMT commented. "Looks like second degree burns on his arms, and third degree on his chest and neck."

His lips looked blue, or was it a reflection from the flashing emergency lights?

As the EMT's covered his burns, I fell to the ground next to him. "Spence, can you hear me? It's Samantha."

His eyes fluttered but didn't stay open. I took his hand. "You're going to be fine. And Riggs is fine. They took him to the vet to get checked out, but I know you'll both be okay." I held back the tears. He squeezed my hand as they lifted the board and carried him to the ambulance.

"We'll take him to the hospital helipad, and he'll be flown to the burn unit in Charleston. It's the best in the state.

They'll take good care of him. I promise," the EMT shouted above the roar of the fire as they lifted him into the ambulance.

"Can I go with him?" I shouted back, forgetting about the   twins.

"Family only. Are you family?" he asked.

"No."

"I'm afraid it's against policy, ma'am. You can drive to the hospital if you want."

The doors slammed shut, and the siren blared as the ambulance sped away.

Chapter 38

Kyle and I strolled down Ocean Boulevard as the sun was setting. The waves were roaring, and the seagulls squawking. A storm was on the way and the wind had picked up.

I pulled my hair back into a ponytail and sinched it with a puffy hair tie I'd been wearing on my wrist. I'd made it a habit to keep one handy for when the wind picked up at the beach, which happened at some point every day. Even with the hair tie, my shorter strands whipped into my eyes and mouth.

"If I'm going to be fighting my hair, we may as well be walking on the beach," I said.

"Sure, sis, whatever you want."

"What I want, is for Spencer to wake up," I said.

"That's outside of my purview." His slight smile faded when I didn't respond. "He will, Sam. Tom and Brandon's church have added him to the prayer list, and a lot of other people are praying for him too." Kyle was always the consummate encouraging big brother.

We walked through the gravel public access area and down the wooden steps to the beach. I took off my sandals and Kyle peeled off his shoes and socks.

"I hope God comes through. I can't lose someone else. Dad's teetering at heaven's door. It's only a matter of time now." I sighed. "Have you done any searching for John recently?"

"No and after you told me about your threats and what happened to Spencer, I'm not about to either. But there is something I haven't told you, sis." Kyle faced me, and we stopped about ten feet from the rising tide.

"That sounds ominous. What is it?" I asked as I turned to face my big brother.

"Several weeks ago, I received a large manila envelope." Kyle paused when I caught my breath. He looked at me wide-eyed.

My heart slammed in my chest. Why didn't I tell Kyle about this sooner? "Don't tell me. It had pictures from your childhood and copies of articles about you from the newspaper," I said.

"Uh, yeah, Sam . . . Did you get one too?" he asked, his voice wavering.

"I did. And there was a key with a weird message on an index card."

"I got one too. It said, 5991, uh, something, something. I took a picture of it. Let me see if I can find it." Kyle scrolled through the photos on his cellphone. "Here it is. 5991 SRI B251."

"That makes no sense to me. I can't remember what mine said, but I'll find it when I get home. Maybe if we put our heads and clues together, we'll figure out what it means." I was determined to unscramble this new clue from the real world. My dream clues hadn't provided much help.

"Sure, Sam. I wish I'd told you sooner. I've been so busy with the doctoral thesis and of course my new bride." A grin lit his face momentarily. "So, I set it aside."

"Of course, don't beat yourself up. I could've told you too, but with everything going on with Dad, and then the threats, and now Spencer, I back-burnered it. One of the pictures in my envelope was of my fifth birthday holding that pink guitar John gave me."

"Ah, I remember. You really loved that thing."

"I did. I even carry a copy of the photo. You know, a

happy memory with him. I put it in my purse when he disappeared and have carried it with me ever since. That photo made me think it might have been from John, but I'm not one hundred percent sure he's even alive. The envelope was postmarked at the--."

"The Dallas Fort Worth airport." Kyle finished my sentence.

"Yes."

Our bare feet were suddenly engulfed in cool water. I squealed and jumped back to keep the wave from catching my capris. The tide was rising. Kyle laughed and then kicked, splashing me with the salty water. I took a few steps back and shook my head.

"A little water won't hurt you, Sam."

"I know, but I'm going to run by the hospital again to see if there's been any progress with Spence." I stepped onto dry sand while Brandon stayed in the shallow water.

"Sure thing. Wouldn't want you to not look perfect for your hunky neighbor."

"You too? Brandon won't stop teasing me about Spence. Please give it a rest. We are just friends." I hoped I was wrong but had no real evidence to the contrary.

"If you say so. Now what were we talking about before that wave so rudely interrupted us? Oh yeah, you mentioned the photo with John. One of my photos was me and John on my seventh birthday, or was it sixth, anyway his arm was around me and the shining red bike he gave me was in front of us," Kyle said.

"Then I'd say the odds are that they were from John. So, he kept tabs on us all this time." My mind raced. "Why reach out now? And where is he?"

"If he was at DFW when he sent those, he could be anywhere now. Do we dare even to try to solve his riddle or code or whatever it is? I don't want you to put yourself in any danger, Sam." Kyle splashed his foot in the shallow water.

I pushed the loose hair that had found its way into my mouth back into the hair tie. "I won't take any chances and promise me you won't either. But it wouldn't hurt to get together and try to decipher the clues he left. That way there won't be an electronic trail for anyone to follow. The code must have significance."

"If we solve the clues, we can enlist the help of the police if they dare after what happened to Spencer," Kyle said.

"I have Officer Abigail McKenna's number. I'll check in with her if we decode the gibberish. I'll make an appointment to see her in person. Who knows if someone is listening to my calls?"

"Good idea. Let me know when you want to get together."

Chapter 39

Abigail was at the hospital when I arrived. She was sitting by Spencer's bed reading to him. I stood by the door and listened to the beeping machines. Spencer's motionless body was hooked up to a ventilator and an IV. And it was my fault. What if he never wakes up? What if he dies? It will be my fault.

I didn't hear most of what Abigail was reading, but then crystally clear, "My help comes from the Lord, the Maker of heaven and earth." I froze. Did I hear that right?

Abigail paused and looked up. I entered the room and hoped she couldn't hear my heart thumping. "Hi Abigail. What was that you were reading?"

"Psalms. If Spencer can hear me, it may bring him comfort. If not, at least it comforted me." She smiled and tilted her head.

"Oh right, that's sweet of you. Any update on his condition?" I asked.

"No, right now they're keeping him sedated. Docs feel that's best for at least another day or two. They're going to contact us if there's any change. For now, he's holding his own."

"He's strong. He has to be okay."

"He will be, Samantha, God willing."

"Yes, God willing." I muttered. *God, please be willing.*

"It's good to see you, Sam, but I need to run. Gotta get dinner for the hubby and kiddos. Hang in there." She gave me a quick hug and exited.

"Hey Spence. I'm not sure if you can hear me, but I need you to be okay. You are my . . . my best friend. I feel so awful that I got you into this. I'm so sorry, Spence." I leaned down and kissed his cheek. No response. I took his hand. It was cool. Warm salty tears streamed down my face and into my mouth as I stood over the bravest person I knew.

I can't believe I never told him how I felt. How do I feel? He's the best friend a person could have. Just a friend? Do I want more than a friendship? Maybe. Maybe not. There's a spark between us, isn't there? Did he feel it? Am I imagining it? I may never find out. And it's my fault. I don't know what I'll do if he dies. Don't die, Spencer. God, please don't let Spencer die.

Chapter 40

Seeing Spencer laying in that hospital bed made me realize that no one knows what tomorrow will bring or whether we'll even have a tomorrow. As angry as I was with Mom, I needed to make things right. She had called and texted a few times since our blowup, but I hadn't responded. We'd both said things we regretted. At least I'd said things I regretted, and I was embarrassed about my childish behavior.

Did she want to hammer me more for putting Spencer in danger or did she want to reconcile? Texts and emails can be misinterpreted, and a phone call misses all the nuances of body language and facial expression. An in-person visit would be the best way to face whatever may come.

As I turned my Jeep down Mom's long, palm lined driveway, the car behind me slowed and parked across the street. It appeared to be the same vehicle that was behind me all the way home yesterday, a gray SUV. Was I being followed or paranoid?

I pulled up in front of Mom's grand home, instead of around the side where I normally parked. It felt safer but that may have been wishful thinking. I glanced around as I got out. A sliver of the gray car was visible through the trees.

The wind was picking up, and the sky had clouded over. A storm was brewing.

I grabbed my black New Balance raincoat from the passenger's seat and made a dash for the front porch. One, two, three, four, and four steps to the door. Perfect.

I pressed the doorbell. Its chime reminded me of church bells as it echoed through the front foyer. As I waited for Mom to open the door, I braced myself for a cold reception.

Mom opened the door, her eyes puffy and red. "Sam, I'm so glad to see you. I couldn't believe it when you texted and said you wanted to stop by." She dabbed her eyes and pulled me close.

I returned the embrace. "I'm sorry, Mom."

"No dear, I'm sorry. I shouldn't judge you for your decisions. It is your life, and it wasn't my place to tell you what you should or shouldn't do."

"It's okay, Mom. I know you're concerned about me."

"Let's go sit in the living room."

"Sure, Mom. It looks like you've been crying."

"Tears of relief, dear. You sit in Tom's recliner. It's the most comfortable chair in the house."

"Thanks, Mom, but you sit there." It didn't feel right sitting in Tom's designated seat.

"No, I insist. He'd want you to – especially if he knew how poorly I treated you."

Mom took a seat on the sofa, and I reluctantly sat in Tom's recliner. She continued, "I heard about Spencer McKenna. Is he going to be okay?"

"I hope so." My eyes filled with tears. "He's sedated for now. The docs feel that's the best step for healing . . . They'll know more in a few days . . ." I sucked in a sob. Mom handed me a tissue. I wiped the tears streaming down my cheeks.

"You really care for him, don't you? Brandon has always said you two would be fabulous together." Mom stared intently at me.

Great, Brandon had mentioned Spencer to Mom. I sighed. "Brandon doesn't give up. He hints about Spence every time I see him. And now Kyle's on the bandwagon too."

"It's possible other people are seeing something you

aren't," Mom said.

"We're simply friends, and he's been superb with the twins, a better father figure than Logan's been. Spence is a special guy."

"Special, huh?" She raised her eyebrows. "The best relationships start with a good friendship. You never know. Keep your heart open, Sam. Oh, here I am telling you how to live your life again."

"No, it's okay, Mom. I know you can't help yourself." I smiled weakly. "Really, I know you want what's best for me. I'll try to keep an open heart. With Spencer in the hospital, I realized that we never know how much time we'll have with someone, and I couldn't bear to leave things the way they were between us." My eyes burned as I held back more tears.

"I feel the same way. I hated the way we talked to each other. But we're good now, right?"

"Yes, of course, Mom. And you were right, I shouldn't have gotten Spencer involved in searching for John."

"Why? Did the fire have something to do with that?" Mom put her hand over her mouth.

"Uh, um, it's possible. It's under investigation." Why did I have to bring that up.? I didn't want to worry her.

"Oh no, are you in danger?" Mom fidgeted with her wedding ring.

"No, no we're fine," I said.

Abigail had told me they doubled up the officers watching my home. They should have been watching Spence's home too. It's amazing no one saw the arsonist. Must be pros.

After our apologies, the conversation moved on to Mom's book club, the twins, and our plans for summer break.

Mom offered me Coastal Chocolate Croissants from the Seacoast Café before I left, and for the first time in my life, I turned them down. I didn't have any appetite and couldn't bear the thought of enjoying my favorite food while Spencer lay in the hospital fighting for his life.

Chapter 41

Dream: Gabriel Grace and Julie Justice-Grace, Faith, Hope, and Charity

I stood in front of the green field. It produced monster size plants and had more variation in color than any of the other plots on Harvest Island. From seafoam green to a luxurious forest green. The parcel itself was smaller than Duke Ryan Rich's, but the produce actually appeared edible. All these plants looked alive and delicious. I reached down, pulled off a piece from one of the darkest green plants, and took a bite. It was like nothing I'd ever tasted. Sweet and savory. My mouth watered for more.

Before I could pluck another leaf, I found myself in a courtyard filled with lush palms that encircled a white marble fountain topped by an enormous angel with outstretched wings. This centerpiece had three scalloped, round tiers of water in an octagonal base that provided the angel's foundation. The splashing water was harmonizing with the birds and crickets in a perfectly choreographed melody.

Four arched openings, one on each side of the courtyard, led to the interior of the stucco home. The low-pitched roofs of terracotta tile perfectly topped the Mediterranean style home. A spicy smell drew me towards the north entrance.

Five gargoyles extended from the roof line keeping watch over the property. An angel with feet of fire, a lamb, seagull, a pair of doves, and a cross of gold. An odd assortment, but Harvest Island is a peculiar place, so I shouldn't have been surprised.

"Hello, Samantha! We have been expecting you. Welcome to our humble abode, dear," a man's voice called out.

"Uh, hello there. I wouldn't exactly call your home humble," I said as I followed the sound of the voice to the kitchen.

"Ah, thank you. So kind, but we can't take credit. It's a gift from The Maker. I am Gabriel Grace, but my friends call me Gabe." He looked up from spreading garlic butter on a split loaf of bread and smiled at me.

I had an overwhelming feeling of acceptance from this forty-something black man.

"I'm Samantha Anderson."

"Nice to meet you, Ms. Anderson."

"Likewise."

A lovely young Hispanic woman entered the room. "Hi! I thought I heard a voice I didn't recognize. I'm Hope, of The Three Sisters."

"So nice to meet you, Hope. I'm Samantha. So, you have two sisters?

"Yes, you'll meet Faith and Charity shortly. They went to the market to get the final goodies for the barbeque. Every inhabitant on the island has been invited. They may not all attend, but there's room for everyone at our tables. We've set up out front, so we can enjoy the ocean view while we eat and socialize. You should join us. What do you say?"

"Thank you. I'd like that." A gathering of all the inhabitants was potentially explosive but might provide some interesting entertainment.

"Good choice! Oh, I hear my sisters outside. I'll go help them. Feel free to stay here and chat with Dad."

"Thanks, Hope."

I turned toward the cook. "What is that delicious aroma,

Mr. Grace?"

"Please call me Gabe. We're all friends and family here."

"Of course, Gabe. You can call me Sam."

"To answer your question, you're smelling my special ribs. I'm baking them before I grill them. The slow cooking helps to keep them tender, but then grilling will caramelize the barbecue sauce. Do you cook?" he asked.

"Not as much as I'd like. I can't find the time to try new things. But I'm solid on the basics."

"You'd be surprised at how often new dishes are as easy as standard fare. It just takes a little faith and perseverance to try the unknown." He placed the garlic bread in a brick oven.

"I'm not so good at getting out of my comfort zone. I stick with the tried and true. A little OCD." In fact, a lot OCD, but I wasn't going to admit that out loud.

"With a little faith comes freedom, Samantha."

I wasn't sure we were talking about cooking anymore.

"Uh, I'd be happy to help if you point me in the right direction," I said.

Gabe had moved on to layering a yummy dessert with fruit, cream, and cake. "No, I'm good here, thanks. Why don't you check with my girls and see if they need help with anything."

I found the sisters singing while setting tables in the front yard. Their voices harmonized wonderfully without any instruments. The song radiated a sense of peace and joy. What I would give to feel that all the time.

I applauded when they finished the enchanting song about the beauty all around us. I'd never heard it before, but the message spoke to me. I had so much to be grateful for, and yet I felt discontented and anxious much of the time.

Hope smiled and introduced me to her sisters, Faith and Charity. Faith appeared to be from African descent and Charity looked Native American. What an interesting, unexpected family.

"I see you are confused by our differing skin tones. Am I right?" Hope asked.

"I uh, . . . um, . . . yeah. I was marveling at how different, but similar you all are. You harmonize beautifully." I hoped I hadn't been staring.

"No worries. We are all adopted. All adopted by The Maker, including Mom and Dad," Charity chimed in.

"Wow, that's amazing." I don't know how that works, but it sounds like The Maker is exceedingly benevolent." I glanced again at each of the three beautiful sisters.

"Indeed, He is." Faith raised her arms and twirled around.

"Most definitely." Charity smiled at Faith.

"One hundred percent. Now let's get busy. Samantha, you can help if you'd like," Hope said.

"Absolutely." I wanted to get to know these women better.

We carried out the salads--one with a variety of beans, one with several fruits, and another with greens, berries, and walnuts. An ambrosia salad was already on the serving table. I'd have to sample that before my visit ended. Other side dishes were prepared and added to the grand feast. The sisters continued to sing in harmony as they worked.

"I'm home. Where is everyone?" The words floated from inside.

"Mom, we're out here," Charity said.

"Ah there you all are." A tall white woman entered the front yard.

"Hi! I'm Samantha." I stretched out my hand.

"We have been expecting you, Samantha. I'm Julie Justice."

"Your daughters have been entertaining me with their gorgeous voices."

"I'm so glad. They are remarkable. No bias here, of course." Her face glowed as she watched her daughters working.

I was comfortable in this home, like I was part of the family. Each member possessed their own radiance, their own unique welcoming aura. The warmth emanating from them reminded me of Mr. Bidding.

"Ms. Justice, what do you do?"

"Please call me Julie. I'm the chief justice. I handle all the major issues in the archipelago. Laws, updating policies as new issues arise, sentencing, penalties, judgements. I oversee several judges and their cases."

"It sounds like a lot of pressure."

"It is, but Gabe helps to give me perspective on the issues."

"Ah. How so?"

"He focuses on finding the motive and heart of the issues, rather than the letter of the law."

"And what is his profession?"

"He's a counselor and an advocate for those in trouble. He has helped hundreds to find a better path. A multitude who have come through my courts go on to be guided by him and his colleagues. We often consult with each other to be sure we take a balanced approach."

"What a complementary relationship."

"It is, but because The Maker is the Supreme Justice with the final say, mercy typically wins over justice. And that's fine by me. I certainly need The Maker's mercy daily." Julie's deep brown eyes settled on me as if waiting for a response.

"I uh, uh, I've never been arrested," I said. What am I saying? "But if I ever find myself in that position, I'm sure I'd hope for mercy." I needed to learn about The Maker. I must read *The Book of Truth*.

"His mercy is wide indeed and covers a multitude of sins. Humanity is in desperate need." Thankfully she ignored my silly comment.

"Of course. Um, tell me about your family."

"Sure. Faith is President of a Christian college, Hope is an angel investor, and Charity is a social worker and presides over of a non-profit that helps in emergency situations. We're so proud."

"You should be. And you and Gabe should be proud of yourselves. What an extraordinary family." I was genuinely impressed.

I breathed deeply, inhaling the scent of ribs that had been put on the grill as the neighbors began to file in. Phillip Phony was first, followed by Fred Fatalist and Paul Passive. Lilly Legalist arrived with a man. I assumed he was her brother, Wally. He had a distinct limp. They offered regrets from Ashley Ascetic and moved to the opposite side of the yard, choosing to sit at a table far from Fred Fatalist. Duke Ryan Rich followed and made a bee line to Lilly, asking about his daughter Ashley.

Mary Mystic and Ellie Ecstasy arrived in similar attire to when I previously met them. Mary's long hooded robe was a navy blue instead of taupe, but it had the same stars and crescent moons embroidered on it. Today she sported a black, spiked tiara instead of a turban. Ellie flaunted a mask resembling a lion's face. The only visible facial feature was her penetrating amber eyes. As she floated into the yard, she scanned the guests and came directly to my side. I smelled sulfur and took a step back.

"So, you've made it this far," She closed the gap between us.

"Yes, I . . . I have," I said.

"So . . ." She paused, appearing to look for the right words. "Have you considered my generous offer to heal your migraines?"

"No, I haven't." I'd love to be free of migraines, but not by sacrificing a cat. I looked away from Ellie's mask to avoid her piercing stare.

"You're kidding yourself, Samantha. You want this more than you're willing to admit." She circled around directly in front of me.

Gabe came out from the kitchen and stood next to me. Had he realized I'd been ambushed by Ellie?

Ellie glared at Gabe, huffed, and glided over to chat with Wally.

George Godfree and Harry Hardhearted arrived without Daniel Dark.

"Is Daniel coming?" I asked Gabe hoping to get a glimpse of Daniel in the daylight.

"No, he's never attended. Too much light for him," he said. "Anna Angst and Felicia Fear have never attended either. Unfortunately, they are imprisoned by their anxiety and fear. And Paige Pleasure has only made a couple of barbeques over the years. I believe she's climbing Mount Kilimanjaro this week. Almost everyone is here now."

Barb Beauty was the last to join the group. I assumed she wanted to make a flamboyant entrance. And that she did, dressed in a long, red, sequined gown with matching stilettos. She looked flawless, like the iconic Marilyn Monroe. Barb crossed the entire group showing off her brilliantly white smile, hair in a loose but attractive updo, and beautiful, but mostly fake, tan. She turned every head in the group as she passed by.

Gabe began, "Thank you all for gathering with us today. Those of you still standing, please have a seat."

"A round of applause for the Justice-Grace family," Duke Ryan said.

"Hear! Hear!" George said, and everyone clapped.

"Before we dig in, I wanted to take a few moments of reflection. Actually, not I, The Maker assigned me this task today. He'd like each of us to express that for which we are grateful. If you're willing, please tell us what The Maker has done for you." Gabe added emphatically, "for He is most worthy."

"Sure, I'll start," George said and stood. "I don't believe there is a Maker. But I'm thankful that I live however I want.

I love the life that I've chosen, and I don't want it any other way." He flipped his long braid back over his shoulder and sat down. He nodded to Harry.

Harry said, "I'm not sure if The Maker exists or not. I've never seen him, have any of you?" No one answered. He continued, "Him Who Does His Bidding talks about this Maker person, and Bidding does some hocus-pocus magic, but so do Mary and Ellie. If we are merely talking about being grateful, I'd have to go with being a self-made man. I work out every day. You see these muscles?" He flexed his biceps. "No one is going to take advantage of me. I'm thankful for my physical strength."

"I understand, George and Harry. Thanks for your honesty. If you'd like to talk more about your views after we're done today, I'd welcome that," Gabe said.

George and Harry shrugged. It appeared their minds were made up.

Gabe glanced around the group. "Who would like to go next?"

Phillip stood and said, "I'm thankful for my position as mayor. I'm able to help the inhabitants of Harvest Island and make important decisions. The Maker has assigned me this task that is so well suited to my talents." He turned to Fred.

Fred stood. "My turn, uh, I'm thankful for being the catalyst for Wally Work's charity work."

Lilly gasped. "How dare you!"

Gabe stepped in. "Guests, this is not a time for conflict. Please try to be sensitive to the feelings of others who are gathered here."

Fred nudged Paul to say something to get the spotlight off him.

"I, uh, am thankful that The Maker has everything under control. I don't have to fret or worry. The whole world is in His hands," Paul said.

Wally went next. "It's okay, Lilly, I am thankful that The Maker took a bad situation and turned it into something good. Now I'm the head of a big charity helping others. What are you thankful for, sis?"

Lilly threaded a cloth napkin between her fingers. "I thank The Maker for a wonderful brother who works hard and has a good attitude. Wally makes following the rules much easier."

"Wally is certainly special. Thanks for sharing, Lilly," Gabe said attempting to calm the waters. "Who wants to go next? Duke Ryan?"

"Sure. Hmm. Uh, I'm thankful to The Maker for . . .hmm, it would have to be my splendid palace and field of gold. Although I have slaved for it, so I'm not sure I should give The Maker credit. But it's, indeed, what makes me the proudest. My gold field buys me whatever my heart desires. Except, of course, . . . my uh, you know, um, relationship with Ashley, my daughter. Oh, you all already know about that disaster. No secrets on this island."

It was silent for a few seconds.

"Thank you, Duke Ryan. We all know how much that pains you. My family prays for reconciliation for you and your daughter. Anyone else?" Gabe asked.

Mary stood. "I will share what I am grateful for, but it is not for anything from The Maker. The Angel of Light has endowed me with certain powers which allow me to help people and to live in the most beautiful home on the island. And I'm sure Ellie can echo my appreciation to The Angel of Light."

Ellie, still floating a foot or so above the ground, announced, "I can. The Angel of Light has made our professions possible, and with his help, I've ascended to a spiritual plateau that none of you understand. I am becoming divine. You are all deceived if you don't believe it's possible."

"We have different views on that, Ellie, but I do appreciate you and Mary sharing today. Barb, you are the only island resident who hasn't shared yet, except for my family, of course. Is there anything you would like to say?" Gabe asked.

"Yes, of course. I am thankful to The Maker for making me so beautiful and talented. He certainly did a good job, if I do say so myself."

I involuntarily rolled my eyes, and immediately regretted it. I hoped no one saw.

Gabe turned to me. "Samantha, you are a guest on our island, so if you're not comfortable sharing what you're thankful for, no judgement."

"It's fine, I'd like to. I'm thankful for Mr. Bidding and for all of you, for the insights I'm gaining, and for the clues to help find my father, though I'm still looking. And I'm thankful for you, Gabe, and your lovely family hosting everyone. Your family is truly special. I'm only slightly familiar with The Maker, so I can't comment about Him."

"Thank you, Samantha! My family is special to me. But we are all special because we are all made in the image of The Maker. Even those of you who do not want to offer gratefulness to Him. He sees you as worthy of his love. I'm grateful for The Maker's grace and the undeserved mercy he extends. There is power in *The Book of Truth* that will help you to become more acquainted with The Maker's ways and The Maker himself, Samantha."

Mary huffed and Ellie let out an otherworldly shriek as she waved her wand. Thunder boomed and lightning flashed. They disappeared.

"Julie, would you like to share, dear?" Gabe barely seemed to notice Mary and Ellie's unruly exit.

"Yes, darling. I'm grateful for the laws of the universe that The Maker has created. For everything there is a time and season, a place, and a purpose. He has a grand masterplan that we only dimly comprehend. I'm grateful that His ways are just and upright, righteous, and true."

"Thank you, Julie. That was beautiful. Girls, would you each like to share something for which you are grateful to

The Maker?"

"Yes, Papa," Faith responded. "I am grateful for The Maker's unchanging character. I know I can trust him because he is a good Father, desiring only good for me, His child. How about you, Hope?"

Hope stared at the cloudless sky and then said, "I am grateful that The Maker's son is preparing a place for us to live with Him for eternity, and that our lives here, as wonderful as they are, are but a shadow of the mind-blowing things to come."

Charity smiled at her sister. "Amen, Hope. We expectantly await amazing things to come. But while we are still here, we can represent Him by loving others the way He has loved us. I'm grateful for The Maker's supreme love, the sacrifice of His son."

"Thank you all for sharing," Gabe said. "As for me, I'm grateful for His Truth and Grace. And in the spirit of truth, it is time to eat." Gabe smiled at the cheers from his neighbors and then raised his hands in the air and prayed, "Thank you, Maker, for our neighbors and the abundance of food you have blessed us with. Let this be a time of encouragement and revelation for all present today. In the name of your son, amen."

Gabe exited and came back with a huge platter of freshly grilled ribs and placed them in the middle of the long serving table along with a big basket of steaming garlic bread. Guests filed by and filled their plates, some more than others.

After everyone was once again seated, Julie went from table to table pouring a clear sparkling liquid into each guest's uniquely engraved chalice. After she filled mine, I took a sip. It was the most refreshing drink I'd ever tasted. "What is this?" I asked.

"Water from The Maker's well," Julie said. "It is the purest on the island and available for any who are thirsty."

I thought of the filthy water Harry had served me and

wondered why every inhabitant on the island didn't get their water at The Maker's well.

It was silent for a few minutes as everyone passed the food around and started eating. Slowly quiet chatter started around the tables as the guests relaxed. After everyone had their fill, the layered dessert was served. I ate much more than I should have. It was all superbly rich, yet simultaneously tasted nutritious.

Gabe stood and thanked everyone for attending the annual barbeque. Then he said, "For those of you who would like to stay, The Maker has instructed Julie to ask each of you a question to ponder, no need to answer now. No pressure. Just something to contemplate. If you'd like to leave, you are free to do so now."

The guests shifted uncomfortably in their seats. I expected a few to bolt, but no one did.

"Thank you, darling." Julie stood and made eye contact with each guest.

"George, you are thankful for being able to choose your own path. What good things are you doing with that ability?'" She smiled kindly at him.

George scowled and crossed his arms.

Julie continued asking questions. "Harry, you were thankful for physical strength. Which is more important, physical strength or another kind, a spiritual kind?

Harry glared at Julie but kept quiet.

"Phillip, is it the appearance or the reality that gets results?"

Phillip hung his head, and his face turned crimson.

"Paul, why did The Maker give you talents?

Paul said, "Well, uh . . . um, I---"

"No need to answer now, Paul. Just something for you to ponder," Julie said and continued, "Fred, what's the purpose of your life?"

Fred clenched his fists and frowned at Julie.

"Lilly, is holiness mostly an outward or inward

attribute? Wally, how are you justified with God? Barb, is it more important to be beautiful on the inside or outside?"

Barb shouted, "Who made you the judge?" She threw her goblet on the ground and stormed out.

Without missing a beat, Julie continued, "Duke Ryan, what good is it if you gain the whole world but lose your soul?"

I was stunned at Julie's candid questions.

"Samantha, I know you're on a quest. The Maker honors those who seek truth. I'm confident that you'll find what you are looking for. What is it you really want deep in your heart?"

Was she was referring to the unspoken cry of my heart that Mr. Bidding had mentioned? I was still unsure what that was, but wanted to find out, especially if that was The Maker's question for me. He seemed wise and compassionate.

Julie turned to her daughters. "My children, you are all so special to me. You each have wonderful gifts. The question for all three of you is how can The Maker's family be one body?"

That was a strange concept. How could a family be one body?

Gabe, standing next to Julie, turned toward her. "My love, do you have a question for me?"

"Of course, darling. Why does The Maker extend grace?"

"Hmm." Gabe cocked his head.

Julie continued, "My question from The Maker is 'What did The Maker's son do when he was deprived of justice? These questions might seem unorthodox, but The Maker has chosen them for each of us. The Maker knows us intimately and is offering an opportunity to grow and to know Him better."

Gabe sat silent for a moment and then stood to address his neighbors. "Thank you again for coming to our barbeque and staying for these challenging personal questions. The questions may appear simple, but the answers hold a host of consequences in our lives."

"What are you trying to say, Gabe?" asked Phillip as he shifted in his wicker chair.

Gabe smiled at Phillip. "The answers to these questions are only the start of the journey. What you do with that understanding is found in The Maker's *Book of Truth*.

Paul sat up straighter and asked, "Gabe, what are you doing, selling *The Book of Truth*, or what?"

Gabe chuckled. "No, Paul. We have copies on the table here for anyone that would like to take one—for free. Julie and I will start a weekly study, Sunday at 4:00 p.m. And we're happy to help all of you discover insights to any inquiries you have. Not only the questions from today. *The Book of Truth* is a treasure of wisdom and knowledge about all of life. Please spread the word to those who didn't attend in case they would like to participate. Thank you all again. May you each find God's love and peace in your life."

Phillip approached Gabe for his free copy and reached out to shake Gabe's hand. "I'll take a look to see what you're peddling here, Gabe. Need to protect my constituents, ya know."

"Of course, Phillip. We only want what is best for everyone on the island," Gabe said.

Gabe raised his eyebrows but said nothing as Harry Hardhearted grabbed a stack of books off the table.

"Just getting these for our customers," Harry said.

"You're welcome to do that, and all are welcome to join our study," Gabe said. "God bless you, Harry."

George Godfree jogged over to Harry's side. "Our clients don't need no religion, all that fairytale stuff."

Gabe turned to talk to Fred, and I heard Harry whisper to George. "They're free. We can sell them and make some money. Phillip gave me the idea. Who cares what's in 'em. Gabe is such a sucker."

I turned back to the table of books to see if any other residents would accept the offer. Wally took a copy without comment and hobbled off the property behind the rest of the guests.

Julie approached with a forest green envelope in her hand. "We're glad you attended our little island get-together today. I hope you felt at home and enjoyed the company." She handed me the envelope with seals depicting the five gargoyles I saw on the corbels.

"Yes, it was lovely. Thank you. The food was delicious, and your family has given me a lot to digest, no pun intended."

"We'd love to have you join us for the study, but Him Who Does His Bidding informed me that it's not possible."

"Oh, that's unfortunate. I really need answers." I sighed.

"I know you'll find another way to study *The Book of Truth*, Samantha." Julie's penetrating brown eyes sparkled.

Chapter 42

A gust of wind blew, and I was instantly at the north end of the island facing Mr. Bidding.

"How'd you like the annual barbeque?" he asked.

"Uh, wow, what happened?" I felt whiplashed.

"Your time here at Harvest Island is coming to an end for now, Samantha."

"Too bad, I was beginning to think I belonged here."

"You do and you don't."

"That's about as clear as a polar bear in a snowstorm."

"Yes, that sounds about right, Samantha." Mr. Bidding smiled.

"Uh, okay?" I waited for an explanation.

"People choose where they want to dwell. And while the dwelling may not be permanent, it's their choice at any given time. Where do you choose to dwell, Samantha?"

"Duke Ryan Rich's place was exquisite, and Wally Works and Lily Legalist's cabin was charming and homey, except Ashley Ascetic's room. But I'd have to choose the home of Gabe Grace and Julie Justice. They and their daughters made me feel more welcomed and loved than any other place on the island."

"Stellar choice. And each day, each hour, and each minute you get to decide where you will dwell. Beware of the consequences of your choices."

"Okay. But I thought my time here was over for now."

"Your island visit has been a vehicle for understanding

and insight, spiritual representations if you will," Mr. Bidding said.

"And for clues that have largely been unhelpful in finding John, I might add."

"You will find your father, Samantha, I promise."

"Thank you, Mr. Bidding. I trust your word. That gives me hope."

"All is well, my child. Continue your quest for the truth, and you'll find it. The Maker's son has said to seek and you will find." Mr. Bidding raised his arms toward the sky and slowly lowered them.

"From *The Book of Truth*, I presume?" I asked.

"It is."

I hoped I could find the truth. At the same time, I feared whatever I uncovered may devastate me, but I needed to know.

"All of *The Book of Truth* is trustworthy, Samantha. It's the story of The Maker and humanity from beginning to end. I told you before that some call it the Good Book, but it is truly the best book ever written, so Best Book would be a better moniker. Please do read it, Samantha."

"That's quite an endorsement. So much is going on now, but I'll try to make time." I felt overwhelmed with life but couldn't recall the events of the last few days. It was a hazy jumble.

"When life gets to be crushing, Sam, call on The Maker and look to *The Book of Truth*. They will sustain you in the storm."

"I'll try to remember that, Mr. Bidding." Did he know of a devastating circumstance on the horizon?

"Now it's time to open the last clue," he said.

I tore open the envelope and was stunned at the words I read.

"They All Whisper a Lie"

Chapter 43

"Hey there, stranger," Spence said hoarsely, pulling down his oxygen mask. "Sorry about the voice. Doc said not to talk too much. Rest my vocal cords. You'll have to do most of the talking, you know, like normal." He winked and grinned.

I shrugged my shoulders. "What are you trying to say, Spencer McKenna? That your neighbor talks a lot?" I smiled back at him, and as we locked eyes, my heart did a flip. I looked away but felt my cheeks burning.

"Uh, um, I brought flowers to brighten your room. I was elated to hear you're awake." I set the navy glass vase on the wide ledge by the window. The bouquet contained white and blue carnations with a few yellow lilies and baby's breath thrown in for good measure.

"Thanks, Sam. They're beautiful. Quite an improvement on the décor," Spencer whispered. "Hospital rooms are the most dreary, stark places. Add a few beeping machines and nurses waking me all hours of the night. It's just heavenly."

"Maybe they're hinting. Don't want you to overstay your welcome. You can be a handful, you know." I took a seat by his bed.

"What? Me overstay, not in a million years. I want out of here as soon as possible," he whispered and grinned.

"And when will that be?" I asked, hoping it was soon.

"Doc said about another two weeks. They want to be

sure the inflammation in my lungs and trachea goes down . . . and the skin grafts on my chest and neck heal. But I should be back at work before too long . . . though I'll probably be on desk duty for a while until doc clears me," Spence whispered.

"Whatever it takes, Spence. Stay as long as the docs think you should, no leaving against doctor's orders."

"Is that an order?" He reached for my hand and squeezed it.

"Uh, yes, I guess it is." I returned his squeeze. "But on the other hand, don't stay longer than you need to." The warmth of his hand on mine made me feel protected.

"That settles it. Follow doctor's orders, but no Hotel California for me." Spence responded. He'd remembered I love The Eagles.

"I have good news. Riggs is doing fine. The veterinarian kept him a few nights to be sure, but no serious effects from the fire. The vet didn't know why he was unconscious when they brought him in, but that may have kept him from inhaling more smoke. Does he take medication or anything to help him sleep?" I asked.

"No, but the doc said I had fentanyl in my system. Maybe Riggs was drugged too. It kept us from waking up when the fire started," Spencer said.

"Wow, someone drugged you. That's horrible." I felt lightheaded.

"If they were trying to kill us, it didn't work. I'm on the mend, and Riggs is okay."

"Yes, he's as good as new now. Because you had put me down for emergency contact, the vet released him to my care. We'll keep him at the house until you're better if that's okay. The kids love him, and Riggs and Lucy are getting along like brother and sister. Last night she stole his blanket, and they had a little tug of war. It was super cute. Lucy's a fraction of his size, but evidently, she hasn't looked in the mirror lately."

Spence chuckled and then started coughing. He took a long sip of water from the clear plastic cup on his overbed table.

"The last thing I remember was sitting in my study looking at a file of John's paperwork . . . oh no, John's paperwork," Spence whispered.

"That's not important, Spence. You are the only thing that matters now."

"I appreciate the sentiment, Samantha, but something in John's case landed me here. I need to find out what's going on."

"I know you're right." He'd probably step back into danger as soon as he could. I didn't think it was worth it. Then again, I wasn't an officer sworn to uphold the law and catch the bad guys. "Okay then, what happened when you were looking at his paperwork?"

"I remember taking pictures of a few files and sending them to Abigail. She was going to follow up. I was texting with her when I passed out. Next thing I knew I was waking up in the hospital."

"I'm so sorry, Spence. It's all my fault. If I hadn't gotten you involved in this, none of this would have happened. When I saw your house burning, I was terrified I was going to lose you." My eyes filled with tears.

"You know I'm tougher than a measly house fire." He laughed and started to cough. "It's not your fault Sam. Whoever is doing these things . . . they are the only one to blame."

"But what if—"

"No 'what if's.' The past has happened. And I wouldn't change a thing about investigating the threats you received. Except to have figured out the weakness in my security system." He started coughing again and cleared his throat. "The person who set the fire drugged me and possibly Riggs. And I have no idea how."

"You'll figure it out. You always do. I'm glad you're

going to make a full recovery. I should let you rest now and stop using your voice. I assume whispering is not doctor approved either."

"Probably not." Spencer slowly released my hand.

Spencer's cell phone rang. "Do you want me to get that for you?"

He nodded.

I picked up his phone from the metal nightstand next to his bed. "Spencer McKenna's phone."

It was Abigail. She'd found something and wanted to talk to Spencer. I explained that he couldn't talk, so she was going to email him, and said she'd talk to me about it later. I wanted to press her for information, but there was no point. She was following protocol.

As I was getting off the elevator in the lobby, a gentleman in a fedora and trench coat was walking toward the elevators. As soon as he saw me, he tipped his head down, his hat hiding his face. Was that the same man I saw a couple of months ago when the school bus crashed? I didn't see his face at all then, and this time only a glimpse. Grey hair and a full beard and mustache. Round wire rim glasses. He looked vaguely familiar, but it was hard to say with such a brief view. His apparel was strange for this part of the country, so it might be the same person.

As I stepped out into a heavy rain and jogged toward my Jeep, my phone dinged. The text from Spencer read, "Please text or call Abigail. You'll be interested in what she found. Phone number 555-4444. " Did he know I liked the number 4? No, he must be clapping about what she found.

Soaked and shivering, I checked the back seat of my vehicle. Empty. I jumped in, put in my earbuds, and called Officer Mitchell. "Hi, Abigail, Spence tells me you have some new information?" I pulled onto the street.

"Hi, Samantha. Yes, I dug into Natalie Torres and found an interesting correlation between her and John's disappearance."

"How so?" I looked in my rearview mirror at the car that had followed me out of the parking lot. The same gray SUV, a Subaru? I took a detour towards Walmart. Surely no one would hurt me in broad daylight with people all around.

"When John disappeared, so did Natalie. There's no trace of her after that. No jobs, addresses, or accounts that I could find. No one ever made the connection because she had lived in Missouri and John disappeared from South Carolina."

"Was she ever reported missing?" I asked.

"No. She grew up an orphan in foster care, so she had no family. After the photo she posted with John, she'd posted a few pictures with friends. But then nothing."

I started to feel queasy. Is it possible John staged the whole bloody scene at his apartment to get away from Patrick Jackson and start a new life with Natalie? The phrase "new life" was in one of the clues.

"Have you been able to track any of her friends?" I turned into the Walmart parking lot. The gray SUV drove past the entrance. I must be paranoid.

"Only one, a Mariana Vasquez. She said that around that time, Natalie told her she was moving somewhere up north to get away from Patrick. He'd been stalking her despite restraining orders, and it became too much for Natalie. Patrick always made excuses as to why he happened to be in the same place as her. She was going to make a fresh start and didn't leave any forwarding address. She promised to stay in touch with Ms. Vasquez, but never did."

"Thanks for the information, Abigail."

"Take care, Sam."

Chapter 44

It was three days before the reading of Dad's will. We had buried him the day before and were all in a freefall emotionally. We didn't need another jolt but were about to receive one anyway. As I sat in Mom's living room with Kyle, Brandon, and Brian reminiscing about Dad, Mom dropped a bombshell.

"Samantha and Kyle, I know you may not understand, but let me explain why I did what I'm about to tell you. I did it for your peace of mind. Now that Tom's gone, I'm afraid he may reveal what we know about John in the letters he wrote to each of you. He wanted to tell both of you, but I asked him not to," Mom said. Her eyes darted from the floor to the ceiling. Brandon and Brian hung their heads.

"You know something about John?" I asked incredulously.

"No way, Mom. After all we've done trying to track John down. What do you know?" Kyle's neck muscles strained against his skin.

"Now, I withheld this information for your own good, I promise. It may not have been the best decision, but it was what I thought was right at the time. Tom disagreed, but I insisted he keep quiet."

"I knew you were hiding something. What do you know?" My heart pounded in my chest.

Mom looked at her hands and twisted a tissue. "About three years ago, I had a call from a U.S. Marshal, James

O'Sullivan, and he asked if I'd heard from your father. Evidently, John had been in WITSEC . . . you know, witness protection, for several years and was missing. He wouldn't tell me anything about the bloody scene at John's apartment fifteen years ago. So, either John was attacked and survived, or he staged his disappearance. Who knows?"

"Witness protection," I whispered. That made sense.

Mom continued, "James oversaw John's relocation from the beginning. Your father had witnessed a crime, testified, and was threatened awhile before he was admitted into the program. After he was in WITSEC for about twelve years, there was going to be a new trial, new evidence or something. That was three years ago, and John was supposed to testify again."

Brian stood. "We should probably leave, me and Brandon. This doesn't concern us."

"No, please boys, let me finish. I want you both to understand why we did what we did. We are all one family. Please stay." Mom looked anxiously back and forth between my twin half-brothers as she pleaded with them. More than likely, she knew Kyle and I would be upset, and wanted Brian and Brandon there for moral support.

Brandon said, "I'm with Brian on this. It doesn't involve us. But if it means that much to you, Mom, I'll stay. Brian?"

"Sure, if I have to, but I want my objection on record." Brian sat down.

Mom dabbed silent tears. "Marshal O'Sullivan was going to take John to the attorney to go over his testimony a couple of weeks before the new trial. When he went to pick him up, John was gone. The home he was renting still had most of his belongings in it. They don't know if he left willingly or by force. But there were no signs of a struggle. The marshal said he couldn't give me any additional information."

"Wow, Mom. How could you keep this from us? We

were adults three years ago." Kyle's voice was elevated and his face flushed.

"I know you were adults, and . . . and it's possible I made the wrong choice, but I was trying to keep from opening old wounds. You'd searched for a long time, but by the time the marshal contacted me three years ago, you had both moved on. I didn't want to dredge up bad feelings or have you worry yourselves sick over him again," she said.

"You may have thought you were making the right decision, but you owed it to us, especially knowing how hard we'd searched for him, knowing the effect his disappearance had on us." Kyle brow furrowed.

"We are John's family too. Why didn't the marshal contact us?" I asked. Nausea filled my stomach.

"The marshal asked me if I knew the last time John contacted each of you. I told him it was about twelve years at that time. And that you both had searched but found no trace. I suggested he not contact you because I thought it would upset you. You know how obsessed you get, Sam. I wanted to protect you." A tear trickled down Mom's cheek.

"So, that's it? We still don't know if John disappeared again because he was afraid to testify or if something happened to him. Do we know who he was testifying against?" I asked.

"No, the marshal wasn't at liberty to share that information. He said John inadvertently was privy to a crime that put him in danger. Because he had testified in a federal case, they put him in WITSEC. The marshal refused to give me any more answers, so I don't know much more than when he first disappeared."

"Of course, you do, Mom. You know he survived whatever happened fifteen years ago, and you know he spent years in WITSEC." Warm tears streamed down my cheeks.

"Wasn't he allowed to let us know he was going into witness protection?" Kyle stood and clenched his fists.

"Evidently John could have informed us about entering

witness protection, but he chose not to. He thought it would be easier to leave things as they were, and he didn't want to put us in danger. Marshal O'Sullivan said John talked about you both a lot. Your father really loves you, and he was so proud of you." Mom still refrained from looking me or Kyle in the eye.

"I can't believe this, Mom. How could you? I asked you directly if you knew anything, and you lied to my face. That's more than withholding information." My salty tears continued to flow.

"Now dear, it wouldn't have changed anything, would it? Please don't be angry at me." Mom's voice was shaking.

"But Dad wanted to tell us?" I asked between silent sobs.

"Yes, he thought you should know. Soon after he got the Alzheimer's diagnosis, he started writing letters for each of us to read after he was gone. He wouldn't tell me what he was putting in them, so I feared he would let you know about John that way. I wanted to tell you myself in case you had any questions."

Kyle stepped toward Mom and demanded. "Why didn't you tell us? That's my only question."

Tears rolled down Mom's cheeks. "I'm sorry, Kyle . . ." She sucked in a deep breath trying to regain control. "I uh . . . I've checked back with Marshal O'Sullivan a couple of times since then . . ." Mom wiped her tears and nose with the tissue she'd already shredded. "There's no new information. Even the U.S. Marshals . . . with all their resources don't know . . . where he is now, so you and Sam . . . wouldn't have had a chance of finding him." Mom took deep breaths trying to stop the sobs.

"But they do know the circumstances surrounding him going into WITSEC. That might have given us a clue if we'd known that." Kyle threw his arms in the air.

"I don't know." Tears streamed down Mom's face. "I really messed this up. I'm sorry. I'm so sorry." She put her head in her hands and wept.

'I need some air." Kyle darted out the front door.

I heard his car start and tires screeching. I wanted to leave but waited for Mom to calm down first, so I could make a request.

"It'll be okay, Mom," Brandon cooed. "You were doing what you thought was best." He went to her and put his arm around her shoulder.

After a few minutes, Mom's weeping subsided. She looked up at me, eyes red and still filled with tears.

"I need to go too, Mom. But can I get Marshal O'Sullivan's number first?" I asked.

"Of course, dear. Anything." Mom left the room.

She returned with his number. "Anything else I can do to make this right?"

"No, Mom." Despite being blindsided, I hugged her and left. I didn't want walls between us again. I sat in my Jeep staring blankly at the dash. My mind whirled and my stomach churned. John chose not to say goodbye when he could have. Why would a father willingly leave his children to think the worst, albeit grown children, with no explanation? He owed us that. And Mom and Tom owed us the information they had been given. Mom was stubborn, but Tom should have overruled her on this one.

I felt less worthy than I ever had. My mother, my biological father, and my stepfather had all lied, had deliberately cheated me and my brother out of the truth. *They all whisper a lie.*

Chapter 45

After numerous calls and being put on hold for untold hours, I made brief contact with U.S. Marshal James O'Sullivan. He was heading to an IACP conference in Myrtle Beach in two days and said he'd be happy to speak with me then. We agreed to meet for lunch at Pier 14 Restaurant near the boardwalk in Myrtle Beach on Wednesday, the second day of the conference. I looked up IACP and discovered it is the International Association of Chiefs of Police. Interesting.

I hated waiting to speak with him, but I'd already waited years for information, so what was another few days? He might be more forthcoming in person, or he may not be able to tell me anything new. I tried to quell my expectations.

I called Spencer to give him an update. "Hey Spencer, how are you feeling today?"

"'Bout the same. How are you, Sam? Still reeling from your mom's disclosure?"

"I'm hanging in there. I was able to get an appointment with the U.S. Marshal."

"That's good news. When are you going to speak with him?"

"On Wednesday. He's going to be in Myrtle Beach. I'm meeting him at the Pier 14 Restaurant."

"I'm jealous. I love that place." I heard the smile in his voice.

"I haven't been there in a while, but I'm looking

forward to it. Can I bring you a doggie bag?"

"And miss out on this spectacular hospital food?" He chuckled. "That's okay, Sam. We can go when I'm outta here."

"Uh, sure." Was he asking me out on a date? "I'd like that."

The next day when I arrived at Spencer's hospital room in Charleston, Officer Mitchell was sitting close to his bed talking in hushed tones.

"Hey, guys, how's it going?" I asked.

"We were discussing John's case. Come here and pull up a chair, Sam. Kinda sensitive information," Spence said. His voice was much clearer than it had been the last time I visited.

I nodded and complied, my neck and shoulder muscles tightened. I took a deep breath and blew it out slowly. When I'd settled in the chair next to Spence's bed, he placed a warm hand on my shoulder and then glanced at Abigail and quickly withdrew his hand.

Abigail offered a bemused smile. "We were striking out with the materials we found in the storage unit, so when you told Spencer about WITSEC, he thought John might have shared something with his good friend. Spencer asked me to reach out to his old buddy's wife."

"You're talking about Bobby Baxter, the one who'd reported John missing?" I leaned closer to hear Abigail's whispers.

"Yes, we've been meaning to reach out to Betty, Bobby's wife, but hadn't finished going through all the contents and paperwork from John's storage unit. Then Spencer's fire sidelined us trying to figure out who set it and why. The good news is Betty shed light on what may have happened." Abigail reached for a notepad she'd set on Spencer's nightstand.

"What'd she say?" I asked.

"She said Bobby and your father, I mean . . . uh, John,

served in the same military unit."

"No worries. John was my father, biologically at least. I remember he was in a medical unit, right?" I asked.

Abigail looked at her notes. "Yes, the Naval Medical Research Unit. Betty said they researched and tested biological weapons."

The butterflies I was feeling turned into a lead weight in my gut. "What? John never mentioned anything like that."

"Yes, it was their main focus and Bobby was in the same unit."

"What did Betty know about that? How could that relate to John's disappearance? I don't understand. You told me the police questioned Bobby and he said he didn't know anything."

"They were sworn to secrecy. Probably why John didn't talk about it, and Bobby didn't tell Betty anything until after John disappeared. When he heard about the bloody scene at John's place, he was scared and didn't tell the police anything. He was worried that John's vanishing may have been related to their military service and didn't want to be next on their list. He told Betty if he went missing or if anything happened to him to contact a member of that unit. Bobby gave her a name and phone number and after his accident, she reported it, but never heard anything. I got the name from her, but that commander's no longer in the military. I'll try to track him down." Abigail stood and stretched her back and arms. "Here's where it gets wild." Abigail sat back down.

"That's already wild. Biological warfare. What did Bobby tell her? Was his accident suspect?" My mind was racing.

"One question at a time, Samantha." Abigail's lips curled but her smile quickly faded. "He told Betty there were two dissenters within their unit. They tried to recruit John and Bobby for a big plot they'd concocted to prove that what the Navy was working on was more dangerous than beneficial.

"Bobby didn't "rat" on them because he was worried they would retaliate. He was trying to protect Betty and their baby. John left Bobby out of the allegation he submitted to the chief master-at-arms. Bobby gave John a written sworn statement but asked him to only use it if necessary. John didn't need it. After his report, NCIS gathered enough solid evidence, and the two men were tried and sent to military prison. One died in prison, and one was paroled a few months before John was attacked and entered WITSEC fifteen years ago."

"Do you believe the man was after John for revenge?" My stomach churned.

"That's my theory. Shortly after the man was released, mysterious illnesses started popping up around Denver and Seattle. Betty said the unit commander at the facility reached out to John before he disappeared and wanted him to help investigate. John told Bobby he suspected the cases were related to the biological weapons they'd researched."

"Oh no. That's awful. Here in the states. And the bioweapons are still out there?" I took another deep breath.

Abigail nodded. "Yes, as far as we could determine, the original source has never been located, but we have limited access to such information."

"You can be certain the Justice Department is working to keep it contained," Spence said. "And the man that was paroled was sent back to prison about a year after that. The records are sealed citing national security and classified information issues."

Spence's voice was getting weaker, and he started coughing. I picked up the plastic cup full of ice water on his overbed tray and handed it to him.

He took a few sips. "Thanks, Sam."

Abigail lowered her voice even more. "About Bobby's accident. Yes, it was suspicious. He died in a single car crash. Foul play was suspected because weather and road conditions were not a factor. The brakes failed, but the crash was so bad, they couldn't verify they'd been tampered with. Betty has always believed someone connected with the biological weapons was responsible for her husband's death. And the military suspected a third person was involved in the virus leak but weren't able to prove it."

"This is incredible. I'd been thinking John disappeared to start a new life, and now I find out he was involved in a bizarre biological weapon scenario." I shook my head. "It's a lot." I sighed.

Abigail reached over and placed her hand on my arm. "I'm not finished investigating, Sam, but these are some seriously dangerous men. We believe they may have hurt John fifteen years ago, had Bobby killed, and now set fire to Spencer's home. And that's only what we're aware of. Please be careful."

"I will. Is there anyone you can contact who may know more?" I asked.

Abigail shrugged. "Unfortunately, I've hit a dead end. Everything is top secret, need to know. But I'll keep trying to locate that unit commander."

Spence chimed in, "I have friends in the Justice Department. I'll see what I can uncover."

"Thanks, Spence. This is all overwhelming." I leaned forward placing my head in my hands. Spence reached over and squeezed my shoulder.

"It'll be okay, Sam. We'll get to the bottom of this. The pieces are finally starting to fall into place," he said.

Chapter 46

I'd been to the Pier 14 Restaurant a few times. It was in a charming beachfront building on stilts. When the tide comes in, the water flows under it, giving the impression of being on a boat. If we were fortunate, there'd be seating available outside along the railings with an unsurpassed water view.

The pier extends out about a hundred feet and on a good day hosts a healthy number of fishermen and women hauling in their catch. The last time I was there, a man caught a small shark, much to the dismay of his wife and child. I wasn't hoping for that kind of excitement today.

I arrived first.

"Do you have a table for two, outside, close to the water?" I asked.

"Of course, we're not too busy yet. We opened about twenty minutes ago. Please follow me," the hostess said.

"Perfect." I followed and took a seat in the rattan chair, next to the worn wooden railings. "I'm expecting a Marshal James O'Sullivan soon." It was 11:20 a.m. We'd agreed to meet at 11:30 a.m.

She placed two menus on the heavily varnished wood table. "I'll direct him to your table when he arrives. Can I get you something to drink while you wait?"

"Sure, I'll take a sweet tea."

It was a glorious day—about seventy-five degrees, a

slight breeze, bright sun, and a cloudless blue sky. The waves were slapping the pilings as they crashed on the shore. A red umbrella over the table provided enough shade that I didn't have to squint to see the menu. The waitress brought my ice-cold drink. I sipped on it as I perused the options. Too many delicious choices. Salmon, scallops, shrimp, or crab legs. No, not crab legs. Too messy. Not good for a first-time meeting. Not that I'd probably ever see him again, but a good first impression may help him to feel comfortable and share more details with me.

"Ms. Anderson?" A tall African American man with a wide smile approached the table.

"Yes. Marshal O'Sullivan?" I stood and extended my hand. He returned my gesture with a firm handshake.

"Yes, Marshal James O'Sullivan, but please call me James." He took a seat across from me as I sat back down.

Marshal O'Sullivan wore a black suit, white shirt, blue tie, black dress shoes, and a marshal badge around his neck displaying a star within a circle.

"James, it is nice to meet you. You can call me Samantha. I didn't realize this was a formal attire meeting." I looked down at my capris, sandals, and sleeveless top.

"Oh, not at all. Don't mind me. I don't usually wear a suit, but I'm presenting at one of the workshops today. I'd say I'm the one not dressed for this location."

"Phew, I thought I missed the memo. You look sharp. I'm sure you'll knock it out of the park."

James sucked in a deep breath. "I sure hope so. I'm a little nervous. I don't do a lot of public speaking. I'm mostly a field agent."

"Just fake it until you make it. That's what I've always done." I laughed nervously. Did I really just say that to a U.S. Marshal?

"Do you do much public speaking?" he asked.

"Yes. I'm a teacher, so on a much smaller scale than speaking at a conference. When I was in school, I had teachers that strongly influenced my life, and I wanted to pay it forward and make a difference in young lives."

"That's honorable."

"Thank you. I'd say keeping the bad guys off the street is honorable too."

"I'd like to think so. What do you teach?"

"Secondary English which at our high school includes public speaking. It's ironic. In college I put off the required public speaking class until my senior year. Now I'm teaching the class I dreaded and enjoy being in front of students. Enough about me. What are you speaking about?"

"Actually, what you called me about, the WITSEC program."

"I'm sure you'll do an outstanding job. I appreciate you taking the time to talk to me."

"No problem. I understand your desire to know what happened to your father, John Garcia, but there are things I'm not at liberty to discuss."

"I understand. Anything you can tell me would be much appreciated. I must confess that since we talked, I've been able to piece some things together with the help of the Seagrove Police Department. Perhaps you can fill in a few blanks for me."

"I'll do my best. Let's look at the menu, and then we'll talk."

After a few minutes of deliberation and asking the waitress what was good, James ordered the Blackened Fire Grilled Salmon with rice, and for me, the Fantail Shrimp with slaw and hush puppies. I had hush puppies the last time I ate there, and they were worth the calories. Warm, crispy corn fritters served with honey butter.

"Okay, now that we have that out of the way, let me tell you what I can, Samantha. A lot of information that was restricted initially, isn't now. John Garcia is no longer considered to be in witness protection. We've never lost anyone to date, so we assume he left of his own volition."

"Good to know," I said.

"We searched for him, but since he's not a fugitive, we've stopped looking. It's been three years, and he may be living under another assumed name, at least that's what we hope."

"That makes sense." I pushed my windblown hair behind my ears, hoping it would stay there.

"I would have told this to your mother if she had called again, but I haven't heard from her in a long while. Please feel free to share any of what I tell you with family members," James said.

"I will. Thank you. I'm sure my brother Kyle will be eager to hear whatever you can tell me."

"When John was in the Navy he testified at a federal trial. He had firsthand knowledge of a potential crime. The two perpetrators – I'll call them Joe and Schmo for anonymity's sake -- were put away on conspiracy charges because a crime had not yet been committed, at least they didn't know of one at that point. In court, Schmo threatened John, and the FBI wasn't sure if he had the connections to carry it out, so John was offered WITSEC, but turned it down and lived his life in peace for several years. Joe died in prison. He was stabbed. Then Schmo was paroled for good behavior and prison overcrowding.

"But his good behavior didn't carry forward on the outside. Schmo didn't show up for his first meeting with his parole officer, and he couldn't be located. John started receiving anonymous threats--phone calls and letters. He reported it to the FBI and was once again presented with witness protection. And as before, he declined." James took a sip of water.

"John was, or uh, is such a free spirit. I can't see him changing his name and willingly settling down in one place. He loved to roam."

"I gathered that. Did he move around a lot as a kid?" James asked.

I waited until the waitress brought a basket of rolls and topped off my sweet tea before answering. For some reason, I didn't want our conversation to be overheard even though we weren't yet sharing anything specific.

When the waitress walked far enough away to be out of earshot, I answered him, "Yes, John was an army brat. My late Grandma and Grandpa Garcia were from the south, but Grandpa Garcia was in the army, and John attended nine different schools in twelve years."

James raised his eyebrows. "Wow, that would be hard on a kid."

"The revolving homes created an appetite for the gypsy lifestyle. At eighteen he joined the navy and continued his nomadic wandering doing medical training. Then he was stationed at research facilities overseas. Moving frequently was normal for him."

"That explains a lot. I was assigned to John, and he relocated four times in the twelve years he was in the program. But he was in a big city with sprawling suburbs, so he stayed within a twenty-five-mile radius, and he kept me informed about the moves, that is until this last time."

"That sounds about right. East to west and everywhere in between, he was comfortable and loved exploring the nuances of local culture and food. He was adept at mimicking accents, so much so, people thought he was a local," I said.

James nodded and took a bite of his roll.

I cut open a roll and buttered it. "John bragged about it more than once. He'd say, 'They have no idea they are talking to a southern boy, born in Mississippi.' From that perspective, he was a good fit for WITSEC, and I'm not surprised he moved around even in the program."

"He did fine for twelve years, and he was not alone. But we'll get to that in a minute."

"Natalie Torres," I said.

"Yes," James' mouth dropped open. "How'd you

know?"

"I have dedicated friends in the Seagrove Police Department who are trying to help me solve John's mystery and a few of my own."

"Okay, fair enough. What you may not know, or you might . . ." James smiled. "On your twenty-first birthday, John was planning on attending your party and intended to bring Natalie and introduce her to everyone."

John was going to keep his promise and was going to bring Natalie too. What a different night that would have been. My eyes stung. James saw my visceral reaction and paused.

I took a few deep breaths, one, two, three, four. "Go on," I said.

"When he was late picking up Natalie from her hotel, she called, but he didn't answer. After an hour, he hadn't called back, so she contacted the FBI agent that had suggested John go into WITSEC. Natalie and John had been dating for several months, so she knew all about the threats and the offer from the FBI. She had her own problems to worry about too."

"You mean the abuse and stalking from Patrick Jackson?"

"Wow, you *have* done some digging. Maybe I should be interviewing you." James chuckled.

"No, no, go ahead."

"Okay, Patrick was not only an abusive person, but he was also a drug dealer. He had a large operation going, buying from the Lorenzo crime family, and occasionally stealing from the prison hospital pharmacy. He got connected with the mob through prisoners at the hospital and was bringing in a lot of money for them and for himself. He supplied inmates and had dealers on the streets selling to kids too. Natalie found out about it and testified against him. He threatened her in the courtroom."

"Oh my, the plot thickens. I knew he'd been arrested for

dealing drugs but didn't realize he was connected to the mafia." I took another bite of bread.

"Natalie was told she was a good candidate for WITSEC, but she stopped the DEA agent from making the OEO request."

"The OEO?" I asked.

"The Office of Enforcement Operations in the Justice Department. They evaluate and review the applications for WITSEC. They do stringent vetting to determine if entry into the program is appropriate and timely considering the threat to the individual and their psychological evaluation. The OEO are the ones who initially authorize or deny the request," James said.

"It sounds like quite a process," I said.

The waitress approached with our meals and set the steaming plates in front of us.

"It looks and smells fantastic, thanks," James said.

"Ya'll want a top up on your drinks?" the waitress asked.

"Yes, thank you," I said.

James nodded.

"Sweet tea for you, hun'. And unsweet for you, darlin'. Is that right?"

"Yes," we both answered.

"I'll be right back."

"Do you mind if I give thanks?" James asked.

"No, please," I said. We bowed our heads.

"Lord, thank you for this food. Please sustain our bodies for your work and glory. Help me to fill in the blanks that Samantha needs to find peace. In Jesus Name, Amen."

"Amen. Thank you, James."

I dipped a hush puppy into the honey butter and took a bite. It melted in my mouth. The waitress returned and filled our drinks to the rim.

James continued between bites. "Natalie told her plans to the agent who offered to help her enter WITSEC. She was going to follow John back to Seagrove and stay at a hotel while looking for an apartment to rent. She said she'd pay cash for a while to stay off the radar of anyone who might be looking for her."

"So, they both were in danger for different reasons." I shook my head. "Amazing."

"It is an unusual story for sure. Back to John's disappearance from Seagrove. After Natalie called the FBI agent, he went to John's apartment and found him barely alive. The door was unlocked, and the music was blaring. The agent rushed him to the hospital where he was admitted under an alias. Your mom told me you found out about the bloody scene when the police called you after a neighbor requested a wellness check."

"Yes. Didn't the FBI inform the police they'd found him?"

"No. As is often the case, one hand doesn't know what the other hand is doing among law enforcement agencies. The Seagrove Police had no idea that he'd been taken to the hospital and eventually admitted into WITSEC."

"That left us in the dark too." I sighed.

"When John recovered, he agreed to go into WITSEC at least temporarily until Schmo was caught. He didn't see the person who attacked him, but assumed it was Schmo or someone working with him."

"So, there is only circumstantial evidence that the parolee was behind the threats and John's attack?" I added more sugar to my already sweet tea and stirred it.

"Yes, that's right," James said.

A gust of wind blew my napkin off the table. James jumped up in time to retrieve it before it flew over the edge into the water.

"Thanks, James." I was so engrossed in the conversation that I didn't notice the white seagull with a black head and wingtips sitting on the railing. He was eyeing my meal. As tempted as I was to offer the hopeful creature a tidbit, it was prohibited. Ironically a "Please Don't Feed the Seagulls" sign was posted on a pole over the bird.

James continued, "When John was strong enough to enter WITSEC, he requested that we allow Natalie to join him. They had discussed a future together, so we brought them to a safe house and sent in applications. Both were accepted. They got married a year later."

"John got married. That's something I didn't know."

"Without knowing his and her new names there's no way you'd find that information," James said. "Then the FBI caught up with Schmo and put him back in prison. They had evidence he was working with an unknown third party and convinced John and Natalie to stay in WITSEC."

"Right. May I interrupt your story and ask a question?"

"Of course, Samantha. I'm here to help you find answers, so whatever I can share with you, I will."

"Mom said John could have contacted us about going into WITSEC. Is that true?"

"Yes, he could have, but in his mind, the less you knew, the safer you were. It's not that unusual."

"Hmm. Okay, and now that we're off topic, what can you tell me about the trial?"

"I'm not at liberty to discuss that. And honestly, I don't know a lot of the details. I was assigned to John after his attack. He only mentioned it a few times."

"I understand. Mom said there was a new trial three years ago."

"Yes, the conviction was appealed when Schmo's lawyer said they'd found new evidence, and he was granted a new trial."

"Mom told us that you went by his house a couple of weeks before the new trial, and he was gone. Was there any sign of foul play? Was Natalie gone too?"

"Yes, they were both gone. Many of their personal items were left behind like cell phones and clothes. Interestingly, their ID's were gone. We believe they left

WITSEC willingly. We tried to track them, but there were no hits on their credit cards, no plane tickets, no jobs, or home rentals."

"What do you think happened?" I asked.

"I have my suspicions but no concrete evidence. About four years ago, John contacted me. He said Natalie was diagnosed with stage four breast cancer. They moved closer to a cancer hospital, but in the same region. That's the last location I was aware of."

"Oh no." I set my fork down and looked into James' sympathetic brown eyes. "What happened? Is she okay?"

"I'm not sure. She was still in treatment when John disappeared three years ago. My hunch is he got cold feet about testifying because of Natalie."

"That would make sense. Have you heard of Bobby Baxter?" I asked.

"Doesn't ring a bell. Who is he?"

"He was a friend of John's who served with him at one of the medical research facilities in the Navy. He passed about a year after John disappeared. The military trial John testified at was about biological weapons, wasn't it?"

"How did you--?"

"From Bobby Baxter's wife, Betty. Not me directly, but one of the police officers in Seagrove reached out to her when Mom finally told us that John had been in WITSEC. Bobby and John were fishing buddies and my friend at the Seagrove Police discovered that Bobby reported John missing fifteen years ago. The officer thought John may have told Bobby what was going on in his life. He was right. Bobby had confided in Betty."

"Is that right? What'd she say?"

While I was recounting what Abigail told me, we split a piece of key lime pie. It was creamy, sweet, and tart. Perfect. And a half piece was all I could manage after my big lunch.

"Interesting," James said.

"Is there anything you can tell me about the new trial three years ago? Did Schmo stay in prison?" I asked.

"Most of the evidence from the original trial was mysteriously missing, so Schmo was retried and released. Without the supporting documents, they didn't have a solid case against him, especially without John's testimony. So, Schmo is out there somewhere and could be hunting for your father. John told me he kept copies of the evidence from the trial and additional items that weren't presented at trial."

"That must be who's been threatening me and burned my neighbor's home," I said.

"What?" James gasped.

I spent the next thirty minutes going over the threats I'd received, the storage unit we'd found, and what happened to Spencer.

"We both learned some things today, Samantha. I'm going to follow up with Betty Baxter, and if you discover anything else, please contact me."

"Will do, James. And if you get any more information that you're able to share with me, please call," I said.

"I will. Even though the U.S. Marshal service is not officially searching for John and Natalie anymore, I'd personally like to find closure on what happened to them. After twelve years in WITSEC, I consider them my friends whose safety was entrusted to me. I hope I didn't fail them. I need to know they left willingly."

"Only one more question, if I may?" I asked.

"Shoot." James placed his napkin on the table.

"Were John and Natalie in the Dallas-Fort Worth area?"

"Uh, um, I um, I'm not at liberty to say. You missed your calling." James shook his head.

That was answer enough.

Chapter 47

The room smelled of musty old books and dust. Sitting with Mom, Kyle, Brandon, and Brian, I tapped my fingernails impatiently on the ten-foot long, oval, wood conference table. We knew Tom's parents had left him a sizable amount from their lottery winnings when they passed. Mom had seen Dad's will and said some of that was going to be distributed to us, but I was more interested in the letter Tom wrote to each of us. How was he going to justify withholding information about John?

Finally, Dad's attorney, Charlie Schmidt, my uncle and affectionately known as "Schmitty" entered the room and took a seat at his massive mahogany desk. As a six-foot four, stout, red haired, former linebacker, his presence usually eclipsed everyone in the room. But despite his dominating appearance, he wasn't a showy man. He preferred to remain in the shadows, behind the scenes. And he had a heart of gold.

"Tom was a good friend and brother-in-law, and I will deeply miss him. I know how much he loved each of you, and I am sincerely sorry for your loss," Uncle Charlie said.

We thanked him.

He continued, "Before Tom's disease progressed, he asked each of you what you'd like to have from his possessions, and he passed that list on to me."

He handed each of us a sheet with our requests. "Do each of your lists look correct?"

After scanning our papers, we all confirmed our wishes were accurate. My heart sank as I perused Tom's possessions which were now mine – a collection of signed books from my favorite author, part of his coin collection for Jaz, and his model trains and planes for Jayce. He'd added a few extra items I hadn't asked for—his Bible and spiritual journals. So thoughtful.

"In addition, Tom left trusts for Kyle, Samantha, Brian, and Brandon in the amount of $500,000 each, with a one-year hold on $450,000 of it. He didn't want any impulsive grief spending and assumed a year would give you all the time to think about the money's best use or investment. If for any reason you want to access the trust earlier, Georgia can override the year wait for you. But it is purely at her discretion." Uncle Charlie shuffled papers on his desk as that number sunk in.

I glanced at my brothers and their wide eyes revealed as much shock as I felt. No more struggling to make ends meet. Tom had always offered to help if we needed it, but I'd flatly refused using twisted logic to try to get Logan to uphold his share of child support. I rationalized that if I was in need, he'd be forced to provide for his children. It hadn't worked. And as far as I knew, my brothers never took Dad's offer to help them financially. Self-made men they were. In truth, we were all stubborn.

Uncle Charlie continued, "Tom also left a trust of $150,000 each to go towards Jayce, Jazmine, and Noah's education should they go to college. If not, they'll each receive $150,000 on their twenty-fifth birthday, plus any interest that has accrued. Tom requested that if there are future grandchildren, that Georgia would contribute to their education, if possible."

"Thank you, Uncle Charlie." Brian sounded overwhelmed.

"One more thing, he's leaving a million dollars to Christian charities. He wants all five of you to get together to decide where the money should go. It's in a trust and will be distributed when you all sign off on your decision. He said you can take up to a year to decide which ones — no more than ten organizations, but as few as one if you conclude they're worthy. If you don't come to an agreement, he has left the name of a few recipients to equally distribute the funds to. Tom was a generous soul."

Georgia dabbed her eyes. "For sure. He never spent the inheritance from his parent's lottery winnings. He only collected the interest, and usually for gifts for other people. He wanted to leave it for us. That's why he continued to work even when he could have retired early. I miss him so much."

"He was one of a kind. Of course, the remainder of his estate goes to you, Georgia. That is the gist of it. All the legalese is here in the actual will." Uncle Charlie handed us each a copy. "Any questions?"

Stunned "no's" all around.

"Good, then on to the next item. Tom left five letters, one to give each of you after he was gone." He passed them out, and I began to read silently.

> My sweet, Samantha,
>
> If you are reading this, then the inevitable has happened. The 100% mortality rate has held. I'd like to have been the one to beat the odds, but as I assumed, it was a false hope. ☺ Please don't grieve for me. I have found peace over the last few years in a relationship with God. While this old body has failed me, I am alive and whole in my maker's presence.
>
> I've left a Bible with Uncle Charlie for you to read and a few notebooks with stories about my recent journey of faith which has meant so much to me. I finally found my way in life, Sam. Guess you

can teach an old dog new tricks after all! I wasted years looking for my value in all the wrong places. My prayer is that my journey will encourage you to find peace with God too.

But on to another extremely important matter. I must make a confession to you, Sam. I do know what happened to your real father. Unfortunately, he died recently. And you are currently reading the letter he left for you.

Sam, I am and always will be your dad. I mean your real dad. Your dad who gave you life. Your mother threatened to kill me if I told you the truth, but her threat is now moot. I hope you'll forgive my twisted sense of humor and the very late arrival of this news.

Your mom and I rekindled our friendship the year before you were born. I met her before she met John. We hung out with the same group of friends when I returned from Vietnam. We even went on a few dates. She was 18, and I was 23. Her parents didn't think it was wise for her to date someone so much older, so it never went anywhere. Then thirteen years later, I walked into the Coastal Real Estate office, and there sat Georgia. My ex-wife and I had divorced the year before.

John and your mom were going through a rough patch at the time, on a break in their relationship, and I was a listening ear. A little too available, as it turns out. But God brought good out of our mistake. I wouldn't trade you for the world. Your mom named you, Samantha, in my honor. Samuel Thomas Myers. Samantha—we are both Sam to her.

When your mom told me she wanted to try and make her marriage work, I moved upstate to Greenville, so I wouldn't be a stumbling block and interfere with her wishes. I wanted her to be happy. John and your mom really did try to make it. John knew you were mine, but said he'd raise you as his own for the sake of the family. She put his name on your birth certificate, and he kept the secret all those years, probably fueled by the guilt from his own indiscretions. But as you know, their efforts didn't succeed, and they divorced when you were three.

About a year after your mom and John divorced, she reached out and told me what happened. I missed her terribly and my heart ached to know you, so I put in for a transfer to Seagrove. It took a while, but when an opening came, I jumped at it. Those years without being in your life were hell for me.

By the time I came back to Seagrove, everyone assumed you were John's, and your mom wanted to leave well enough alone. She didn't want to have to tell Kyle you weren't his full blood sister. And she didn't want the humiliation of owning up to the affair. I respected her wishes, but I didn't like it. You deserved to know. I didn't want to let you go your entire life without knowing the truth. Please forgive me.

Over the last few years, after coming to know God, I've realized how important the truth is. How a lie can affect us. So, I know it's a little late. And I wish I could be there to hold you as this stunning reality dawns on you. You were always wanted by your father. You were always cherished. You were always mine. I love you and look forward to seeing you again one day in the life to come.

As I prayed about leaving this letter for you, I kept hearing God say, "He is The Maker and the Lord of the Harvest." I'm not sure what that means to you, if anything, but I felt I should share it with you in this letter.

Be happy, Sam. Please don't cry. Your father loves you. Your search is over.

Love you through eternity,

Dad

Stunned and yes, crying, I could scarcely believe what I'd read. I looked at Mom. She kept her head down.

"What's wrong, sis?" Brandon asked.

"I can't believe it," I said. "So, Kyle's my half-brother? And Brandon and Brian are my full brothers? John isn't my real father? Dad is! Mom, how could you keep this from me all these years? Haven't you seen the agony it's caused to feel I was unimportant and neglected by my father?" The words spilled forth as I absorbed the reality of this revelation.

Kyle, Brandon, and Brian sat in stunned silence.

I'd been living my life believing a lie. Not just any lie, but a lie that cost me much happiness. A lie that made me feel unloved and abandoned. A lie that made me feel less than. The truth could have saved me so much heartbreak.

"Mom, all I remember of your marriage to John was yelling and screaming at each other. I'd hide in my bedroom closet and cover my ears. You led me to believe I was the product of two miserable, bickering parents, but I was a love child. A child who was wanted and cherished by a man whom I adore."

"Sam, you have to look at it from my perspective. I was married to your father, or—you know, not your father, but to John. He didn't mind womanizing, but I couldn't stand word getting out that I had cheated on him, like he'd cheated on me. I was humiliated that I'd stooped to his level—I was as guilty as him. You know I did and do and always will love Thomas. He is the best thing that ever happened to me. I'm sorry I've hurt you." Mom straightened her newly blond locks and fidgeted with her wedding ring. She hadn't removed it—she never may. Tom was the love of her life. And she was his.

I understood, sort of, but was so deeply confused and hurt and grateful to know the truth all at the same time. She reached out for me, but I pulled back.

"We'll talk later, Mom. I can't do this right now," I said.

"Did you know about this, Uncle Charlie?" I asked, wondering if my whole world was lying to me.

"No, Samantha, but I won't deny that I've had suspicions. You looked so much like Tom, I wondered, but never asked," he said.

"I need to go." I collected the Bible and notebooks and rose to leave but remembered Mom had picked me up on her way there.

"Brandon, may I borrow your car? Brian can drop you off, right Brian?" He nodded. "Thanks, guys. I'll drop your car by later," I said.

Outside Brandon's car, I dropped the fob, my hands still shaking. Finally in the car, a scream of anguish erupted and then morphed into an explosion of tears followed by a sobbing tirade against God. I'm not sure how long it lasted, but finally the rage subsided. I wasn't sure if anyone saw my outburst, but at that moment I didn't care.

When the trembling stopped, I started Brandon's vehicle, and the radio came on. The words of the song stunned me.

> *So many little words, so many little lies that have followed you all of your life, looking for the truth . . . even when you were running, even when you were hiding, never*

been a moment that you were not perfectly loved, when you barely believed it, when your eyes couldn't see it, every single moment, you've always been perfectly loved . . . . you've always been perfectly in the hands of the Infinite, as the wounds of the world became his, see the kindness Heaven has for you, and he's always drawing you in . . . you're perfectly human, made from the dust, you've got a heart broken and scarred, yet perfectly loved . . ..

As the song ended, the DJ, announced, "You heard it folks, you are perfectly loved. Don't ever doubt it. That was Rachael Lampa with Toby Mac singing, you guessed it, *Perfectly Loved.*"

Tears started flowing again. Gentle tears. Silent tears. The song moved me in a way as never before. I needed to find out if it was true.

Chapter 48

A week later, Brandon knocked on my door. I hadn't talked to any of the family since the day of the "big reveal."

"Hey, Sam. Thought I'd check on you."

"Aw, thanks. Come on in."

"How are you doing?" Brandon asked.

"Honestly, I'm still reeling."

Brandon gave me a hug and then followed me into the living room. I sat on the recliner, and he took a seat on the matching sofa.

"It may take us a while to absorb the truth, Sam. It's a lot. Especially for you."

"I'm sure it was hard on Kyle too. He recently found out that John was in witness protection and then that I'm not his full sister. It might be as hard on him as it's been on me."

"I talked to Kyle a couple days ago. He was angry but trying to work through it. You know Kyle, he'll get over it," Brandon said.

"Yes, he's a strong person. I haven't called him yet . . . I don't know what to say. So, what's new in your world?" I asked.

"Guess." He waited for me to answer.

I chuckled. "I have no idea."

"Okay, you'd probably would never guess anyway. If you hadn't received that letter from Dad, you would have found out about Mom and Dad's secret this week. I received the results from my DNA test, and it showed 100% sibling match with you.”

“Wow. That’s certainly not what I expected to find when I first sent in the DNA test.”

“So, the truth would have come out, but I’m glad you found out the way you did. That news was better coming with Dad’s explanation,” Brandon said.

“For sure. It would’ve been a lot harder to understand what happened. God was working in the situation, wouldn’t you say?” I asked and couldn’t help smiling.

“I would.” Brandon smiled back.

“I’ve started reading through Dad’s journal notes, and he saw God working in little ways in his life. Some may call them coincidences, but he was sure it was God’s hand. It’s encouraging me to have faith too,” I said.

“Yes, I’ve been reading Dad’s journal notes too. After you left his office, Uncle Charlie gave me, Brian, and Kyle copies of Dad’s journals. At Dad’s request, of course.”

“I’m glad. They’ve helped me to understand his heart. I’ve only started reading them, but it’s like he’s still here with me. You know, I never let him talk to me about spiritual things. I’d always cut him off. I believed I was too busy to go to church or get involved with so much already on my plate.”

“You do have a lot on your plate, single mom, full time job, attractive friend next door to entertain.” The edges of his mouth curled up.

“Thanks, matchmaker. You forgot to add nosey pushy brother.” I smiled. “On a more serious note, I have a question to ask you.”

“Shoot, sis.” His blue eyes were filled with compassion.

“I know the revelation about who my real father is came as a shock to all of us. How do we, or more specifically, how do I forgive Dad, Mom, and John for keeping that secret all these years?”

“Sam, I’m sure it’s heartbreaking for you.” Brandon’s voice was tender. “We were all thrown by that revelation.

Brian told me his head's been spinning all week. After Mom admitted knowing that John had been in witness protection, I didn't think I could be more shocked, but I was."

"So how are you handling it? The forgiveness part especially." I looked back at him hopeful that he knew a secret on the topic.

"It's a tall order, for sure. I noticed in Dad's journals, he regularly asked God to help him to forgive and do the right thing. He admitted that there were times he didn't want to but asked God for His help. And he received it." Brandon rubbed his neck. "I can't imagine how this is for you. I must admit, Dad seemed pretty perfect, so this revelation is not like him. As for myself, well, let's just say I'm another story. I know I need forgiveness and . . . often. That's where I go when I need to forgive."

"I'm right there with you. And I've always admired Dad, and still do. One mistake doesn't define him. I'll have to dig a little deeper into his journals and, of course, the Bible he left me. I'm still in shock."

"Completely normal, sis. You know you always have someone to talk to if you need it."

"Thanks, bro."

"Oh no, I wasn't talking about me, I meant Spencer. Your handsome neighbor." Brandon smiled.

I punched him in the arm. "Ha-ha."

"No really, sis, I'm here for you. Anytime, anywhere. I'm only a phone call away."

After a few weeks of letting the truth sink in and the shock wear off, I started on a path to understand The Maker and his son, a.k.a. God the Father and Jesus. Brandon suggested we do a Bible study starting in the book of John. While I had a perfunctory knowledge of the Bible, I never read it, much less studied it. I recalled the lessons about Adam and Eve, David and Goliath, Noah's ark, Job, and stories about Jesus, but not the depth of wisdom buried in each chapter. It was a new journey for me. After thirty-six years, I was finally finding truth. Truth about this life and truth about the one to come. If Mr. Bidding was watching me, I thought he'd be thrilled that I was finally making time for *The Book of Truth*, better known as the *Bible*.

Chapter 49

I sat on the canopied swing on Mom's back patio watching the moss on the live oaks sway in the breeze. Mom was inside making dinner with the twins. I pulled out my yellow lined legal pad. I could have done this on the computer, but I've always thought better with pen in hand.

I wrote each clue and underlined it.

Clue 1. It Began in the Isle of Palms

After the big secret was out, Mom told me she first met Tom on the Isle of Palms when she was eighteen. Her two lifelong girlfriends, Bev and Kristin, were going to an art walk and invited her. They met up with Bev's brother, Bruce, and his two friends at an oceanfront Isle of Palms restaurant. Mom raved about the Café with a view of the pier. I'd have to check it out sometime. Tom was one of Bruce's friends she'd met that day. They had such a good time, the group started hanging out together. Clue one: check. Under the clue I wrote, "Mom and Dad first met there."

Clue 2: In His New Life, He Works No More

I assumed new life referred to Tom's salvation. Working no more could be about his retirement, or it might be a spiritual reference. Like he doesn't work for salvation but trusts in what Jesus did. It could be either or both. Clue two: check. Under clue two, I wrote, "Dad's Salvation and/or Retirement."

Clue 3: Find Your Cue in the Color Blue

That was easy now that I understood the clues were

referring to Tom. Blue for police. He'd served for decades on South Carolina's police force. Brothers in blue wearing blue uniforms. There's the thin blue line flag representing the solidarity of police officers who keep society orderly and out of chaos. As I considered all the ways blue related to police, I realized 'blue' was in the title of my favorite TV series, Blue Bloods about a family of police officers, detectives, and police commissioners in New York City. Clue three: check. Under clue three, I wrote, "Dad's Life Work, Police Service."

Clue 4: From the Mountains to the Valley

Hmm. I wasn't sure about this unless it's a spiritual reference. The mountains – spiritual growth and training, where Moses met God. I remembered that from my summer vacation Bible school as a kid. The valley could be the Valley of the Shadow of Death from Psalm 23. That fits. Clue four: check. Under clue four, I wrote, "Dad's Spiritual Growth and Imminent Death at the time I received the clue."

Clue 5: The Light is Flickering

This clue must be about Dad's physical and mental decline. He shined so much light when he was healthy. And it grew brighter as he drew closer to God. I noticed, though I didn't understand at the time that he was radiating God's light and love. Even when he was ill, light flickered through his being. And now he is in the presence of pure light. It comforted me. He's home. Clue five: check. Under the clue, I wrote, "Dad's physical and mental decline, but spiritual life shining through."

Clue 6: The Answer is in His Name

I had been sure this clue was about John, that we'd finally started making progress when this clue inadvertently led us to John's storage unit. From Dad's letter, I now know this clue means I was named after him. Samuel Thomas Myers. Samantha, we are both Sam. Clue six: check. Under the clue, I wrote, "Samuel and Samantha, both Sam.

Clue 7: Three, three, zero, four, five

Not the zip code for Key West. Mom had appeared startled when I mentioned those numbers to her after that dream.

I got up and walked inside. "Wow, it smells heavenly, guys."

"Your grandma's Low Country boil recipe," Mom said.

"And I'm making an Ambrosia Salad, Mom," Jaz said, her face beaming.

"It looks yummy, honey," I said. "What are you working on, Jayce?"

He didn't turn around. "It's a surprise. It will be the best dessert you ever ate," he said. His body blocked the view of the counter where he was working.

"It's a peanut butter chocolate ice cream pie," Jaz whispered.

"Yum," I whispered back.

Mom asked, "What are you up to, sweetie? You're missing all the excitement."

"Oh, I'm tying up loose ends. May I ask you a personal question?"

"Sure, dear. Dinner is almost ready, so make it quick." She stepped into the dining room. I followed.

"Remember when I asked you about the numbers from my dream. You seemed to recognize them. Do they have significance to you?"

"Oh, Sam, you aren't still obsessing about those dreams, are you?"

"Please, Mom, I'm trying to piece it all together." I wasn't going to back down.

"Um, I'm sure it's a coincidence, but that was Tom's badge number." She shook her head, turned, and went back into the kitchen.

I stood motionless, trying to process that. His badge number. I numbly walked back to the patio. Did I ever know Tom's badge number? Could that be a coincidence, or something buried deep in my subconscious? But why would that have surfaced? I thought I was getting clues to find John. Not Dad.

Under clue seven, I wrote, "Dad's badge number."

<u>Clue 8: They all Whisper a Lie</u>

No explanation needed. Under clue eight, I wrote, "Mom, Dad, and John, all lied about who my true biological father was."

If I were to bet on it, I'd say the clues were supernatural, not a figment of my imagination. Beyond the clues, the insights from Harvest Island helped me to understand myself and the spiritual world. Mr. Bidding said the island and its inhabitants were spiritual representations. I'm sure if I spent some time, I could gain more knowledge. That will be a task for another day.

Chapter 50

Michaela was working that day, so Kyle suggested we meet at his apartment to discuss the envelopes we'd received. He said he didn't want Michaela to fall into his rabbit hole. I understood that.

Kyle and Michaela lived in a cute complex with winding paths with lots of flowers, palm trees, and live oaks that provided ample shade. If the units weren't so small, I'd consider living there with the twins. No yard work, a community pool, and an easy walk to the waterway. I hadn't been there since they got married and moved in. Michaela was a superb decorator, so I was looking forward to seeing what she'd done with their flat.

That car again. A late model gray Subaru Forrester had been behind me since I left home. I turned left onto 9th Avenue. The SUV followed. I turned right three streets earlier than I normally would onto Maple Street. The vehicle followed, so I zig zagged to Kyle's apartment. Left, right, left. right, left, and right into Kyle's parking lot. The Subaru followed and then drove past the complex. The windows were tinted, so I couldn't see who was driving.

I parked and sat in my vehicle with the doors locked for a couple of minutes to make sure the car wasn't going to circle back. When I thought the coast was clear, I grabbed the manila envelope from the passenger seat and made a dash for Kyle's door. I knocked lightly, not wanting to disturb any neighbors.

"Hey Sam. Come into our humble abode." Kyle bowed slightly and waved me in.

"Wow. I love what you guys have done here." The apartment had modern furniture with clean lines and light blue-grey paint on the walls. It was an uncluttered minimalist décor, but homey, and welcoming.

"Thanks, but it's all Michaela. She's a true artist, whether she's styling hair at the salon or decorating. I'll give you a tour."

I followed Kyle and every room was perfectly designed--simple and elegant. "Michaela did a beautiful job. Please tell her that I'm blown away."

"Will do. She'll be happy to hear that. Her confidence is lacking but it shouldn't be. I keep telling her how talented she is. She assumes I'm biased."

"Probably, but it doesn't mean you're wrong. Artistic personalities are some of the biggest self-doubters. I should know."

"Yup. You and Michaela, two peas in a pod. Beautiful and talented but don't know it."

I shook my head and smiled at my brother.

Can I get you something to drink?" Kyle asked.

"Water, please. It's hot out there today. I was going to stop and get a drink at the convenience store but was sure I was being followed.

"Oh no. Sam, what happened?"

"A gray Subaru tailed me until I pulled into the apartment complex. It took every turn, even when I zig zagged to get here."

"Better let the police know, so they can be on the lookout."

"I will."

Kyle walked into the kitchen to get me a bottle of water. I followed.

"Why don't we sit here?" Kyle asked. "The white board should help." A small white board about a foot and a half long sat on a tabletop easel on the kitchen table.

"Sure. I'm glad we're finally getting a chance to figure this out."

"Honestly, when you discovered that Tom was your real father, I thought you may give up trying to find John." Kyle handed me a bottle of water.

"I've spent so much of my adult life wondering what happened to the man. Father or not. I'd really like to solve the mystery, now especially for you, Kyle."

"Thanks, sis." Kyle gave me a warm hug.

We sat down at the table with our two identical manila envelopes. While going through the contents we'd received, we reminisced about the photos and articles and then turned to the mysterious messages on the cards.

Mine read: TINU EGAROTS GA 54321.

Kyle's read: 5991 SRI B251

He wrote both cryptic messages on the white board.

"Let's brainstorm for a couple of minutes and see if anything makes sense," I suggested.

"On the surface I can't see any connection to any of the photos or newspaper articles. Can you?" Kyle asked.

"No," I said.

"Tinu Egarots – possibly a person's name," Kyle said.

"GA, someone who lives in Georgia," I said.

"54321 – a zip code?" Kyle mused.

"Okay, let's look that up and see. Tinu Egarots." I pulled out my iPhone and searched on Google. Eno'tinu Egarots a character in the final fantasy XIV. Never heard of it. No other people with that name.

"So probably not a person. Let's check the zip code theory." Kyle entered the number into the US postal service webpage on his phone. "The message says, 'You did not enter a valid ZIP code.' So not a zip code." Kyle sighed.

"There's a TINU syndrome listed. It's an auto immune disease. Hmm." I took a sip from the bottle of water.

"Okay. But what does it mean?" Kyle asked.

"I don't know. Let's try another approach. If these were from John, which it appears they were, what could it mean to him?"

"Hey, didn't he play a cipher game with us when we were kids?" Kyle asked.

"I vaguely remember something like that," I said.

"You were pretty young, so he made them simple. One of his codes was to write the alphabet forwards and then start with Z being A and go backwards," Kyle said.

"Okay, let's see what that would be." A seed of hope began to blossom.

Kyle wrote the alphabet forwards and underneath backwards and then deciphered the message. TINU equals GRMF. EGROTS equals VTZILGH.

"That can't be right," Kyle said.

"No that's even worse, but let me look it up in case," I said.

I searched for GRMF. "It could be Gospel Rescue Mission Fellowship or Geothermal Risk Mitigation Facility or Graph Regularized Matrix Factorization. Good grief." I looked up VTZILGH. "A bunch of sites about Vitiligo, a skin condition, come up. That code's a dead end," I said.

"Okay there is one other cipher I remember. And it's a lot simpler." Kyle erased the reverse alphabet code. "John sent messages written backwards for us to decode, remember?"

"Not really, but worth a try."

Kyle took a green marker from the pile laying on the table and wrote:

12345 AG STORAGE UNIT

I stared at the message, my mind spinning.

"Sis, you look white as a ghost. You okay?"

"I know what that means," I finally said.

"You do? What?"

"Remember the storage unit I told you about with all of John's collections in it?"

"Yes," Kyle said.

"His code to get in the gate was 12345. And it was rented under John's middle name, Alvin Garcia, initials AG."

"Wow, now we are getting somewhere."

Kyle wrote the reverse message from his card on the white board.

152B IRS 1995

"The unit's number was 152B. It's the largest storage facility in the area, so if we'd searched, we probably would have found it."

"Unbelievable."

"And Abigail told me they had to cut off two locks to access the unit. I bet the two keys taped to the index cards would have opened those locks."

"That leaves IRS 1995." Kyle pitch grew higher. "Were there any tax files in the unit?"

"I don't know. Spencer and Abigail took all the files from the cabinets back to the station. There were a lot of files. They haven't managed to finish going through everything yet."

"Are the files still at the precinct?"

"Some, I imagine. Spencer had a batch of them at his home when it burned. He said they were initially looking at the antiquities and art files for possible clues. I doubt he had any related to tax returns at his house. I think the rest of the files are still at the station. I'll call Abigail. She can check it out for us."

Abigail answered on the first ring. I explained what we were looking for and why. She confirmed there were tax files found in the unit. The returns from a few years before John's disappearance had been examined, but she hadn't reviewed the older ones yet. Abigail promised to check the other files as soon as she got to the station the next day.

"Hey, sis, tell her about the car that's been following you," Kyle said.

"One more thing, Abigail. I'm sure I've been followed a few times recently."

"Oh no, Sam. Text me a list of dates, times, and places that you remember and anything you recall about the vehicle. I'll see if I find any traffic or store cams to get a license number."

"Will do. You're an angel, Abigail."

"No worries, I'll let you know what I find out. But please be extra careful."

"I will," I said and hung up.

Kyle stood. "We may have answers soon, sis. Let's go celebrate. I'll buy you lunch."

"Sounds good." I hoped he wouldn't be disappointed.

Chapter 51

I tossed and turned all night. The dreams came in waves. One with John playing with me and Kyle when we were kids. Another with Dad at church in his wheelchair watching Jayce and Jaz in the Christmas play. The dream morphed into Dad's funeral service at the same church.

Ding, ding, ding. "Huh?" Ding, ding, ding.

I reached over to the nightstand and picked up my phone. Abigail Mitchell's name showed on caller ID. Clearing my throat, I touched the green button. "Hi, Abigail, did you find something?" I didn't want to sound like I'd been sleeping.

"Samantha, I'm sorry. I woke you, didn't I?"

Drat. She'd heard the frog in my throat. "It's okay. I need to get up now anyway."

"Could you call your brother and see if he's available to join you at the station today?"

"Sure. What time?"

"Anytime this morning would be good if you're both available."

"Okay will do. That means you found something?"

"Yes, you'll both want to see this," she said.

I could tell she wasn't going to offer any more information on the phone and probably shouldn't. "Alright, I'll give him a call and see you soon."

I called Kyle, and we agreed to meet at the Seagrove Police Station at 10:00 a.m.

I leaned against my Jeep as I waited for Kyle in the SPD parking lot. His late model red Ford Mustang convertible pulled into the spot next to me. The Mustang was Tom's wedding gift for Kyle and Michaela last year, but Kyle drove it the most. When he was by himself, he kept the top down if it wasn't raining. Michaela didn't like her hair being blown around, except on days when she wasn't working. On those days, they both enjoyed cruising down by the beach, feeling the wind and sun on their faces.

"Here we go. The moment of truth," Kyle said as he got out.

"Let's not get our hopes up, Kyle. We've been disappointed before."

"I know, sis. But this time the clue is directly from John."

"True. Let's see what Abigail found."

We walked through the front double doors and then passed through the metal detector before accessing the rest of the station. An officer took my purse and put it through the scanner. I had removed the handgun Spencer talked me into keeping and left it in my vehicle's glovebox. Since I wasn't an officer, I assumed they would not want me to take it into the police station. Spencer never had a chance to teach me how to use the Taurus Ultra-Lite 38 special, so Abigail had stepped in and gave me lessons, and she helped me to get a concealed carry permit while Spencer was recuperating.

Kyle dinged the metal detector as he went through. He took off his belt and tried again. The second time he was clear. The screening officer directed us to the information desk.

We walked by four uniformed officers working at cluttered desks. Two of them had individuals sitting across from them while they typed information into their computers. They were probably taking statements about crimes or missing people. Life is difficult for so many. I'll never know their stories, but realizing others were struggling with issues big enough to seek police helped to normalize our situation, at least momentarily.

The front desk attendant looked up from typing. "Can I help you?"

"Yes, we're here to see Officer Abigail Mitchell."

"And whom should I say is asking to see her?"

"Kyle Garcia and Samantha Anderson," I said. The woman glanced at her screen and pushed a couple of buttons on her desk phone.

She let Abigail know we'd arrived and then directed us to sit in the small waiting area with a half a dozen navy blue fabric armchairs crowded together on one wall. They were facing a large television, probably seventy-five inches, mounted on the opposite wall. The seats looked comfortable, but I soon discovered they were as hard as rock. There must have been a sale at Big Discounts, the local overstock and return store.

Kyle drummed his fingers on the iPad he'd brought. I tapped my foot on the tile floor. One, two, three, four, pause. One, two, three, four, pause.

After what felt like an hour, but was probably only about ten minutes, Abigail appeared and led us to her desk at the back of the station. Her small cubicle was piled high with boxes. They appeared to be the ones Spencer and Abigail filled with files from John's storage unit. The side and tops of each box had the initials J.A.G. The date we were at the storage unit was underneath.

"Thanks for coming in. Sorry for the wait. I was on the phone when you arrived," Abigail said.

"No problem." My butterflies were in overdrive.

"Hi. I'm Kyle." He extended his hand.

Abigail shook his hand. "Nice to meet you, Kyle. Officer Abigail Mitchell. But you can call me Abigail. Have a seat." She pointed to the navy blue, armless, padded chairs across from her desk, and then sat down in front of an open laptop surrounded by stacks of files and folders of various sizes. The chairs were as unbelievably uncomfortable as the armchairs in the waiting area. Must have been the same sale.

"Before I get to the main bit of news, I wanted to let you know that we've made progress on the vehicle that was following you," Abigail said.

I inhaled and let out a long breath preparing myself for bad news. "Who was it?"

"It was a couple of Charleston goons hired by Epps Gallery. We got the license plate from security cameras on a few businesses. We cross-referenced multiple videos to be sure we had the right vehicle. The same SUV appeared several times behind your car on different days."

"Good work. Why were they following me?"

"They were hired to find out where John's antiquities and art collection was being stored. You told the curator that the person who owned had an extensive collection in a storage unit?"

"I did. He asked a bunch of questions. I thought it was kind of weird at the time," I said.

"He hired these guys to find the unit and steal as much as they could. Of course, you didn't give them the name of the person who owned the pieces, so they were following you hoping you'd lead them to the unit."

"What's going to happen to them?" I asked.

"Since they had prior stalking charges, the penalty could carry up to a ten thousand dollar fine and/or up to fifteen years. In reality, they'd probably never get that if they went to court, but they didn't know that. They took a plea deal in exchange for testifying against the curator, Carl Johnson. We're investigating further. They'll probably serve a year or two. But if we can convict Curator Johnson and Epps Gallery on numerous counts of grand larceny and unlawful business practices, it will be worth it to shut them down," Abigail said.

"Wow. I can't believe it," I said.

"They had no intention of hurting you, Sam, which is a relief. It's a good thing they were so conspicuous trailing you. Most criminals aren't known for their brains."

Abigail reached across the lowest pile in front of her and grabbed an expanding file from the top of a stack. "Now to the bigger news. John's taxes from 1995."

"Was there anything suspicious about his return that year?" Kyle asked.

"No, it was straightforward like all his income tax records. But I found something at the bottom of the file in the back slot. I wouldn't have known it was there if I hadn't been looking for something, anything, out of the ordinary."

I held my breath. Kyle leaned forward.

"There was a small envelope with both your names on it. Inside was a thumb drive." She showed us the envelope, which now appeared empty. John had written our names in calligraphy just like he used to on our birthday cards.

"And did you look at the contents of the drive?" I asked, gripping the edge of my seat.

"Yes, since everything we collected was considered 'evidence,' I was able to look at it," Abigail said.

"And?" Kyle asked, leaning even further toward Abigail's desk.

"And there are pictures of documents that are related to the biological weapons he worked on. There are numerous scientific medical reports and an affidavit from John and one from Bobby Baxter stating what they saw and knew about the plot. John also left documents of his research from fifteen years ago when he was assisting the Navy in their investigation of the strange illnesses popping up."

"I'm surprised it didn't make the news back then," I said.

"If the virus was a leak from a Navy facility as we believe, I'm sure they tried to do everything they could to keep it quiet," Abigail said.

"Makes sense. No awareness means no public outrage,

no liability, and no required compensation. They swept it under the proverbial rug," Kyle said.

"Yes, that sounds about right." Abigail glanced from Kyle to me, and then back at the thumb drive plugged into the side of her laptop. She took a deep breath and said, "There's also a video to you two from John. It's only about a minute long."

"What? No way!" Kyle said.

She turned her laptop around so we could see it. It was paused. The silhouette of a man was on the screen. No details of his face or clothing were visible. She clicked on the play button with her mouse.

"Kyle and Samantha, I'm so glad you got my message. I assumed you would share the clues I mailed each of you. Both still smart as a whip. This thumb drive contains information that I'd like you to pass on to U.S. Marshal James O'Sullivan. He's out of the Beaufort office. I recently removed a box containing the hard copies of the documents on this drive. Just in case you noticed a disturbance in the dust at my storage unit, it was me.

"Please don't worry about me. I'm fine, at least at the time of this recording. And I'm going to do my best to keep it that way. I'll contact the marshal soon, but I am not in a position to do so right now. I'll explain more when I see you in person, Lord willing. I love you both and am proud of the wonderful adults you've both become. God bless you and your families. Congratulations on the new bride, Kyle. And, Samantha, you're a wonderful mother. I knew you would be. Keep up the magnificent work. Oh, and one more thing, I'd like you and Kyle to split the contents of the storage unit. I have no need for those items anymore. Keep or sell whatever you want."

A lump in my throat grew. I'd wanted that kind of acknowledgement from John for so long.

Abigail broke the silence. "Can you confirm that's John Garcia's voice?"

"Yes," we answered in unison.

"But he's different," Kyle said.

I added, "Yes, he mentioned God which he never used to. And he said he was proud of us. I don't ever remember hearing that from John."

"Me neither." Tears filled Kyle's eyes.

"People change. It's been fifteen years. But you're sure that's his voice?"

"Yes," we both answered again.

"Okay, let me call the U.S. Marshal and see if he's interested in picking up the thumb drive. I'd hate to email or snail mail anything as sensitive as these documents."

Chapter 52

Dream

"The clues you sought were given, and the mystery has been revealed. Now you know your father is Tom, Samantha. You tried so hard to find your biological father, but he was there all the time, loving you as a father should." Mr. Bidding spoke softly and then continued, "Finally, Samantha, this leads us back to your heart's cry I spoke of when we first met. I will no longer speak in mysteries. While you certainly wanted to find your father, more than that, your heart's cry was to be valued, to have significance.

"You are right. I've never felt good enough," I said. A seagull flew overhead and squawked at us.

"In addition to Tom's love, your heavenly Father, The Maker has been showing you that you are a highly valued child. You don't have to do anything to earn His love. He lavishes it freely. You were created in His image, and thus have innate value beyond your comprehension. You are perfectly loved," Mr. Bidding said.

"I am so grateful to finally have answers and closure. It's hard to not feel cheated out of the knowledge that Tom is my father, my real, biological father. I wasted so much time worrying about John's broken promises, believing there's something unlovable about me."

"Yes, worry is a waste, Samantha. The truth is and was that both your earthly father and heavenly father have always loved you. And John did too, in his own way. But he had his own demons to battle that kept him from being a consistently loving parent."

"I realize that now. But wish I had a time machine to go back with this knowledge and stop so much of my anxiety and feelings of not being good enough. Just think how much I would have saved on therapy."

Mr. Bidding smiled. "Even if John was your biological father. It wouldn't change anything. Your worries were chains that kept you imprisoned. They were not based on your true worth. Truth does set one free, Samantha."

"I know you're right, Mr. Bidding. I see now I've placed my self-worth in an external value. I believed I was only worth as much as John cared for me. I so wanted to please him, to be cherished by him. Now I've discovered that the object of my wishful thinking was misplaced," I said.

"Samantha, it's not uncommon for humans to search for acceptance and even joy in places that can't meet those needs. Most of those you met on Harvest Island were looking for meaning in poor substitutes or were bound by their own set of false truths. They missed their intrinsic value. Samantha, tell me, what have you learned from your visits to Harvest Island?"

My first thought made me laugh. Mr. Bidding would be a brilliant therapist. Always asking questions. Always wanting me to come to my own conclusions. But it seemed to be a solid strategy, and it worked. I certainly changed my perspective during the "therapy" with Mr. Bidding. My Bible studies with Brandon over the last few weeks helped to clarify some of the things Mr. Bidding was sharing.

The waves crashed on the shore as I considered my response. I hoped to finally get it right. "I see myself in several people who live on Harvest Island. I learned that I must be aware of my personal lies and guard against them with The Maker's help. And I related to a lot of the inhabitants in one way or another. Given different circumstances, I could have fallen into most of the deceptions they represented. And I know I need to learn a lot more about *The Book of Truth*, the *Bible*. Some of the inhabitants held partial truths that were not balanced. It may take a while for everything to sink in."

"Bravo, Samantha! You are learning these lessons well. In time, those realities will travel from your head to your heart. Growth is a process--rarely an epiphany that changes everything. In earth's fast-paced society, quick fixes are everywhere. But the human soul takes time to heal and flourish. Go easy on yourself." His voice was gentle.

"Thank you, Mr. Bidding." I sighed.

"The two greatest mysteries in your life were solved at the same time. The Maker is wise," Mr. Bidding said.

I heard the awe in his voice and hoped to attain that deep reverence for The Maker one day.

"Another lesson I learned was about my purpose," I added without my angel psychoanalyst prompting.

"How so?" Mr. Bidding quickly jumped at the learning opportunity.

"By valuing the wrong things, all the inhabitants of Harvest Island were missing their purpose, their reason for being," I said.

"And what is that reason?"

"To have a relationship with The Maker and to do the good things He has planned for each of them. I was distraught by the lack of love from my father and wasted precious time and energy that could have been directed at others, others who truly loved me and others who may have needed someone to love them."

"Yes, Samantha. You've discovered spiritual truths. If you follow this knowledge, your life will never be the same again."

"I'm counting on it," I whispered.

"One last question, Mr. Bidding."

"Anything, Samantha."

"Why the South Pacific?"

"Why indeed." He smiled and then was gone – again.

A ringing phone woke me from my dream. I glanced at an unknown number.

"Hello, this is Samantha." The frog in my throat croaked.

"Hi Sam, this is John."

Chapter 53

I sat next to my half-brother, Kyle, waiting anxiously for the arrival of the man I'd let dominate my inner life for far too long. Kyle ordered another coffee, and I silently counted the ceiling tiles while I sipped my sparkling raspberry tea. From the small booth in the back corner of this busy café, I watched the door for John's arrival. It had been fifteen years. I wasn't sure I'd recognize him.

A man in a fedora and trench coat entered. What? That's not possible. I'd seen this man before, once in Seagrove hospital and again at the hospital in Charleston. I stared at his face. I recognized him. It was John behind the beard, mustache, and glasses.

He approached our table, arms open wide. "Kyle, Samantha, I can't believe I'm finally getting to see you again after all this time. What a blessing."

Hmm. Here he was—the long searched for John, but with a brighter countenance. And he never used to say 'blessing.' Time can certainly change people, and so can circumstances, and marriages, and divorces, and God.

Kyle and I updated John on what was going on in our lives over hamburgers and onion rings. He insisted on hearing about us before we heard his story. I told him about the threats and Spencer's fire. We condensed a lot of events, and he already knew about anything big enough to hit the newspaper or our social media accounts.

John said, "I know you both probably have a lot of

questions, so feel free to ask me anything."

Kyle didn't waste any time. "So, why did you leave WITSEC, John?"

Kyle had told me he'd made peace with the fact that John didn't want to put us in danger when he first went into WITSEC but couldn't understand why he hadn't contacted us since he'd left.

John's brown eyes filled with tears. "Natalie was going through treatment for breast cancer and was extremely fragile. I understood more clearly why Bobby didn't want to testify all those years ago. I needed to protect Natalie, like he had needed to protect his wife and baby. I wanted to be sure I didn't put her in harm's way. And she needed me to care for her, so I didn't want to jeopardize my life either."

"That makes sense." Kyle took another bite of his sandwich.

"I'd heard Bobby died in a single car crash under suspicious conditions. I've always assumed those thugs that stole the virus were responsible. They're dangerous men," John said.

"That's what Betty Baxter thinks too," I said.

"They are evil. Atif Bashir and Milton Bridges were sentenced to thirty-five years in prison. Atif died in prison. Stabbed, they said. Milton was out on early parole when I was attacked. I never saw the person who stabbed and then shot me, so I don't know if it was him or someone he hired. When they caught up with Bridges, he was in violation of his parole and was sent back to serve the remainder of his sentence. Then he was released three years ago after the appeal and new trial."

"Right, when evidence went missing," I said.

"Yes, I thought they could convict him without my testimony. I didn't know most of the evidence had disappeared. Probably paid someone off. He was released after the new trial when they couldn't prove beyond a shadow of a doubt that he was guilty." John slowly shook his head and hunched his shoulders.

"It's not your fault, John. You didn't know," Kyle said.

"Thank you, Kyle. I appreciate it, but I failed." John sat up straighter and resumed his story. "Jamal Gaber was also involved in the plot, but Bobby and I didn't work with him, and never met him as far as I know. He was the mastermind and a terrorist rather than a misguided whistleblower," John said.

"We know bits and pieces of your story but didn't know the thieves' real names. Marshal James O'Sullivan called them Joe and Schmo," I said.

John laughed a deep belly laugh. "Sounds like James. When I talked to him last week, he told me about your meeting and all you'd found out on your own. Even more than he had. You'd make a crackerjack detective." John smiled the smile of a proud parent.

"Thanks, John." I wished he'd been that proud of me when I believed he was my real father.

"Sam, remember that conversation the last time I spoke with you fifteen years ago?" John asked.

"Sort of."

"When I mentioned George Purnell, it was because he was one of the patients infected with the virus created by my military unit. The cover story was drugs, but I wasn't happy about that. He didn't deserve his family being fed the overdose story. He did pass out and died in a car crash, but it wasn't from drugs."

"Betty Baxter mentioned you'd been recruited to help investigate the outbreaks in Denver and Seattle. What a small world. It's hard to fathom that an acquaintance from Seagrove was one of the first victims of the stolen virus."

"That's right, hard to believe, Sam. And the school bus accident in Seagrove was caused by another victim of the virus. The truck driver blacked out and hit the bus, which hit other cars and caused multiple injuries. Fortunately, no one was killed in that one."

"So that *was* you on the elevator that day," I said.

"Yes, I was shocked to see you, so I turned away. I'd been eluding detection for almost three years and then walked right onto the same elevator as you. And then I saw you again in Charleston. There's been an outbreak there recently. Pretty coincidental, huh?"

"No doubt. But thanks to the school bus accident, the education board is now considering installing seat belts on all the buses. They claim they don't have the money, but I bet they'll find it. Even a bake sale or car wash would raise enough to cover the cost if all the kids get involved." I paused as the waitress approached and filled our glasses.

"Can I get you youngins anything else?" she asked and winked at John.

"You still have those fried pies?" John asked.

"Sure do, apple or peach? And with or without vanilla ice cream, darlin'?"

John's eyes lit up. "Peach, with ice cream. Thanks. Oh, and a coffee too, cream and sugar, please."

"Got it. How about you two kids?"

Kyle and I declined. Though fried pie sounded pretty good. If we were there another hour, I'd reconsider.

After the waitress walked away, I said, "Tell us about the virus."

"We call it Zed Virus X10. It wreaks havoc on the neurological system—causing people to black out, and then attacks their respiratory system and heart rate. There's no test for it currently. It can only be determined by an analysis of the patient's blood. That's where my research comes in. The virus is prone to mutating and unfortunately is becoming more contagious. I can tell from our research if it's a derivative of the biological weapon the Navy created."

"That sounds scary."

"It is, and there's no known cure. It has to run its course which takes up to three months. Often the blackouts cause more fatalities than the virus itself—fainting is the first major symptom. One man was flying a small Cessna 208 Caravan when he lost consciousness. His passengers called for help on the radio but none of them knew how to fly. The plane crashed, and all nine passengers and the pilot lost their lives."

"That's terrible," I said.

"One of the positive things, if you can say there's anything positive about this strain, is that it's symptoms are less severe than the original virus."

"That's . . . somewhat comforting." A shiver ran down my spine. The prospect of passing out without warning was disturbing.

"So, what about Natalie?" I took a sip of my tea.

"You know we were married under our WITSEC names and were thrilled to be Mr. John and Mrs. Natalie Gomez. They told us keeping our first names was allowed and would be helpful, so we'd answer to that name if someone was trying to get our attention. The name Gomez allowed me to have the same initials. Of course, Natalie had to get used to a new last name, which she would have needed to do anyway. We were talking about getting married before I was assaulted. But that's probably not what you're asking about."

"No, did she survive breast cancer?" I asked barely above a whisper.

"She fought it for over three years but passed about ten weeks ago." He touched the wedding band on his left hand. "I wish you could have met her. She was incredible."

"I'm so sorry for your loss, John," I said.

"That's rough." Kyle reached over and patted John on the shoulder.

"Thanks, fortunately I had time to prepare. And about seven years into our marriage we discovered a church that changed our lives, well, actually God did, but He used that church. We leaned on God's comfort as we went through her trial. But that's a story for another day."

"I glad you've had divine support, John," I said. "I've

recently started a similar journey."

"Me too," Kyle said.

The waitress brought John's pie. "Careful the plate's hotter than a Billy goat with a blow torch." The vanilla ice cream was melting quickly.

John took a bite. "Mmm . . . You guys want some of this?"

We both declined.

John continued his story. "After Natalie passed, I started investigating cases of the virus on my own. I wanted to have more evidence to present and needed time to get my head on straight before coming forward. I went to the storage unit and retrieved the hard copies of what I'd put on the thumb drive that I left for you."

"But the storage facility owner said your code hadn't been used in fifteen years," I said.

"I was trying to avoid anyone knowing where I was, so I parked outside the gate and waited for another person to open it and followed them in when I retrieved the documents and again when I went back to place the thumb drive in my tax file."

"I should have guessed. I did the same thing when I first met Spencer and Abigail there, but only because I didn't know your elaborate code."

John's deep laugh filled our corner of the café again. "Pretty creative, huh? Anyway, with Natalie gone, I figured I could spend time looking at new cases."

"I understand. It must have been so painful losing Natalie." I reached across the table and put my hand on John's hand.

He set his fork down and placed his other hand on mine. "I'm sure you understand with Tom being gone now."

I nodded and looked away. Tom's absence was a gaping hole that I still felt in the pit of my stomach.

Kyle broke the silence. "How were you able to find cases?"

"I have a connection at the CDC, Justin Jasinski, from when I started looking into cases of Zed Virus X10 fifteen years ago. He knew my need for anonymity and was willing to use my new alias, John Gonzalez."

"You must be one of a few that know all about that virus." Kyle took a sip of his Coke.

"That's right. Jasinski informed me about unusual cases with no known cause. Especially when there was a mass casualty from the illness. Jasinski gets me into hospitals to investigate under my alias. I turn my findings over to him. And I keep copies of course.

"When I called Marshal O'Sullivan last week, he said Officer Mitchell called him, and he picked up the thumb drive with all the old evidence. It contained known associates of Bridges and Bashir. The marshals were able to apprehend Bridges with the virus in his possession. They were still engineering it, trying to make it more deadly."

"That's incredible." I was relieved to hear Bridges was in custody.

John continued, "Bridges gave up Gaber to avoid the death penalty. Both are behind bars now, and their trials are scheduled for this fall. This time it's not conspiracy charges but terrorism resulting in death that they're charged with. Neither one will see the light of day again, and Gaber could get the death penalty."

"So, you're safe now?" I asked.

"Yes. We are safe now. The prosecutor said it's a slam dunk."

"That's such a relief," I said.

"Now that I don't need to hide anymore, I can investigate cases of the Zed Virus X10 under my own name. Seems kind of strange being John Alvin Garcia again." He cocked his head. "I kinda dig it. It's like a long-lost friend."

"I bet. But why did they target Samantha and Spencer?" Kyle asked.

John took the last bite of his pie and then said, "Last

week an FBI agent filled me in on Bridges confession. In it he stated three years ago his lawyer told him I was scheduled to testify at his new trial. Bridges believed I was dead, so was shocked to find out I was alive."

"If he thought you were dead, he must have been involved in your attack fifteen years ago." Kyle leaned forward placing his arms on the table.

"Yes. When Bridges told Gaber I was alive, he hired a professional to hack into both your computers and phones. They were keeping tabs on you guys in case I reached out. When you started searching for me, Sam, they were alarmed. As long as I was in hiding, everything I knew was secret. But if you succeeded in finding me, they were afraid I'd tell you about them and go to the authorities. They didn't know whether or not I'd kept copies of the evidence. But my testimony alone would have been damning. Bridges and Gaber hoped to find and kill me before you found me, so I'd never be able to testify against them."

"Your experience in WITSEC must have helped you to stay under the radar," Kyle said.

"One hundred percent. I thought I was being followed a few times when I took Natalie to the Mayo Clinic in Arizona, so I abandoned my usual military cut. I grew a full beard and mustache, stopped coloring my gray, trimmed my bushy eyebrows, and added these wire rim glasses. My phone doesn't even recognize me."

Kyle and I chuckled.

"And your new outfit?" I asked.

"A fedora and trench coat completed my disguise, and I've kinda grown to embrace it, a regular Humphrey Bogart with a little extra facial hair and spectacles." John winked at me.

Kyle and I sat across from John for another hour talking about the events of the last fifteen years. He explained how a few of his antiques, appraisals, and authentication paperwork were ruined in a flood at Uncle Jerry's and Aunt

Mabel's property. When John learned about his aunt and uncle's fatal accident, he retrieved his undamaged property from their farm and put it in storage.

When we asked about the artifacts he'd pulled from the Epps Gallery, he said he'd discovered their practices were not above board and didn't want to get in any deeper with them.

We let John know that the big secret he'd kept all those years about Tom being my biological father was out. He said he hoped I would have found out sooner but was glad I finally knew. He assured me he always loved me as his own and still did. I knew he did in his own way. The same way he loved Kyle. Though I objected, he still wanted me to have half of his collections. So did Kyle.

Chapter 54

Spencer's healing didn't go as quickly as we all had hoped. Complications added a few weeks to his stay. He'd contracted pneumonia and when that started clearing, he developed an infection on his chest and neck. The skin grafts were redone after the infection cleared. It was four weeks and four days when he was finally able to leave.

A few days before he was released, I offered to pick him up. At first, he refused. He didn't want to put me out. But after bribing him with something he couldn't refuse, he relented. I told him we'd stop at Friendly's for his favorite ice cream, Hunka Chunka Peanut Butter Fudge, and mine, Vienna Mocha Chunk. Win. Win. After that I'd take him to the hotel he booked, or if I could convince him, to my guest room, which I'd offered, but to that point he'd refused.

On the day of the great escape, discharge time was pushed back to that evening. Spencer's doctor, Sanjay Bakshi, and the other burn docs were recruited to treat a couple dozen people who were injured in a bus that crashed and caught on fire. Several others died at the scene. The call to help victims came right after Bakshi started his rounds. Spencer couldn't leave without the doctor signing off, so he told me to wait for his text before heading that way. Mom offered to watch the twins overnight, so I didn't have to keep them out late on a school night.

I got Spence's text about 6:45 p.m. "Samantha, doc will be on my floor in about an hour. Nurse Ratched says I'm on the last wing of his rounds, so it'll be about another hour before he gets to me. According to her, this is the biggest burn unit in the state and the worst cases are flown here. They are currently at capacity. She said I should be grateful for even being admitted. Which I am. Sorry for the delay. I can always get an uber if you have other plans. "

Cute. I texted back, "Wouldn't want you to miss your   .   I'll head to the hospital now. I want to look at the full   over the   on the way."

He replied: ♥

Was that a heart for me or for the full moon and ocean? I hoped it was for me, but Spence had a few pictures of the ocean around his home, one in the moonlight. Who wouldn't love a full moon over the ocean?

I took my time as I drove to Charleston, cutting over to Ocean Boulevard to check out the picturesque scene. I opened my window so I could hear the waves crash on the shore as I drove along and then pulled into a public beach access between the high- rises. The moon's reflection on the water was breathtaking. It made me feel small and insignificant, yet simultaneously grateful and awestruck.

I arrived at the Charleston Hospital and headed to the elevator. As I got on, a man with a fedora and trench coat was getting off.

"John, good to see you again so soon."

"It's a relief not having to hide anymore, Samantha. The feds have all the evidence now. And I can once again assist the navy in the cases that don't have an explanation."

"I'm happy for you, John. So, what was your mission today?"

"Did you hear about the bus that crashed and caught fire?"

"I did."

"According to witnesses, the driver passed out and slammed into a concrete barrier and then was hit by a semi.

The bus's gas tank was full. Boom. The CDC suspected the bus driver was infected with the Zed Virus X10 when every other test came back negative. I looked at his blood sample. Sure enough, they fit the profile."

The elevator door started to close, so I hit the open-door button.

"That's so sad. I'm glad you're able to help. Stay safe, John," I said.

"You too. Now that the perpetrators are behind bars, we are free, Sam. No looking over our shoulders all the time. God bless you, dear."

"You too, John." I let the elevator door close.

When I arrived at Spencer's room, he was in khaki shorts and a police dog t-shirt sitting on the edge of his bed, a bulging backpack next to him. A dimpled grin lit his face when he saw me. My heart skipped a beat.

"Doc left a few minutes ago," Spence said.

"Fantastic, so you're all set then?" I asked.

"Pretty much. I'm waiting for the nurse to bring in the release paperwork," Spence said.

"I know you booked a hotel, but I'd love for you to stay at my home. It's the least I can do. You were injured because of me. I have the guest room ready, so no need to sleep on the sofa to be the first line of defense anymore."

"Samantha, I don't want to be a bother. My insurance will pay for accommodations while my house is being rebuilt."

"But you won't have anyone to look after you while you're recovering. Please stay at least as long as you're out of work. You don't want to get your burns infected again, right? I'll help you with changing bandages and medication, meals, laundry, or whatever. Then if you want to go to a hotel after that, I wouldn't be as worried about you. But you're welcome to stay until your house is rebuilt. Being right next door would help you to keep an eye on the progress."

"You missed your calling. You should be in sales." He

laughed. "I'm a big boy. I can look after myself, but I do appreciate the offer."

"Spencer McKenna, I'll call your boss if I have to, so he can order you to stay with me." I smiled at the amusement on his face.

"Only if you let me help you in some way or pay you." His resolve was waning.

"Don't be silly, Spence. You've done so much for us. And your research is what finally unraveled the mystery of the threats against us. Without that we'd still be jumping at our own shadows waiting for the other shoe to drop. We owe you big time."

"One thing, Sam." He stood, took my hand, and pulled me toward him.

Looking straight into my eyes, he asked, "Do you know how I feel about you?"

"I think so, but why don't you tell me?" I wanted to make sure we were on the same page.

He leaned down and kissed me. My knees felt weak. How could I be so lucky? This brave detective cared for me.

"I do." Awkward silence. "What I mean, Spence, is I do know how you feel now for sure. I feel the same way." I nervously twirled my hair.

He chuckled. "I've wanted to tell you for so long, but I wasn't sure you felt the same way. I feared you'd never see me as more than another brother." Spence cocked his head. "You're so beautiful, Samantha Anderson, not only on the outside, but your big heart, it's gorgeous."

He pulled me closer. The warmth of his embrace was exactly what I needed. I nestled my head on his shoulder. I couldn't remember a time when I was so content.

The nurse stepped into the room. "Hm-hm, what is that dog doing in the hallway?"

"Oh, I forgot. Rigg's, come. Surprise!"

Rigg's pranced in, tail wagging, and started licking his owner's knees.

"Aww, Riggs, it's been so long." Spence bent down and embraced his dog.

"It's okay, he's a police dog," I said to the nurse.

"Sure, I can see he's hard at work." She huffed and continued, "I have your discharge paperwork here. The care instructions that Dr. Bakshi gave you verbally earlier are here too. You need to sign this, this. and this."

"I'm not signing away my life, am I?" He glanced at the paperwork and signed without reading it.

"I sure hope not. If you are, I've taken a lot of lives." She didn't crack a smile. But I could see in her eyes she was charmed by Spencer. Who wouldn't be?

Spence picked up his backpack and headed for the door, with me on one arm and Riggs on his other side.

"Woah there, Casanova. Not on my watch. Sit." The nurse pointed to the wheelchair. "Hospital policy. No exceptions."

I took his hefty backpack. "Bricks?" I asked.

"Of course, what else would I need while recovering?"

When Spencer was allowed to get out of the wheelchair at the front entrance, he grabbed the backpack I was struggling with and flung it over his shoulder like it was full of feathers. My hero was as strong as ever.

As we stepped outside the hospital, fireworks lit the sky. The full moon just above the bursts. The Charleston Spring Music Festival was ending.

"Aww. Fireworks for me?" Spence asked, and leaned down and pressed his lips against mine. More fireworks. Riggs nuzzled our legs and barked his approval.

A perfect ending to a perfect night.

Epilogue

Over the next several months, I dreamed about Harvest Island on several occasions, especially when my life was becoming unbalanced, and I forgot about my heavenly father's extravagant love for me.

In my dreams, I would find myself in one of the Harvest Island homes. Most often it was in Anna Angst's and Felicia Fear's home. Of course, that's the home Mr. Bidding said had been my favorite dwelling for years, so that pattern is the hardest to break. I also found myself in Duke Ryan Rich's palace a few times and Paige Pleasure's home too. I even woke up in Wally Works' log cabin a couple of times.

Like I said, I am a slow learner, but at least I'm learning. The Maker is patient. And slow movement in the right direction is better than standing still. It has taken some painful stretching and will continue to take intentional decisions each day, but I'm convinced that in the end, it will be worth it. Now my hope is to one day stand before The Maker, my true Father, and hear, "Well done, Samantha!"

Questions for Book Clubs

1. What were the obstacles in Samantha's faith journey?

2. What do you think the main catalyst was for her to find faith?

3. Have you ever come to the wrong conclusion even though accurate information was given?

4. Samantha's search for her father had several impediments. What were some of them?

5. Does your view of your father impact your view of God the Father? If yes, how so?

6. What did Samantha believe John valued most while she was growing up?

7. What did Samantha believe Tom valued most?

8. Where did Samantha place her value at the beginning of the book? At the end of the book?

9. Have you ever struggled with forgiveness? How did you work through it?

10. Do you think Samantha's OCD could be related to her relationship with John?

11. Have you or someone you know ever had a dream with symbolism in it or a dream that came true?

12. What biblical stories have dreams that contain symbolism or predict the   future?

13. If you remember your dreams, what is the craziest dream you've ever had?

14. Whose Harvest Island dwelling do you find yourself in most often? Choose the top two or three.

> **a. Daniel Dark**
> **b. George Godfree**
> **c. Harry Hardhearted**
> **d. Phillip Phony**
> **e. Fred Fatalist**
> **f. Ashley Ascetic**
> **g. Wally Works**
> **h. Lilly Legalist**
> **i. Barb Beauty**
> **j. Brad Brainiac**
> **k. Paige Pleasure**
> **l. Mary Mystic**
> **m. Ellie Ecstasy**
> **n. Ryan Rich**
> **o. Rita Rich**
> **p. Anna Angst**
> **q. Felicia Fear**
> **r. Uncle Unforgiveness**
> **s. Aunt Anger**
> **t. Gabriel Grace**
> **u. Julie Justice**
> **v. Faith**

      w. Hope
      x. Charity

15. How does our culture promote unhealthy values?

16. In which of the following do you place your significance? (Circle all that apply)

      a. Job/Position
      b. Power
      c. Money
      d. Appearance/ Being physically fit
      e. Intellect
      f. How others view you
      g. Your accomplishments
      h. Your service, helping others
      i. Your experiences
      j. Number of friends
      k. Number of likes or Happy Birthday's on Facebook
      l. Number of followers on social media
      m. Being self-made
      n. Being made in God's image and loved by Him

17. What symbolism did you see in the book?

18. Were you surprised by the ending of the story?

Author's Note:

I hope you enjoyed the Mystery of Harvest Island. While Samantha's quest for her father was the primary focus of the story, the underlying mysteries found in Harvest Island are universal. All of humanity is lost in the darkness of Daniel Dark, George Godfree, and Harry Hardhearted's home, until they allow the light of The Maker, God Almighty to penetrate their souls.

People strive to find meaning and value in various ways, often from multiple sources. The homes Samantha visited represented some of those avenues. While many of the inhabitants of Harvest Island were not evil or in the clutches of Satan, most were not living in the fullness of life that God offers to all.

I have often wavered in embracing God's love as enough, seeking to find my value in relationships, things, money, or careers. Please be encouraged that no matter where you find yourself on your journey, you are greatly loved and highly valued by the creator of the universe. And if you ever veer off the road, he will patiently coax you back to the path.

Amazingly, the articles about the Medical Center for Federal Prisoners were all true except the one about the Lorenzo crime family. Who knew that severely ill inmates could cause such chaos? It makes me wonder what havoc healthy inmates create.

Thank you, Cynthia Hickey and Winged Publications, for taking on my project and believing in me.

I have never-ending appreciation and love for my husband, Doug, who unwaveringly supports my writing and allows me to bounce ideas off him.

Thanks to Cherryl Feighn, my sister and best friend,

who always encourages me in my writing and other areas of my life.

Special thanks to Bev Riggins and Kristin Burdine who read my manuscript and gave me excellent feedback and much encouragement.

Special thanks to Essential Music Publishing, LLC, Sony Music Holdings, Inc. for granting permission to use some of the lyrics from Perfectly Loved, artists - Rachael Lampa feat. Toby Mac; written by Ethan Hulse, Andrew Ripp and Rachael Lampa.

Some of the names in the story came directly from scripture.

The **Old Testament** declares **God** is **Maker or The Maker** 27 times.

John 14:17, 15:26, 16:13 all refer to **The Holy Spirit** as **The Spirit of Truth**

Psalm 103:20 describes **angels** as those **"who do his bidding**."

John 10:10 calls **Satan "The thief."**

2 Corinthians 11:14 says **Satan** masquerades as an **"angel of light**."

The Book of Truth is a moniker I created for the Bible because it is indeed a book filled with truth. See: II Timothy 2:15, John 17:17, Psalm 33:4, Psalm 119:142, 151, 160. The phrase "Book of Truth" is used only one time in scripture in Daniel 10:21, and this passage refers to a heavenly record of future events.

Scripture is filled with **dreams**. See the following for some interesting reading. Daniel 2, Genesis 20:3-6, Genesis 28:12-15, Genesis 31:10-13, Genesis 31:24, Genesis 37:5-9, Genesis 40:5-22, Genesis 41:1-32, Judges 7:13-14, I Kings 3:5-15, Daniel 2:1-47, Daniel 4:4-37, Daniel 7:1-28, Matthew 1:20-25, Matthew 2:12-23 (3 dreams), Matthew 27:19.

Thank you, readers. I pray you were encouraged by reading *Harvest Island*. We are all image bearers of God our Maker. Never forget that you are perfectly loved.

And last, but not least, I am grateful to my Lord and Savior, Jesus, for walking with me and my family through the trials and treasures of life.

Lissa Raines has had a varied career path including missionary, educator, real estate agent, and business owner. A graduate of Southeastern University and AG Theological Seminary, Lissa has a passion for sharing biblical truths through her stories. She lives in Missouri with her husband, Doug, and their dog, Stormy. Between them they have three sons, two daughters-in-law, and five grandsons.

https://www.facebook.com/AuthorLissaRaines

www.lissaraines.com